S0-BFD-335

Adam walked into the bathroom and shut the door to keep the warm air in. "I told you to call me if you needed anything," he said roughly as he grabbed the towel from the hook and threw it over his shoulder. He stepped to the tub, keeping his eyes leveled on her face and reached out to help her up.

She jerked away from him. "Wait." Her wide eyes met his. A flush filled her high cheekbones as she licked her succulent, wet lips. She had no idea how damn provocative her simple action was and he went hard instantly. Thank God he was hunched over. "Aren't you going to close your eyes?"

He snorted. "Then I won't see what I'm grabbing. Besides, it's nothing I haven't seen before."

"You haven't seen *me*!" she said angrily, her eyes blazing.

Yet, he thought. He shook his head. What the hell was wrong with him? "Fine. I'll close my eyes and you lead my hands, but if I knock you into the sink, it's your own fault."

"Okay," she uttered meekly.

He closed his eyes and felt her pull his hands into the water and place them on her rib cage. She fit perfectly in his hands and he took his time lifting her out of the water, reluctant to let go of her sleek, soft skin. When he set her down, he let go unwillingly and grabbed the towel from his shoulder, holding it out to her with his eyes still shut.

She took it from him. "Thank you. You can open your eyes now." Evangeline stood before him with the beige towel wrapped around her torso, her hair dripping wet, sending droplets down her shoulders.

This woman would be the death of him.

To my fabulous Ralphie

Tortured Soul

by

Julia Laque

Tortured Series, Book One

Love! Julia Laque

This is a work of fiction. Names, characters, places, and incidents are either the product of the author's imagination or are used fictitiously, and any resemblance to actual persons living or dead, business establishments, events, or locales, is entirely coincidental.

Tortured Soul

COPYRIGHT © 2013 by Julia Laque

All rights reserved. No part of this book may be used or reproduced in any manner whatsoever without written permission of the author or The Wild Rose Press, Inc. except in the case of brief quotations embodied in critical articles or reviews.
Contact Information: info@thewildrosepress.com

Cover Art by *Debbie Taylor*

The Wild Rose Press, Inc.
PO Box 708
Adams Basin, NY 14410-0708
Visit us at www.thewildrosepress.com

Publishing History
First Black Rose Edition, 2013
Print ISBN 978-1-61217-876-9
Digital ISBN 978-1-61217-877-6

Tortured Series, Book One
Published in the United States of America

Dedication

To my family and friends, for your unwavering support
and always putting a smile on my face.
To my nephews, my good luck charms,
for making my life complete.
To my father,
for Irish lullabies and fairy tale stories before bed.
To my mother,
my rock, my educator, my inspiration.
To Omar,
for believing in me
and giving me the extra push I always need.
And last, but certainly not least,
to my sister, Jessica,
my writing partner and better half...this one's for you.
~Julia

Acknowledgements

To all the authors who have inspired me over the years.
To my sister and friends, for putting up with
my incessant questions about everything under the sun.
To Debbie Taylor,
for the lovely image that graces the cover.
And a very special thanks to Rhonda Penders,
Callie Lynn Wolfe and Lill Farrell,
for taking a chance on a newbie like me.
I thank you.

Chapter One

Evangeline Wolcott raced quietly across the red-carpeted hallway, careful not to knock into the oversized vase sitting on a table just outside of her father's office. The hallway was dimly lit and adorned with family photos. As she neared the door, she turned to make sure no one saw her ill attempt at stealth. Not that it mattered. She just didn't want anyone giving her away. Pausing for a moment, she listened to the goings on in her father's two story home. She could hear her mother and sister talking in the back of the house and knew they were in the kitchen preparing dinner. What she was doing was beyond childish, but she couldn't think about it right now.

She had some eavesdropping to do.

Her years as a ballet dancer paid off as she tiptoed the last few steps to listen in. On her way out, the family's cleaning lady had informed Evangeline her father was talking with Maxwell Jones, lawyer and co-founder of the Illinois Mediation Committee for the Human and Supernatural Society.

Maxwell might have been a good friend of the family, but she had her suspicions as to why he'd come over unannounced on a Tuesday. There was definitely something going on in the supernatural community and she was determined to find out what.

Ever since she had been a little girl, Evangeline

Wolcott daydreamed of meeting a vampire or werewolf. She was fascinated by their mystical ways and stayed updated on famous supernatural figures in the media and by reading numerous books on their way of life. She instigated countless arguments with friends on the history of the werewolf and the alleged involvement with witches centuries ago.

On several occasions Maxwell Jones had contacted Evangeline herself to inquire about certain aspects of the paranormal from a werewolf's reaction to the moon phases to a vampire's appetite after transitioning. Unfortunately, she was no help when it came to witches. The only mention of witches she encountered in her books was from a werewolf's perspective. With the exception of fictional witches portrayed in books or movies, real witches had no literature whatsoever on their race.

Despite her years of research she had never actually met anyone from the supernatural society. She had seen, from a distance, a vampire in town a couple years ago. He was a large, scary-looking man, getting into a black BMW. There was also the time she glimpsed the back of the Vampire King of North America at a fundraiser with her father. It seemed every time she was in the vicinity of a vampire, they slipped out of view.

But she would never forget the night she saw from her bedroom window, the pack of werewolves running together across the Midewin prairie beneath a full moon. Evangeline had run quickly to find binoculars to get a closer look, but by the time she did it was too late. They were too far away as they headed across the creek toward the woods. But what she had managed to see from her bedroom window was one of the most amazing things she had ever beheld.

Now Maxwell Jones, mediator extraordinaire, was in her home and she just knew he came with news about the clash between her two favorite species. Evangeline was aware there were more covens and packs around the world, but things were heating up in her neck of the woods. Literally.

Just then, Evangeline heard her father's voice rise from inside his office.

"I see no other way out of it. I owe him—"

Maxwell's voice cut in. "Have you thought this through? Do you realize what you're asking of her? She'll never forgive you."

Evangeline flinched and quietly moved closer to press her ear to the cold oak. She had never heard her father and Maxwell argue like this. They may have had their difference of opinion when it came to the supernatural, but they had no qualms about stating their points in public. Why were they behind closed doors?

"You don't understand, Max. He can basically do whatever he wants at this point. He knows what I've done." Her father's voice shook as he spoke. She could tell he was pacing across the hardwood floor. It was Geoffrey Wolcott's telltale sign something was seriously wrong.

"Let me speak to him." Maxwell's voice was urging. "He can be difficult, but I'm sure we can come up with some sort of arrangement."

Who's he? Evangeline thought with mounting frustration. What were they talking about?

"No. He warned me not to get you involved. I'm sorry I even called you, but I didn't know what to do.

I'm out of options here," Geoffrey said.

There was silence in the office for a moment, and then she heard Maxwell ask quietly, "How much?"

Somberly, her father uttered, "Three million."

"Fuck, Geoff! What were you thinking?" Maxwell shouted.

"I was thinking about my family. I had no other choice. These are grim times. My accounts are empty, most of my investments have bellied up...hell...I almost lost the house for fuck's sake. I did what I had to for my family."

Shuddering at her father's words, Evangeline braced her hands on either side of the door to steady herself.

"When, in your plan to save your family from poverty, did you think it was wise to embezzle three million dollars from a vampire?" Maxwell sounded as shocked as Evangeline felt.

"I was going to put the money back as soon as I got back on my feet—"

"By gambling no doubt," Maxwell said bitterly.

"Watch it, Max. I called you here as a friend. I know what I did was stupid, but I only started gambling again a few months ago when my funds were low. Tell me, what would you have done? Would you let your family lose everything?"

Evangeline's father came from old money, but he had made several investments over the years to maintain their fortune. Geoffrey was City Hall's Director of Finance and also served on the Vampire Rights Council in Wilmington and had evidently stolen money from one of the vampires on the council.

"I'm sorry, Geoff, but did you have to embezzle

from the king?" Maxwell asked mournfully.

Her stomach leapt at Max's words. Evangeline stood frozen against the door. *Tell me I heard wrong. Tell me I did not hear that my father stole from the Vampire King of North America.*

"We received the commission for the new Vampires in Transition facility," her father was saying, "I panicked. Stupidly, I thought I could place a few bets to earn the money back, but I can't do it anymore. I've been losing miserably and I just can't do this to Rachelle again. I've managed to stop. I've put the properties in Chicago on the market, but they're not selling."

Evangeline heard the desperation in her father's voice and her heart went out to him. She was hurt, of course, that he had fallen back into gambling, but like he said, he was doing it for his family. He was desperate.

But to steal from the vampire king...

She was really scared now. What would the king do to her father?

How on earth could they pay him back if her father's accounts were indeed empty?

"He came to my office a couple days ago..." There was a heavy note to her father's voice. "Told me he knew and threw his ultimatum on the table." She'd never heard him so despondent before.

"You have to tell her, Geoffrey. She needs to know soon so she can take the time to let it all sink in. It's asking a lot, of course, but Evangeline will see reason."

Evangeline furrowed her brow in confusion at the mention of her name. Surely her father was worried to tell the entire family about what he'd done. Why did

Maxwell only mention her?

"I'm going to tell her tonight. God, how could I do this to my precious daughter?" Geoffrey Wolcott's voice was thick. "Tell me the rumors aren't true, Max. Tell me I'm not marrying my Evangeline off to the most ruthless womanizer on the entire continent."

****

Maxwell Jones sat in an armchair in his friend's office with both elbows resting on his knees, hands clasped. The tension building in the back of his neck was excruciating now when he thought of the events of the past few months.

Maxwell's work on the Mediation Committee was extraordinary. He and his colleague formed it twenty years ago and had managed to maintain the peace in Illinois until now. The disputes among the werewolves and vampires in Wilmington were getting way out of hand. He'd managed to keep the human population ignorant for a while, but talk in a small town spread faster than he could blink.

It had started a few months ago with the murder of Tyson Maury on the Midewin hunting grounds. Tyson was a member of the Blacktail werewolf pack and the bite mark on his neck indicated he had been bitten by a vampire and then shot with a hunting rifle. From then on it had been one strike after another. Members of the Blacktail pack going missing along with a few Wilmington vampires.

Maxwell was working overtime to get to the bottom of all the kidnappings, but tension continued to flare between the two species.

Now his good friend was in trouble with none other than the head of the North American vampires.

Cyrus Stewart. *The king.*

He truly felt for his friend. Maxwell hoped Evangeline's fascination with vampires might intrigue her to at least consider the marriage. Hell, she invested most of her time researching the supernatural. She might even enjoy being married to a vampire.

Who was he kidding?

Evangeline was so headstrong. Geoffrey would be lucky if she ever spoke to him again.

There was a sudden bang as the door to the office flew open and slammed against the wall. Evangeline Wolcott stood on the threshold looking shocked, hurt, and confused all at once. Max stared for a moment at his friend's daughter, forgetting in an instant what was going on.

Evangeline was one of the most beautiful women he had ever seen.

Her deep burgundy hair contrasted strikingly with classic features causing even the women in town to admire her beauty. Her nose was straight and dainty above full lips, but it was her olive green eyes, which simply melted a man's soul.

Maxwell was a happily married man with a son about Evangeline's age. He felt slightly guilty for staring at Geoffrey's daughter. He had known her since she was a little girl, but even then, her beauty was astounding. Anyone, man or woman, was hard pressed to look away.

Standing tall in the doorway, her chest heaved in rapid succession. She wore jeans that seemed to be made for her toned body and a black V-neck top. The heels she wore brought her to nearly six feet in height.

"What did you say?" Evangeline moved slowly

into the room, her eyes wide and glued to her father.

Walking over to his daughter, Geoffrey raised a hand toward her, but she waved it away.

"I want to know what is going on and I want to know now!" She glanced at Max during her tirade and her long, thick hair spilled over her left shoulder.

"What did you hear, Evangeline?" her father asked. Resigned to allow his daughter the space she needed, he stepped over to stand by his mahogany desk.

"Everything from stealing three million from Cyrus Stewart." She looked miserably at her father for a moment. "Why did you keep the fact you're broke away from your family? My God, Daddy, we could have tried to help you come up with a feasible solution."

"Angel, I didn't want to worry my girls. Please, let me explain—"

"Explain to me how marrying me off to some stranger is going to help pay off Cyrus Stewart. Has this...what did you call him... *ruthless womanizer* offered to pay the three million on your behalf?"

Maxwell and Geoffrey both looked at her for a moment then turned to one another. She hadn't heard the *entire* conversation.

Their shared glance was not lost on Evangeline. "What? What am I missing here?"

"Evangeline, Cyrus Stewart has offered to let me keep the money."

Her eyes narrowed. "Why would he do that?"

"Because *he* wants you to be his wife."

****

Evangeline was trying her damnedest to get a hold of her emotions. She stared at her father as if she were looking at a stranger. He seemed shorter to her, not the six-foot-two-inch man he was. He didn't look like the man who'd stayed up late with her to play scrabble or to read her stories when she was a little girl. His gray hair seemed more pronounced than it had this morning when they had shared breakfast on the terrace. Geoffrey Wolcott had aged a decade in a matter of a day.

Maxwell had intervened during her father's explanation, playing mediator as always and urging her to sit down and listen to what had transpired with her father and the vampire king.

"Why on earth would Cyrus Stewart want to marry me? He's never even met me." Evangeline was eerily calm. She decided she should get all the facts first then blow up later.

"Evidently, he's seen you on several occasions." Her father was sitting down as well, choosing the chair Maxwell had vacated, while Max stood by the window behind her father's desk. "He first saw you at the Wilmington Education Fundraiser last year, then a few times in town. I believe he was also at your recital last month."

Evangeline cringed inwardly at this news. At last month's recital the director of Valentino's Dance Studio made all the instructors dance with the children. She'd fainted the instant she'd left the stage. "Unbelievable," she breathed. "He's been spying on me?" The men in the room chose not to answer this specific question.

The whole situation was still not sinking in. It was almost comical what was happening. She was waiting for her father or Max to tell her this was all a joke. The grim expressions they both wore, however, gave her no hope of that happening.

Taking a deep breath, she said, "He can't force this on me, can he?" She looked around at Maxwell, flustered. "There are laws...hell...I have rights."

Maxwell came toward her now and leaned back on her father's desk with his arms crossed. "Technically he is not breaking any laws. Cyrus Stewart can replace the money for the Transition Facility out of pocket so there will be no need for an investigation." Maxwell looked like he had been thinking long and hard about the situation, assessing every angle. "Now, as you know, humans and vampires can marry." He put up his hand before she could cut in. "As for forcing you to marry, our laws don't exactly apply to the vampire king and the vampire legislature have no power when it comes to him. They have no laws against blackmailing anyway. As your father said, he can basically do whatever he wants. He can't force you down the aisle, not if he wants to maintain his political status, but he has put you between a rock and a hard place. Now, that's not to say he can't see reason. I propose you meet with him tomorrow evening—"

"Are you serious?"

"Yes. Listen, your father and I may not be able to do anything about this situation, but you can. His Grace has asked you to join him for dinner tomorrow at his coven. Talk with him, Evangeline. I believe, if he is as enthralled with you as he says he is, then he'll see what this is doing to you and he may have a change of heart."

"He doesn't have a heart, Max," Evangeline said forlornly, looking him dead in the eye.

Maxwell didn't say anything more. She was glad, too. Every word he said was disheartening and unfortunately true.

Evangeline leaned forward to put her head in her hands. The room was becoming extremely warm and she was beginning to feel dizzy. A thought came to her then and an anxious laugh rose out of her. She glanced up at her father and Max, who looked like they were seriously worried she was losing her mind.

"I have a date tomorrow with Richard. We're supposed to go to the movies."

"Angel..." Her father reached for her hand and refused to let her pull away.

She nodded at him, letting him know he didn't have to explain. There wasn't going to be a date tomorrow night with Richard. She was going to meet the vampire king. She had been picturing this moment for years, and now she had the chance to meet a vampire in the flesh and all she could feel was anger and anxiety. This was all wrong.

Evangeline continued to sit motionless, staring dejected at the floor. "What if I refuse?"

Geoffrey looked at her poignantly. The creases around his eyes more pronounced now than ever. She knew what would happen if she refused the king, but she had to hear it. Somehow, hearing the words from her father would give her the push she needed to go through with this.

"Then, I will be called before the vampire tribunal." Evangeline squeezed her eyes shut as her father continued, fighting the tears now threatening to spill. "I think you know what will happen there, but as I am human, I'll be sentenced to a human prison. There will be no more income and your mother and sister will be left with nothing. We will lose everything."

He was right. They had no other family and nowhere to go. The Wolcott family had been a part of Wilmington for years, but gambling and a bad economy had swallowed up their fortune. Their good name was all they had, but if her father went to prison, it would be gone too.

"I can pay him back. I'll start up more classes. I can help out with the bills," Evangeline put in weakly, knowing full well her meager salary at Valentino's could never support her entire family and pay Cyrus Stewart the money her father owed.

Geoffrey's hands shook in hers. He looked as if he were fighting a battle in his head as his eyes glossed over. He remained silent, staring miserably at her.

She never disrespected her father by cursing in front of him, but now seemed to be the perfect time to toss her manners out the window.

"I can't believe this. I can't *fucking* believe this."

****

Mona Vance closed the bedroom door behind her and stepped into the elaborate master suite in the King's Coven. Her body reacted instantly to the man sitting in front of the fire with stunning urgency. The king sat with his beautiful profile to her. The fire, blazing to his left, cast him in a silhouette of massive, sexual masculinity.

She felt herself moisten in excitement at his large frame filled so alluringly with self-confidence. Mona both loved and hated how her thoughts always returned to the enigmatic king.

Cyrus Stewart looked up from his favorite lounger and stared languidly at her. His black eyes gleamed in the dim light. As usual he seemed distracted, in a different place, never giving her the attention she craved.

She didn't care. She wanted this powerful man and she wanted him now. Twice a week, she would sneak away from her weak, balding husband and give herself to this man in any way he desired. Mona had done things she had never dreamed in a million years she would do.

Staring longingly at the massive king-sized bed behind him, she wished he would go to her, lift her up in his arms and take her there. Alas, Cyrus simply turned his head and continued to gaze forward.

Mona walked slowly over to him in the skimpy red dress she had worn just for him, swaying her hips provocatively. Bending down in front of him, she gave him an ample view of the D-cups spilling out of her dress. "I've been dying to see you all day." Her breathy voice shook with excitement.

Cyrus did not return the smile. Instead, he simply continued to stare at her as she knelt in front of him. "Really?" he asked as he took a long swig from the glass of amber liquid in his hands. He continued to hold the glass as he placed an arm on each side of his chair. He looked at her with little interest. She felt insignificant, ignored, alone.

Mona tilted her head to the side, trying with all her might to entice him. She wanted to hear more of his sexy voice. He spoke from a different time and it drove her crazy. Cyrus Stewart was born in Painswick, England in 1750. He had been turned during the American Revolution when he fought against the colonists at the age of 25.

The king continued to look bored, but his stony

expression did not deter Mona. Cyrus looked good enough to devour. Having discarded his suit jacket and tie, he lounged with his delicious pecs peeking through the top of his dress shirt.

He watched as her hands slid slowly over his thighs and up his body. As usual, Cyrus kept his body temperature warm by keeping near fires and sipping hot drinks. Mona guessed the drink in his hand was Grand Marnier, heated. She looked down at his pants then up at him.

Cyrus knew what she wanted and gave a small nod of his head to indicate she could proceed.

Mona did not waste another second, and reached forward fervently. She unbuckled and unzipped with skill then reached up to pull down on his briefs. His erection appeared in all its glory, huge and golden in the firelight.

Smiling to herself, she grasped the base of his member and slipped it in her mouth, taking him to the hilt. She took long draws, relishing the feel and smell of him. Her head bobbed over him again and again, the skin of his shaft sliding easily over her tongue. The only sound coming from the room was the sound of her wet mouth moving over his slick sex. She waited to hear moaning or feel a hand on her head, urging her to go on, but none came. Feeling a little perturbed, she made her movements faster, sucking him hard, filling her mouth with him until her jaw locked.

Her efforts were rewarded when she heard the click of his fangs elongate, a wonderful sign he was very aroused. She moved her hair to one side and glanced at his hand. It gripped the arm of the chair and when his knuckles turned white, she knew he was about to finish.

His thighs tightened underneath her arms and his hips jerked up.

Instead of releasing him to let him spill himself on her chest, she kept him inside her mouth, letting him fill her up with his juices. As he pumped once, twice, and once more into her hot mouth, she felt her own body climax and she reached around to grab his ass, loving him in her arms and in her mouth.

When they were both spent, Mona lazily lifted her head to gaze at her lover. Cyrus watched her lick her swollen lips and smirked.

"Well, aren't we eager today." His voice was smooth and laced with conceit.

His fangs retracted as he reached down to zip up his pants and stood up, leaving her on the floor in front of the chair.

"The Alderman is a lucky man, Mrs. Vance." Cyrus slipped his shirt in his pants and walked over to the bed to retrieve his jacket.

"I don't want to talk about my husband with you, Cyrus." She stood up gracefully and moved toward him. The king usually fed from her when they were together and she couldn't wait for him to be inside her again with his glorious fangs sheathed in her skin.

Cyrus put a hand up and said, "You should refrain from calling me Cyrus from now on, Mrs. Vance. It's Your Grace."

Her face fell. "Uh…if that's what you want. I'll call you whatever you like."

"You won't have to call me anything, my dear. You're services are no longer needed. As of today, I am spoken for." He turned back to the side table near the chair he just vacated to pick up the glass. He downed the rest of his drink and slammed it back on the marble. To add to the chill she felt run through her, he willed the fire in the hearth to die out with his mind and the room's cozy atmosphere instantly vanished.

"What are you talking about?" Mona asked. Hurt and anxiety filled her chest.

"I am engaged to be married and I have no further use for you." He put both hands in his pant pockets and looked at her. She saw his Adam's apple shift up, then down.

"Engaged?"

"Yes. My intended will visit tomorrow night." Cyrus put on a look as if he were actually moral bound and placed a hand on his chest. "How could I face my fiancé with another lover waiting in the wings? No, no. That won't do."

The shout burning to come out was stifled by a knock on the bedroom door.

"Come in," Cyrus called out.

The king's enormous nineteenth-century manservant walked in, filling the entire doorframe. He scared the hell out of Mona. His expression always gave the impression of a cold-blooded murderer and his deep baritone was even scarier than his face.

"Your Grace, Mr. Wolcott just called to confirm dinner tomorrow with his daughter. Evangeline will arrive at eight." He waited for a response.

Jealousy oozed through Mona like a heat wave. How could the bastard do this to her? He was *engaged* to Evangeline Wolcott, that spoiled ballet dancer, but he had let Mona blow him off one last time?

Prick.

"Wonderful, Victor. Thank you." Cyrus marched to

the door to precede his manservant out of the room. He paused for a moment to look at Mona. "Victor, will you see Mrs. Vance out?"

"Of course, Your Grace."

Chapter Two

The sun had descended over Wilmington, falling out of sight on the other side of the west woods. Jason Linus drove south through the summer evening, heading toward Adam's octagonal home on Water Street. The black pick-up cruised at about fifty miles per hour with the windows rolled down and the radio off. Jason preferred the quiet hum of his truck to any loud nonsense on the radio. His shoulder length hair blew in the wind and his natural scowl was in place.

He had no idea why Adam summoned him. His friend didn't give any details when he'd called twenty minutes ago. Jason had been on his knees working on a leaky pipe under the kitchen sink of his apartment. When he'd pressed the end button on his cell, he'd tossed back the last few sips of his beer and grabbed his keys. When the alpha called, you went, plain and simple. There were no arguments and no questions. Even if Jason didn't want to go, he was still honored bound to the alpha of the pack. As the Blacktail beta, it was essential for Jason to stand next to his master at all meetings.

Jason pulled up to the front of the round house. He got out, stuffed the keys in his jean pocket and walked up to the front door. As he waited for one of the pack members to answer the door, Jason thought about Tyson. The Blacktails, in retaliation of their pack member's murder, had captured and killed two vampires. But there was something still nagging Jason from that day. Tyson did not have any evidence of a vampire encounter, other than the bite marks on his neck. Why had they not been able to smell a vampire on his clothes? Why was he shot in the chest when a vampire could kill with their bare hands?

Nevertheless, the two bloodsuckers they had managed to capture deserved what they got, a long and gruesome death, befitting a nasty species.

After Tyson was found, two of his fellow Fighters cornered a vampire in a deserted alley one night. Before the vampire could teleport, they grabbed him and morphed enough to bite him, making it impossible for the son of a bitch to travel anywhere.

Adam caught the second vampire during the last full moon. Jason witnessed the grisly encounter. Luckily, what was left of the bloodsucker had incinerated in the sun.

Since then, two members of the Blacktail pack had gone missing. One of them was Adam's younger sister, Serena Perez. The other missing werewolf was Benjamin Michaels, the town's librarian. The pack had taken up searching for them in pairs, rotating shifts.

Jason finished a four-hour shift last night with no luck. There was no hint of Serena or Benjamin anywhere around Wilmington. Their hopes of finding their pack members alive grew dimmer by the day.

He was jerked out of his thoughts when Adam answered the door. Jason nodded his head in greetings. "Hey."

Adam Perez was huge with black wavy hair and piercing blue eyes. His face was grim as usual these days and he sported dark shadows like he hadn't slept. The alpha resembled his mother in so many ways, but Adam's dark coloring and black hair were from his Mexican ancestors, along with strong facial features permanently sculpted in a stressed expression.

The pack leader was usually in control, a Fighter through and through. But from the moment Serena had gone missing, Adam lost it.

He searched everywhere, day and night, pushing the pack to find her. He believed his sister was still alive and his desperation to find her was weighing on all of them.

The man standing in the doorway was a complete mess.

"Hey, J. Come in." Adam moved aside to let Jason through and closed the door behind him.

"Why are you answering the door? Where's Ramo?" Jason asked, his deep, solemn voice was always at the same pitch, low and subdued. He looked around at the empty foyer. The octagon house, dubbed "the round house" by his pack had a wide spiraling staircase placed directly in the middle, which spanned up to the second floor. The foyer, living room, kitchen, and dining room encircled the stairs on the first floor. It was quiet in the house, which was not the case when the pack Fighters came together.

There were twelve—eleven now with Tyson gone—in the Blacktail Fighters and they worked together to protect their pack. Six—now five—members resided in Wilmington with the alpha while the other six patrolled in Chicago, taking care of the remaining Blacktails in the city.

"He's not here. I didn't call anyone else." The

alpha's voice echoed somberly in the hall.

"I thought we were having another meeting…" Jason started.

"It's just you and me," Adam said brusquely as he walked around Jason and marched through the dining room to the left of the foyer and into the spacious, empty living room.

Jason followed his friend, growing more curious by the minute. His friend's presence in the quaint home always baffled Jason. Adam looked like an enormous beast that didn't belong.

They entered Adam's cozy living room decorated in reds and browns with thick velvet drapes and plush sofas. The paintings on the walls hung there since the nineteenth century and depicted watercolors of the countryside.

Adam stopped in the middle of the room and motioned for Jason to have a seat on one of the sofas. Jason sat and waited for Adam to explain what was going on, but his friend simply stared at the floor with his hands on his hips. Jason wasn't the chatty type either, but what was the sense of him coming over here if his friend wasn't going to speak.

"Adam, what the fuck? Talk man."

Adam looked up and nodded seriously. "Ok." The look on his face was freaking Jason out. And Jason never freaked out. Whatever Adam had to say must be serious, because the guy looked like he was about to kill his best friend.

Oh, shit.

"Adam—"

"I have an assignment for you," Adam finally said.

He relaxed a little. "Sure, ok. What do you need?"

Adam looked away again, focusing on the end table to the right of the sofa. "You're going to judge me, but, fortunately for me, you have to do it."

Jason raised an eyebrow.

"We've been hitting dead ends out there, but I haven't lost hope…" Adam stopped and raised his hands like he'd given up. Without further preamble he said, "Fuck this. You're kidnapping Cyrus Stewart's fiancé tomorrow night."

****

Jason's usual stern expression suddenly shifted. For the first time in a long time, Jason looked totally baffled.

Adam sat on the love seat across from Jason, elbows on his knees, hands clasped tight in deep concentration.

Tension ebbed through his shoulders. He sat across from his long time friend and beta, wishing to God there were another option.

He thought about the call he'd received an hour ago.

Mona was a crafty bitch. He'd met her two months ago in Joliet, at some dive bar where she flirted with him outlandishly. He knew who she was and knew her husband, the Alderman, associated with vampires. Before making her acquaintance he'd followed her for days, learning her secret rendezvous with men, women, and the supernatural. After a very long and strange conversation, Adam offered Mona five grand to seduce Cyrus Stewart and become his new plaything while collecting information for the pack. Mona didn't hesitate and agreed on the spot. He suspected Mona had her eye on the king anyway, as did a lot wives in

Wilmington. His little trust in her had dwindled, however, until today.

He didn't hear from Mona for nearly six weeks. He was sure she had fallen in love with the vampire king and had no wish to fulfill her duties to the Blacktail pack. Adam didn't worry she'd sell him out. The vampire king would kill her instantly if he knew what she had agreed to do. Adam had recorded their entire conversation.

Finally tonight, Mona called with some interesting news.

Cyrus Stewart planned to marry Evangeline Wolcott, daughter of one of Wilmington's prominent and wealthiest men. Adam had never met Evangeline, but he knew who she was, as did everyone. The moment he'd heard the news, the wheels in his head started turning.

It was crazy to even contemplate kidnapping a human, but Adam was running out of ideas. He was certain Cyrus was behind his sister's kidnapping. Serena and Benjamin were not Fighters. They were easy prey for a monster like Cyrus. As Adam saw it, the only way he was getting his sister back, was to take something of the vampire king's.

"What?" Jason spoke up from across the coffee table, where he lounged on the sofa with one arm draped around the back and the other in his lap. Jason wore his usual garb of blue jeans and a black t-shirt. His beta's hazel eyes watched as he waited for Adam to explain.

"Cyrus plans on marrying sometime soon and I want you to kidnap his fiancé. I know where she lives and the general layout of her home." Adam stopped at the look on Jason's face.

"Are you joking?" Jason asked incredulously.

"No."

Jason sat up. Clearly, he'd realized Adam meant business. "You want me to kidnap a female vamp and—"

"She's human."

"What?" Jason nearly shouted and leaned toward Adam. "Are you out of your mind? Do you know what kidnapping a human would start?"

"Yeah, I'm very aware." Adam stood up again and began pacing the room, running his fingers through his hair. His first plan was to gather all the Fighters and storm the King's Coven during the day, but vampires didn't necessarily sleep when the sun was up and breaking into the coven was virtually impossible. Even if they managed to break in, what if they couldn't find her? Adam ran the risk of losing pack members. "Look, I am going out of my mind imagining all kinds of shit my sister is going through. I know the bastard has her and the only way I'm going to get her back is if I threaten his fiancé. It's the only solution I've got. If you were in my position, you would do the same thing."

Jason just stared at him. He knew exactly how Adam felt. Werewolves, especially the Fighters, could feel the other's emotions. Slowly but surely, Jason was beginning to see things through Adam's eyes.

Damn emotional bond.

"Adam, are you sure this is what you want to do? If you give me your final word then I'll do it, but I want you to be absolutely fucking sure."

Adam had to give his friend credit for being a little more understanding as opposed to the other Fighters.

He could just hear Ramo's big ass mouth telling him how stupid the plan was. Jason, however, was a dedicated Fighter. He did what was necessary for the pack and Adam knew he'd do anything to bring back Serena.

Adam nodded gravely. "I want you to keep this between us for now. If I think about it any longer, I'm going to go fucking nuts. So here's the plan…"

****

Evangeline lifted her head from the crook of her arm and watched her sister come into her room through swollen eyes and a runny nose. The spacious room was purple with beige furnishings. A queen-sized bed lay between her two nightstands adorned with books and a chaise near the window. Her sister shut the door quietly and turned to face Evangeline.

Katherine's angelic face softened. She stood for a moment by the door in her skinny jeans and loose, cotton V-neck with concern written all over her face. The tables had turned on the girls. Katherine was three years younger than Evangeline and it was usually Evangeline swooping into *her* room trying to solve a problem Katherine managed to find herself in.

At the age of nineteen, Katherine Wolcott was a bit too curious in her family's opinion. Her sweet face belied the fact she was nosey, outspoken, and irrational and the Wolcott family counted their blessings every day that Katherine lived to be the young woman standing in front of her. Ten years ago her sister nearly died of leukemia. Memories of the awful ordeal caused the family to frequently overlook her outlandish ways.

She sat on Evangeline's four-poster bed and wrapped her in her arms. Evangeline savored her sister's hug and unleashed more tears. Her soft cries were muffled in Katherine's honey-colored hair. She soothed Evangeline with soft words and gentle rocking.

The Wolcott sisters were both beautiful in their own way. Evangeline looked like their mother with deep red hair and green eyes while Katherine took after their father, sharing the same honey-colored hair and dark eyes. Katherine was also shorter than her sister at five feet, four inches tall and had a little more meat on her bones, whereas Evangeline was fit and statuesque, Katherine was more curvy and voluptuous. The only similarities between them were their full lips and almond-shaped eyes.

Evangeline finally pulled away from her sister, closed her eyes briefly and took a deep breath. "I guess everyone knows now."

"Yeah. Dad just told us at dinner. Needless to say, none of us ate. Mom's been crying ever since. I think she's too scared to face you." Katherine rolled her eyes. "I can't believe this is happening." Katherine reached for the Kleenex box on the nightstand and handed it to her sister.

Evangeline wiped her eyes again and blew her nose. At first she'd wanted to be present when her father gave the family the news. She wanted to be there for her mother, to reassure her everything was going to work out fine, but her emotions had other plans. The fact was she didn't know if everything was going to be fine. Hell, how did they know Cyrus Stewart would keep his word? She kept imagining the worst possible scenarios; locked up in the King's Coven, while her father rotted in jail and her mother and sister wandered the streets begging.

Evangeline retreated to her eerie calm mode again. She kept telling herself crying wasn't going to solve anything, but as soon as she thought of the plans she had made for the future, or leaving her family's home, her tears got the better of her.

"I'm so mad right now I could scream. What was Dad thinking, gambling again? We were so past that. It's like he was possessed," Katherine said, her eyebrows furrowing over her deep brown eyes.

Evangeline looked up at her sister, a thought coming to her. Katherine stared back questioningly. Evangeline chose to keep the thought to herself. She could tell Katherine was very upset and she worried about getting her too excited. She'd been in and out of remission but, for some odd reason, whenever Katherine would get overly upset she'd be back in the hospital. For the past three years she'd managed to stay in remission, and luckily chemotherapy, surgery and Evangeline had kept her sister from reliving that dreadful time.

It was then Evangeline discovered *her* supernatural power.

A simple, yet devastatingly draining act of placing her hand on Katherine's chest healed her sister when she'd been at death's door. Unfortunately, Katherine still couldn't handle a lot of stress. Over the years Evangeline would heal her sister to spare her from going to the hospital, but her healing efforts severely weakened Evangeline and would render her useless for extraordinarily long periods of time.

The Wolcott family decided to keep Evangeline's healing capabilities quiet. God only knew what would happen if word got out she could cure the sick and wounded.

"What?" her sister asked.

Evangeline shook herself. "Nothing." She leaned back against her headboard, determined to toughen up for her sister's sake. "Look, I'm going to meet the king tomorrow night and hopefully I can persuade him to forget this stupid plan and allow us to pay him back over time. I mean seriously, what century does he think we're living in?"

Katherine shrugged and shook her head. They both stayed silent for a while as they thought about the crazy predicament their family was in. Katherine traced a pattern on the bed with her finger and Evangeline stared off into space with her arms crossed.

Of course, Katherine broke the silence.

She looked up, her expression hesitant as if she was sure Evangeline was going to blow up any minute. "I have a feeling Cyrus Stewart won't let you go."

Evangeline's panic-stricken face did not deter Katherine.

"Come on, Eva, you're the prettiest girl in town. The guy had to settle down some time and once he sets his sight on something, it's usually his for the taking. I'm not saying it's right, and I'm really pissed he thinks he can take you away from us, but aren't you a little curious?"

"What the hell are you talking about, Katherine? Curious about what?" Evangeline stared at her sister as if she'd lost her mind.

"Aren't you curious about how it would be to live with a vampire? What's more, *married* to one? You've been fascinated by them for most of your life, and now you'll be married to one of the most powerful vampires in the world." Katherine's eyes grew bigger and bigger as she became more excited.

Evangeline had to remind herself that her sister could be very naïve at times. She sat up and ran her fingers through her hair, down her neck and finally clasped them together in her lap, hoping the gesture would calm her nerves. "I know you want to make me feel better, Kat, but please, stop talking."

"Okay. I'm sorry." Katherine had the decency to look sheepish and got up from the four-poster and walked over to the window.

Before Evangeline could slip into her I-hate-my-life state of mind, Katherine whirled around.

"What the hell are you going to tell Richard?"

Chapter Three

Henry Wolcott, Evangeline's great-great grandfather purchased the two-story house in Wilmington, Illinois back in the nineteenth century. It sat on a vast expanse of land on the north side of a creek just fifty miles south of Chicago. Evangeline walked through the first floor hall next to Richard in a daze. She'd called him over to tell him the bad news in person and they were now heading out through the back terrace and into the gardens. She didn't stop along the extended path, but continued on, turning left toward the creek, all the while silent as the grave.

The day mocked her sorrowful mood. The sun was still out this August evening with no cloud in sight and a light breeze in the air. It would have been a nice night for a stroll if she didn't have to ruin it with a break-up.

Richard was a high school math teacher at Wilmington High. His daughter was in one of Evangeline's ballet classes for five and six year olds.

Evangeline hadn't had many boyfriends. Men were too intimidated by her wealth and beauty.

After a year of mild flirtation, Richard finally asked her out. They had only been dating three weeks, but things had been going smoothly. Relaxed and well mannered at the age of thirty-one, Richard was of medium built and stood only about an inch or two taller than Evangeline.

She glanced in his direction and smiled nervously, having no idea how to broach the subject. Should she tell him the truth or make up a lie? Getting more people involved made her uncomfortable, but Evangeline didn't want to hurt him either by lying. She decided to go with half-truth and let the cards fall as they may.

They were out of the gardens now and headed toward a small wooden bridge. The view from the middle was picturesque. From where they stood, they could see the sun begin to set behind the house, the gardens, the creek, and the woods. The bridge stretched about eight yards over the creek and onto the other side where it met a thin trail into the Midewin woods.

"You look beautiful as ever tonight," Richard said.

Evangeline silently cursed herself. She'd told Richard over the phone she could not make their date tonight, but needed to talk to him in person. Now, here she was, in a black strapless, cocktail dress and stilettos. Richard probably thought she was blowing him off for another guy. Well…wasn't she?

Richard grabbed her left hand from the bridge's rail and turned her toward him. "What's wrong, Eva? Talk to me."

She looked at his soft eyes and imagined what it would be like to marry a man like Richard. He was a good father, sweet and caring and she knew he would take good care of her. Their relationship, if she could call it that, was just barely taking off with few dates a week and a couple of make out sessions. Evangeline was attracted to him, but she wished there were a little more heat between them. She thought they'd have time to build on this, but it looked like fate had other plans. Scratch that. Not fate, but Cyrus Stewart.

Evangeline held onto his warm hands as she spoke. "Richard, I'm sorry, but I'm not going to be able to see you again." She hoped she didn't sound cold or heartless. She had never broken up with someone before. Her last real boyfriend had been her first and he ended up taking off without a word.

Richard stiffened and he frowned. He looked down at their hands before speaking. "Why?" His voice came out different, deeper than it naturally was.

She took a deep breath. "My family is going through a rough time right now and unfortunately, it has put me in a very difficult position. I can't bring you into this and I think it's best if we just remained friends." There, she wasn't exactly lying and it wasn't too harsh.

He looked up at her. "Whatever it is, I'll help you through it, Eva. Let me be there for you." He gripped her hands tightly.

Damn it, she knew this was going to be hard. She wished she could give him a better explanation, but what could she say? *My family is broke so I'm going to marry the vampire king. It was nice knowing you.* Maybe she should tell him the real truth, but she wasn't ready to face reality yet and she couldn't let him hang in the balance while she attempted to sort the situation out. As if she had any say in the matter. Her sister was right. Evangeline had little hope of persuading Cyrus Stewart to call off the engagement.

She looked at him with a small smile and hoped her expression looked less tense. "I really wish things were different. I wish I could tell you more, but I can't. I don't want to drag you into this mess. I'll understand if you don't want to be friends, but I hope you'll still bring Jalynn to her lessons."

She tried to back away slowly, but Richard reached around her and pulled her into his arms. His slight force surprised her. Richard was always gentle with her. "I'm not going to fight you on this. You do what you need to do for your family, but I'm not going anywhere."

"Richard, you can't—"

"Don't," he warned as he reached up and held her chin in his hand, his other firmly held her against his body. He was lean and hard. It was the first time she felt a measure of excitement in his arms. *Now of all times...*

He leaned in and placed a soft kiss on her mouth. Evangeline let him kiss her, thinking this might be the last time she'd enjoy it.

There was a sudden rumble of some kind, a low growl and they both jumped. They looked around and saw nothing. Richard half turned and looked into the woods, his gaze searching. Evangeline looked too, but the trees were thick and all she saw was green everywhere.

"You heard that, right?" he asked.

"Yeah. It sounded like a growl, but I don't see anything."

"Let's get you inside." He grabbed her hand and they walked back toward the house, completely unaware of the wolf hidden beyond the trees.

****

What the hell is wrong with him?

The Blacktail alpha silently turned and trotted off further into the Midewin woods. Adam ran, in full werewolf form, at a slow pace. Always in stealth mode, his paws lightly hit the forest floor as he went.

Contrary to fantasy belief, true werewolves were

able to shift whenever they wanted. It was only during the full moon they had no say in the matter. They had to shift.

He shook his furry black mane from his eyes. Adam had gone to assess the layout of the Wolcott estate on his own. Jason was setting up at the cabin in the far northwest region of the woods. They were meeting up to plan the strategy of getting Cyrus' fiancé out of the house. Adam had located a side entrance to the Wolcott estate which would be easy enough to open. Once inside, Jason could sniff out Evangeline's bedroom. Earlier, they had broken into Evangeline's studio and found her locker with a sweater and a pair of worn out slippers inside. They'd use her scent to locate her in the house.

What Adam had not anticipated, was running into Evangeline herself. He'd caught sight of her with some guy as soon as they'd left the house. Werewolves had great vision and even as far as she was, Adam could see she was stunning.

He should have left the second he saw her, but something compelled him to get a closer look. Standing on his hind legs, as werewolves were basically man-shaped wolves, and not shapeshifters, walked along the forest edge as they came closer. His gaze remained riveted on her.

As he drew closer, he reached out with his extra hearing senses to listen to their conversation. She was dumping the poor bastard.

He snorted to himself. She was probably a spoiled little heartless bitch. Engaged to Cyrus Stewart now, so she had to let go of all her other lovers. He thought of leaving until she spoke again. Without realizing it, he made several more steps closer to the couple.

Her voice was melodic and Adam found himself staring at her, hard. His nostrils flared as he took a deep breath. Yep. The sweater in the ballet studio was definitely hers. Adam's eyes felt heavy in an instant as he breathed in her sweet scent. *Jesus*.

He shouldn't have cared, but he wanted to feel her emotion, to see if she was as genuine as she sounded. As soon as he was close enough, he picked up on a pretty strong feeling. Surprised at what his senses read, Adam took in the overwhelming sorrow that engulfed her. She was hurting, bad.

Before Adam could process her feelings, he picked up on Ol' boy's emotion. The guy went from devastated to aroused in a second. He watched as the guy grabbed her, pulled her tightly against him and planted one right on her full lips.

Adam wasn't aware of his reaction until he saw the two of them jump and glance in his direction. He realized too late the rumble they'd heard had come from him.

Why the hell had he reacted like that? What did he care if this girl wanted to get her fill of a man before she married another?

Adam picked up the pace and reached the old cabin deep in the woods about fifteen minutes later. He could have made the trip in two minutes if he wasn't all up in his head.

Jason stepped out of the cabin and down the wide steps leading up to the small front porch. His second in command watched as he shifted back into human form. The process was never a pretty sight. The sound of shifting bones and tendons reverberated in the air as

Adam shrank back to his six foot six inch frame. When it was done, Adam's huge naked body was on all fours. He stood up fast, used to the pain involved and brushed it off without a care.

His beta held out a pair of jeans and t-shirt. Adam took the clothes and put them on. "Everything set?" he asked as he thrust one leg into the jeans.

Jason stuck one hand in his back pocket and gestured toward the house with the other. "Yeah. I put bars on all the windows. The back door is nailed shut and she's not getting past me to the front door. The bedroom is clean and there is food in the fridge. We'll have air conditioning and water too, but it looks like the weather is gonna be cool."

Adam had flinched a little at the mention of "bedroom" and "*we'll* have air conditioning." Before he could stop himself he stepped, barefoot, up to the cabin's steps. "Change of plans. *I'm* getting her."

****

Evangeline asked her family to give her a little space as she prepared to leave for the King's Coven. She sat at the vanity in her bedroom, checking her make-up to be sure there were no signs of tears. Her father had asked her to dress in appropriate attire, but all she wanted to do was throw on her favorite jeans and t-shirt. She knew Cyrus would probably see this as an insult, but what did she care?

She reminded herself she was doing this for her family. Besides, perhaps the famous vampire king would have a change of heart and release her from the engagement. He did have a heart. It just didn't beat.

Evangeline forced herself to get up and walk out of her room. In the hallway she ran into her mother. They had spoken earlier that morning. She'd tried to soothe her mother's worries, but Rachelle could not stop crying. Before they could both succumb to another bout of tears, Evangeline bent slightly and kissed her mother's cheek. "I'll be back, Mom."

Evangeline sounded as if she was just stepping out to get the paper, but she didn't want to worry her mother. She was so fragile. No, Evangeline was going to put on a calm façade...all was well. There was no point in crying over the matter anymore.

Rachelle didn't say anything. She returned the kiss, ran her hand over Evangeline's hair and let her go.

Evangeline was driving herself to the King's Coven. Her father had insisted he go along, but she refused. She didn't want to meet Cyrus Stewart veiled behind her father.

He was waiting in the foyer for her with Katherine. When she came down the last step, he came toward her. "Are you sure you don't want me to go with you? You've never been inside a vampire coven. It might be frightening for you."

In truth she was both scared and curious to see the inside of a coven, but she'd never tell her father of her fear. "I'll be fine, Daddy. They can't hurt me."

Geoffrey flinched. He looked at his daughter. She saw the anger, and panic he felt. Her father wanted to kill Cyrus, because he knew, as she did, the terms of a vampire betrothal, and it made him *sick*.

Chapter Four

The King's Coven was located on the west bank of the Kankakee River. In the nineteenth century it was once The Soldiers Widows' Home, founded by The Women's Relief Corps. In 1963 the ladies were moved to Quincy, Illinois and the home was left abandoned. In 1972, Cyrus Stewart purchased the home before it could be burnt down. The king had traveled for centuries and upon receiving the title of King of North America, decided to take up residence in the most quiet and remote places in the Midwest.

Evangeline had always admired Cyrus Stewart for saving the old home from destruction and choosing to live in a quaint little town like Wilmington. Those cozy feelings were now dead and gone, replaced with rage at his audacity and superiority.

The King's Coven, as it was referred to now, was three stories high with a winding porch along its perimeter. The king had made several renovations over the years and even added a wing to provide a better view of the river. On the outside it looked like a simple mansion with freshly cut grass and rosebushes on either side of the front steps. No one would ever suspect it was home to a number of vampires.

Evangeline drove past the open iron gates, taking a curious glance at the empty post where she assumed one of his guards were supposed to be on duty. She pulled into the long driveway and turned off the ignition. She sat for a moment before getting out of the car. Looking to the left, she saw a man walking away from her. He passed behind a tree and never reappeared. He simply vanished. Her heart leapt. The king had several vampire guardsmen. He must have been one of them. Evangeline wondered where the others lurked.

She turned to look in the review mirror and instantly felt eyes on her. They were watching her. The hairs on the back of her neck stood on end and she shivered slightly. Shutting down her cowardice, she stepped out of the car, hoping she wore her most calm expression. Evangeline refused to show her fear. After all, she had wanted to meet a vampire for ages and now she was going to meet a whole coven. She wasn't going to take out her hatred on vampires who had nothing to do with her predicament. There was only one vampire she hated.

As she approached the steps, a woman opened one of the two heavy front doors. Evangeline guessed she was about to meet her first vampire, if the woman's porcelain skin and cool demeanor were any indication. She had dark long hair and dark eyes, wearing a black scoop-necked silk blouse, and a white pencil skirt. Her high heels were the same Stuart Weitzman's Evangeline wore. She was beautiful, more than beautiful. Perfect. Her pale, fair skin seemed to sparkle and her hair had not one strand out of place. Evangeline thought she recognized the woman from television, but then she noticed the woman's avid expression.

They stared at each other appraisingly for a moment, one beautiful woman to another before she spoke. "Welcome, Miss Wolcott. Won't you come in?" Her voice was deep and husky. The woman didn't smile or sound as inviting as her words.

Evangeline nodded at the first vampire she'd ever seen up close and walked forward. She lifted her chin slightly, showing the female vampire she wasn't afraid and that she came willingly...kind of.

She stepped into the foyer with its gleaming hardwood floor and high ceilings. The staircase was something to behold. It took up the entire foyer with two separate flights of steps coming together at the top. The chandelier above looked like it once graced a European castle. Evangeline hadn't known what to expect, but clearly, the king fancied audacious décor. She guessed if anyone could get away with a castle-like home, it would be the vampire king.

As Evangeline took in her surroundings the door slammed shut behind her at the same time the female vampire instantly appeared in front of her with barely an inch to spare. Startled, Evangeline jumped back.

"Mary, stop showing off," a sweet voice said. Evangeline turned, her hand over her racing heart. A petite blond stood in an open doorway. She had kind blue eyes and a warm smile. By the looks of the tan line over her collarbones, she was also human. "Never mind Mary, Miss Wolcott, she's just trying to scare you. Please, come in and make yourself at home." She gestured toward the room she'd been in and Evangeline obliged, still a little shaken. Evangeline gave Mary a hard stare before turning toward the room, but the woman's flawless face didn't change from its serene expression.

With all these beautiful women in the coven, what

does Cyrus Stewart want with me?

She strode into a large modern parlor. Royal blue covered the walls and a massive brown U-shaped sectional sat in the middle of the room across from a large flat screen. The stereo was turned on and Evangeline recognized the overture to *The Marriage of Figaro*.

She turned to face the women. The dark-haired vampire, Mary, had followed them. She walked over to the sectional and sat, crossing her long legs.

The blonde woman held out her hand to Evangeline with a kind smile. "My name is Jane and this is my wife, Mary."

Oh.

Evangeline shook Jane's hand and turned to smile weakly at Mary. She knew most vampires didn't shake hands with humans. Mary didn't smile, but inclined her beautiful head. "It's nice to meet you," Evangeline said, more to Jane than to her bitch of a wife.

Jane gestured to the couch. "Please have a seat." She wore a blue A-line dress with spaghetti straps. It reached just above her tanned knees. Jane looked like she had once been a head cheerleader. "We were just playing a game of chess. Do you play?"

Evangeline sat on the other side of the sectional, crossing her legs at the ankle. A beautiful jeweled chessboard sat on the marble coffee table. "No, I've never learned."

"That's too bad," Jane said as she sat next to Mary, who leaned back casually against the cushions with one arm draped on the back of the couch behind her wife.

Jane, who seemed eager to have a houseguest, sat up straight, smiling at Evangeline.

"My goodness, where are my manners? Would you like something to drink? Wine, perhaps?" Jane was standing.

Evangeline wanted to refuse alcohol, but the woman was being so kind. She didn't want to appear rude. "Wine would be great. Thank you."

"Wonderful." Jane's lovely smile brightened.

"I'll get it, my love." Mary's sultry voice spilled over them as she stood, towering over Jane. She ran her porcelain hand down Jane's arm. The blonde shivered and gave her wife the most alluring smile. Jane stared after Mary for a moment, a warm blush on her cheeks.

Evangeline had thought she was in love once, but it was nothing compared to the love these two women obviously shared. Evangeline felt like she'd walked in on the two women making love. She felt her own cheeks burn and looked away to survey the artwork around the room. There were a lot of Picasso's and other works she didn't recognize. She noticed a huge sideboard just below one piece, complete with crystal decanters of some dark liquor and crystal glasses.

Mary walked over to a wall encased with small round holes where bottles upon bottles were shelved. It reached from the ceiling to the floor.

"So, I hear you're a dancer. How fantastic," Jane was saying and Evangeline returned her attention to her. "I took lessons when I was little, but I'm afraid I wasn't very good."

Dancing was the furthest thing from her mind right now. She wanted to ask Jane a million questions. She wanted to know how Jane came to live in a vampire coven. How did she meet Mary? Was she planning on turning herself? What did it feel like to be bitten? The questions were endless, but she couldn't ask her outright. She needed to be tactful. "Yes, I've been dancing since I was a little girl here in Wilmington. Did you grow up in our little town?"

"Oh, yes. I was actually born in the bedroom just above us."

"Really." Evangeline wore her sweet conversational smile. She glanced over at Mary and saw the woman was staring at her. Jane's wife smiled stiffly and lifted the two glasses she'd poured and walked over. Mary handed her a glass of red wine, her eyes never leaving Evangeline's.

Jane went on to explain happily how she came to be here as Mary handed her a glass and resumed her seat. "My parents are vampires and they adopted me. The king actually named me," she said with a bright smile. "My birth mother was only fifteen when she had me. She lives in California now. My mother is the king's lawyer and my father is on the Vampire Rights Council. He's on the Transition Committee and helped organize the new Vampire's in Transition facility."

Evangeline squirmed at the mention of the facility her father had stolen from. She wondered what this sweet girl would say if she mentioned that bit of news.

"Now I'm a supernatural researcher for the king, but I'm also getting my masters in finance," Jane continued as Mary gazed at her proudly. "Mary is one of the king's publicists. We met about three years ago when she interviewed for the position." She turned to smile at her wife. "I've lived here for twenty-five years. We have a condo in Chicago, but when we're working, we stay in the King's Coven. After all, I was born here," the girl ended breathlessly.

"And her blood type is O positive." Mary spoke, finally to tease Jane and spook Evangeline. She was surprised the woman knew how to joke.

Jane giggled and took a sip of wine.

Evangeline couldn't help her eyes from roaming over Jane's neck and down her arms. There were no visible bite marks. She knew vampires fed from their spouses and wondered if Jane covered them somehow. When she looked up, she saw Mary's eyes grow dark.

Oh, shit. Evangeline hoped Mary didn't think she was checking out her wife.

"I'll go see what's keeping His Grace," Mary said in a stern voice.

Jane turned to Evangeline. "You'll have to excuse my wife. She's very overprotective."

"I can hear you." Mary's voice carried from the foyer.

"You were meant to." Jane called out. She shook her head and smiled. "She wasn't supposed to answer the door, but when we saw you get out of the car, well…you're gorgeous and I said so, which made Mary jealous." She shrugged. "Anyway, His Grace asked me to greet you and keep you company so you wouldn't feel scared or nervous."

Evangeline gave her a small smile and nodded in assent. Meeting the two women had certainly distracted her, but now she was beginning to feel nervous again.

"I can tell you have a lot of questions you're dying to ask," Jane said with a twinkle in her eye. Evangeline liked her. She was sweet and intuitive. The king knew what he was doing when he suggested Jane greet her.

The truth was she had a million questions; some she wanted to confirm and some rather inappropriate.

She decided to confide in her new acquaintance. "Do you know why I'm here, Jane?"

Jane glanced down at her lap and clasped her hands together. The look she gave Evangeline showed she knew, and wasn't quite happy about it, but wouldn't say anything against her employer. "Yes, I do."

Without thinking about her next words, she asked, "Is there anything I can do to persuade the king not to do this?"

Jane looked worried. "Miss Wolcott—"

"Thank you, Jane." A cool voice rang out from the doorway and both ladies jumped.

Cyrus Stewart the Vampire King of North America stood, towering in the doorframe in a tailored dark blue suit.

The vampire king. Her future husband.

Oh, God.

Evangeline froze. She felt like she was on the verge of a serious panic attack, her heart pounding against her ribs. She told herself to calm down and suck it up. She didn't want to show him how much this was affecting her. It was best to be cool and collected…at least that was what she was attempting.

Evangeline thought about how her demeanor changed when she was in front of her ballet students. She was no longer Evangeline or Eva, she was Miss Wolcott, instructor. Putting on a different persona with the king might do her some good. Her chances of persuading him to forget his insane marriage plan had quickly dwindled the instant she laid eyes on him. There was no deterring this man. So why not put on an *All-right-I'll-marry-you-when's-dinner persona*? When they were better acquainted and relaxed, she would spring on the *What-the-hell-why-are-you-doing-this*?Evangeline straightened and took her fill of him. "Hello, Your Grace." Her eyes looked up into his. Way up. He stood about six feet five inches and her eyes lingered on his long neck.

He was very tall with classic features. Evangeline read some years ago he was turned while fighting for Britain during the American Revolution.

The traitor in her noticed how handsome he was with dark blonde hair reaching just below his jaw and black eyes. He was pale of course, with the same glow Mary's skin bore.

As she stared at the king, Evangeline wanted to feel joy and excitement over meeting the man she'd yearned to meet for years, but all she saw was the stranger who would be her husband. The frightening words repeated in her head: *This is going to be my husband. This is going to be my husband.*

"You have been a wonderful hostess, but I think it is time for Miss Wolcott and I to become better acquainted." Cyrus stepped further into the room with an easy swagger and one hand in his pant pocket.

Evangeline watched Jane walk out and close the door behind her, wishing she could stay and help break the ice.

His lids drew down over midnight eyes, a boyish smirk on his wide full lips. "Miss Wolcott, I am very happy to finally meet you."

She tried, but couldn't summon a smile for him. Evangeline chose to study him instead and noticed a hint of an accent, a mixture of southern and British. His stubble across both cheeks and chin contrasted strikingly with his dark Valentino suit and Prada shoes.

He was a fascinating combination of rugged meets chic.

Ordinarily she would appreciate a handsome man as the king certainly was. But instead of attraction, she felt loathing.

As he stood there, with his hand still in his pocket, Evangeline thought she saw a glimmer of apprehension behind those midnight eyes. But as soon as the thought came he blinked and stepped forward with purpose.

"I'm glad you could make it. I hope Mary and Jane served as polite hostesses. I hold them both in high regard." He stopped in front of her, leaving only about two feet between them, too close for her liking.

"Uh…yes, they're both lovely." *Except for Mary,* Evangeline thought.

"I see you already have a drink." He motioned to her untouched glass of wine with his free hand and turned to the side to pour a glass of dark gold liquor. His big, long arms skillfully handled the delicate crystal. "Please, have a seat."

She took one step away from the sofa. "I'd rather stand." *Damn it.* She was trying for cool and collected and giving off bratty.

Cyrus paused to stare at her for a moment with the decanter in hand. "All right, we'll stand." He sat the decanter down and picked up his drink. He took a long swallow, his eyes locked on hers.

She'd read vampires ate and drank like everyone else, but for different purposes. They ate food for enjoyment, not sustenance, however, raw meat provided a little. They drank coffee and tea to keep their body temperature warm to the touch and liquor to…for fun. Liquor had the same effect on vampires as it did humans, even more so when they haven't fed. To her understanding vampires needed to feed about two or three times a month, depending on how old they were.

Crap, why was she thinking about feeding right now when she was standing in front of a vampire? For years she wondered what it might be like. Would it hurt? Was it pleasurable? Now, just the thought of it made her heart leap with anxiety. Thank goodness vampires couldn't read minds, but they could hear with amazing acuity and Cyrus' eyes shifted to her chest and back up, curiously.

"Are you all right?"

"I'm fine," she said too quickly.

She forced her damn heart to calm down by cautiously taking slow pulls of air and looking about the room with feigned nonchalance. When she returned her gaze, he was still staring with his brow furrowed over dark inquiring eyes. "Were you ill recently?"

Evangeline's head jerked a little with surprise, her expression matching his. "No, I don't get sick. Not really."

The only time she was sick or rather incapacitated was after healing. Other than that, she'd never had a cold or the flu. She didn't count all her curious fainting spells as being sick, just extremely weak.

Turning to explore the room, Evangeline tried to keep him from staring at her, but she still felt his crude eyes all over her body.

The music had changed from Figaro's overture to Nina Samone. Man, great art, classy music and fine wine; the guy had great taste. If he weren't forcing her to marry him, she would have been on the couch, feet tucked under her and on her second glass of wine, joking with the king about the recent theft at the

Museum of Modern Art in Paris. They could have been good friends.

Just friends.

Alas, age-old vampires with egos the size of the continent they reigned over, don't play by her rules. Humans, especially women, were treated like booty, ass and loot.

A knock sounded at the door and they both turned. Evangeline's quick intake of breath was not lost on Cyrus. He glanced quickly at her and she didn't know what was more frightening: the scary-looking giant at the door or the fact Cyrus' voice had just told her to *Mind her manners...*inside...of...her...head.

****

Cyrus found it nearly impossible not to stare at Evangeline. Every single inch of her was striking to the eye. His own body hadn't reacted like this in a long time. Cyrus placed his fork down on the small dining table they shared in his study and reached for the glass of Zinfandel he'd opened for them, giving him a chance to stare at her again.

She was his.

This beautiful creature was going to be his wife. And if things went as planned, those long, firm legs of hers would be wrapped around him in a week.

They sat in his study where Cyrus preferred to take his meals. There were bookshelves embedded into the two parallel walls and a large glass case of Egyptian artifacts encased the wall by the door. The wall behind his desk was all glass with double doors leading out onto the terrace.

The rest of the coven took their meals in the formal dining room where all nine of them could eat comfortably at his thirty foot mahogany table. Some of them had already had their first meal of the evening and were conducting business in their office or out for the evening.

As they'd walked through the house toward his study, he watched Evangeline take in her surroundings, eyeing an office where Armando and Gabe, his coven's financial advisors, worked at their computers and a reading room where Florena, his personal assistant and advisor, sipped coffee and read the day's Sun Times.

He didn't know what Evangeline expected, but he was glad she wasn't afraid. Her beautiful face looked around with curiosity and made him want to kick Florena out of the reading room so he could take Evangeline on the chaise by the window.

Evangeline's sexy alto interrupted his thoughts. "Can everyone here communicate telepathically?"

He placed his drink down and regarded her. She was holding his stare. The girl had great eyes. He would be happy to have her stare at him for as long as she liked. "Yes, they can. I insisted everyone here should learn this method of communicating, with the exception of Jane. It's a very convenient ability to possess." He hesitated. "I apologize for spooking you earlier. We're accustomed to the method and sometimes we forget it's rude to use it on others who are unsuspecting. I've tried to limit the amount of telepathic communication in my coven. You see, some of my staff use it to gossip about someone in the room and it's waning on my nerves."

Evangeline's face became worried for a moment. "You can only hear what the other person is, 'telling you' though, correct?"

She was worried he might be able to read her mind,

which bothered him. He wanted to know what was going on in that glorious head of hers. "We cannot read minds, Evangeline." It was the first time he'd ever said her name and he felt a rush of ownership at the sound.

She looked relieved, which doused his feeling of possession and irritated him again.

"Are you through eating?" he asked. She'd barely touched her filet mignon and had only taken a few bites of asparagus.

"Yes. Thank you, it was very good," she said stiffly. He wanted her to loosen up, become relaxed with him, but he supposed it was going to take time.

As Girard, the cook, came in to take away their plates, he caught Evangeline eyeing him. Girard looked like anything, but a cook. He was a very good-looking French vampire with hazel eyes, brown hair and tattoos covering half his body. Cyrus didn't like the way Evangeline noticed his good looks and wanted to strike Girard for smiling at her.

Girard left and closed the door behind him. The silence in the room made Cyrus uncomfortable. Evangeline stared at her hands in her lap. He didn't know what to do to put her at ease. It had been over two hundred years since he last courted a woman. He didn't have a clue what he was supposed to do.

Evangeline spoke something under her breath.

"I'm sorry?"

Her head came up and those eyes bored into him once again. *Fuck.* Her face reminded him of why he chose her.

"I said, why me?" Her voice was cold and she was practically glaring at him.

Ok, small talk over. Good. It was time to get down

to business. He waited, trying to think of something clever and romantic to tell her, but nothing came. "Truthfully, and I'm quite sure you won't like this, but, I just simply had to have you." Her eyes widened at him. "I really don't have a reason other than my own selfish needs."

She was angry. "I'm not some fancy car or a piece of meat. You're forcing me to do something I don't want to do." She leaned forward and placed her arms on the table, making her collarbone jut out enticingly.

He sat back in his chair, his arms resting on either side, with his head tilted as he regarded her. "In time, you will get used to the idea of being my wife." She looked at him aghast. "I can give you a good life here, Evangeline."

Astonished, she hesitated for a moment then whispered, "You're insane."

"Watch it, my dear," he snapped.

Her lips pursed and they glared at each other for a while until she asked, her voice stern, "Did you compel my father to steal the money?"

Clever girl.

Very few people knew vampires had the ability to coerce humans to do their bidding. He considered what to tell her. "If I said no, you wouldn't believe me and hate me for lying. If I said yes, you'd still hate me." He waved a dismissive hand in the air. "There's no point in discussing this. It does neither of us any good." In truth, Cyrus only compelled Wolcott to consider stealing the funds, knowing of his dire straits, and low and behold, it worked. Cyrus needed something to hold over the Wolcott's' heads. He knew he wouldn't have been able to get Evangeline to marry him so quickly, save from compelling her, and that was something he refused to do.

Cyrus needed a wife and queen to strengthen his status as king. The moment he saw her at a fundraiser with her father, he knew she was the one.

"It would do me some good." Her voice was growing louder. "My father is not a thief—"

"Enough!" he snapped again. The evening was taking a wrong turn and they had business to conduct. Straining for calm, he said, "I don't want to resort to more threats, but do I have to remind you what will happen if you do not cooperate with me, Evangeline?"

Her eyes were tearing up. *Christ, don't cry.* She sucked it up though and lifted her chin. If need be, he would go so far as to out her father as a thief and compulsive gambler. There was no way he was letting her walk away from this and the stricken look on her face told him she knew it too. "No, Your Grace."

"Call me Cyrus, please."

Rolling her eyes, she turned away from him, looking out the back windows. He let her sulk for a moment before he brought up the inevitable.

"I understand you know the procedure for a vampire betrothal contract." He sat up, clasping his hands on the table as if he were in a meeting with his subordinates. The fact her expression went from angry to anxious told him she knew of the contract. "I will get you an engagement ring soon enough as I was once human and those traditions still stick, but I'm afraid we will have to proceed with *our* tradition so no other vampire can claim you." His stomach knotted as he asked quietly, "Have you ever been with a vampire, Evangeline?"

She shook her head.

"Good." He relished that no one else had tasted her as he slowly stood.

Eyes wide, she jerked back against her chair.

"Relax." It was a short distance to her, but he didn't want to move too fast.

Visibly shaking, she grabbed for the arms of her chair. "I can't do this." Before she could get up, he reached her and laid his hand on her bare shoulder, gently pushing her back down. He reached for the chair perpendicular to hers and sat down to face her with only the corner of the table between them.

"Yes, you can. You're stronger than you think." He was leaning forward, getting very close to her skin.

Evangeline shook her head slowly, eyeing him with disgust. "You bastard."

"Actually, I am," he replied and reached for her hand. She tried to snatch it back, but his patience was waning and tightened his grip. He was getting this over with.

She gasped.

"I'm sorry," he said and loosened his grip, but only just. He was exasperated with the whole evening. What did he expect? Did he really think she was going to come over here ready and willing with a smile plastered on her face? *No.*

She was trembling and he cursed.

"Listen to me, Evangeline. As my fiancé you might become a target for my enemies. If I have your blood in me, I could find you and protect you."

She was looking more worried by the minute.

"It's all right. Nothing is going to harm you. You and your family have the protection of my coven now.

Do you understand?"

"Yes." Glancing down at their joined hands, her eyes were shining when she brought them up to stare at him and his stomach knotted again. "Do *you* understand I don't want any of this and will hate you for the rest of my life?"

"No, you will not and do you know why?" Cyrus practically hissed and didn't wait for an answer. "Because, once we are together, I will show you the kind of passion which will render you limp and sated for weeks. I will do things to you that will make you weep and beg me for more." Mouth parted in stunned disbelief, Evangeline was speechless. "And if you're relaxed and willing when my fangs break your skin, you will feel a jolt sidle up your arm and down to your very core and when I drink, your body will be hard pressed not to climax." The rush of blood filling her face combined with her scent made him go hard in his pants, his fangs ring out and his eyes flash silver.

Ok, a little too much for her. She was really shaking now.

Shutting his eyes, he calmed his irises to return to their natural state. He left his fangs out though, to get her used to them. When his eyes were back to normal, he opened them slowly.

His lips tightened. "A compromise..." he began. "I will only break the skin to get you accustomed to the feel of it. I won't drink from you tonight." Her look of relief pissed him off. "But, the next time we meet, Evangeline, there will be no discussion on the matter. Am I clear?"

"Yes," she answered, breathlessly.

Without further ado, he flipped her palm up, made

and held eye contact with her, and broke the skin at her wrist. The sound she made as he'd punctured her almost made him come in his pants.

It was over too quickly. He came up, letting go of her wrist, and tried to judge her reaction.

She was staring at the marks on her skin with no reaction whatsoever.

God, he'd wanted to feed from her so bad. His tongue flicked out to see if any remnants of blood were there. *What the...*

There was the tiniest speck of blood on his fang and it made his tongue tingle. He was 260 years old and he had never tasted anything like it.

He looked at her in shock. "What are you?"

Chapter Five

Evangeline turned off the faucet, stepped out of the shower and reached for the terry cloth towel. She dried herself off, still a little dazed at the night's events.

When she was dry, she put on deodorant and then grabbed her jasmine-scented lotion and rubbed it all over her body. She rinsed her hands and ran her moisturizer over her face.

Unclipping her hair, she brushed a few times and then headed out of the bathroom to her walk-in closet and the drawers inside. She threw on a pair of black yoga pants and a white camisole, and then tried to get cozy on her chaise.

For years she'd wanted a dog or cat, anything to cuddle up to, but her mother had refused because of her allergies. Evangeline wasn't the teddy bear type and had given away all her stuffed animals and dolls years ago to charity. Wishing she'd kept something to hang on to, Evangeline now felt cold, empty and worse, completely and utterly alone.

Why didn't she stand up for herself better? She should have argued more, yelled more, hell...she should have struck him in his self-righteous face, but what good would any of it have done?

You couldn't predict a vampire's moods or reactions and she'd tested him tonight just by cursing at him. Had she been a man or, worse for vampires, a werewolf, she would have been dead.

Her door opened and Katherine's dark gold head popped in. "Are you up for some company?" She smiled nervously at her.

Evangeline was thankful for her sister's presence. She would even put up with Katherine's nonsense right now, anything to fill the growing void in her chest.

"Come on in." Evangeline stretched, loosening the muscles in her back and arms.

Katherine shut the door and jumped on the foot of the chaise, making Evangeline bend her legs at the knee to make room.

"So...how'd it go?"

Evangeline shook her head slightly at her sister's expression. "I guess you could say it went okay. I wasn't killed or drained of all my blood."

Katherine shrugged and assessed her. "Yeah, you look all right."

Evangeline looked down at her wrist. "Do I?"

Katherine gasped and grabbed her hand. "What a prick!" she yelled.

"Yeah, it was." She was surprised she could joke about it.

"Did it hurt?" Katherine was running her finger over the two tiny crimson holes.

Narrowing her eyes at the memory, she answered truthfully. "Not really. Cyrus told me to relax and be willing and it wouldn't hurt so much. When I was finally willing, I couldn't relax. It stung for about half a second and then I felt this jolt. It was all too fast though, because he didn't drink, just wanted to break the skin."

"So does this mean the contract is fulfilled?"

Katherine gave her back her hand.

"I'm not exactly sure. It can't be binding because he didn't drink, but he certainly left a mark."

"It's all right. You're a fast healer."

Vampires usually lick the wound to help it heal faster, but good ol' Cyrus neglected to complete that part. A mark like this was going to stay with her, but not as long as he'd like. Her ability to heal others meant she could heal quite fast. She didn't know if vampire venom could heal her faster than she could, but the guy could have tried. Their venom runs in the secretions of the mouth. It was also an intricate tool during transition.

Katherine tilted her head and studied her. "You seem...calmer...more resigned. Are you beginning to accept all of this?"

"What choice do I have, Kat? He can ruin our family and Lord knows what would happen if Dad was taken before the vampire tribunal." Eventually, her father would be transferred and his official hearing would take place in a human court, but to be fair to vampire laws, he'd have to answer to their magistrate, whose methods of punishment were terrifying.

Katherine got up and cracked the bay window. The night was cool so the air conditioner was off, but on the second floor, their rooms could get stuffy. "Let's look at the pros here," her sister started.

"Kat—"

"No, listen. If you're going to have to live with that asshole then I want to be sure you're okay over there or else I'm going to go crazy worrying about you. So just do this for me, please."

"Ok, Kat," Evangeline said calmly. She didn't like to see her sister get all worked up. She especially didn't want Katherine worrying herself sick over her. Evangeline decided right there and then to stop being such a whiney baby about all of this and try to look on the bright side, if there was one.

Katherine looked satisfied. "Okay...I think the first pro is the fact you won't be far from home. The King's Coven is only ten minutes away. "

"I agree. If I'm not chained to a wall, I'll come home to visit as much as possible," Evangeline said and winked at her.

"Ha ha," Katherine said lamely. "Now, tell me about the estate. Was it nice?"

"Actually, it was beautiful. He has great taste."

"Good. Pro number two." Katherine paced in front of the bay window, holding up two fingers. "Now, how was the rest of the coven?"

Evangeline crossed her legs and arms. "I didn't meet the whole coven. I met two women; one was rude...the other, very nice, but she was human. I wasn't formally introduced to anyone else, but I ran into the king's infamous henchman." Evangeline raised her brows at Katherine. "His name is Victor and he's huge and frightening. And then I saw the cook. He seemed nice and pretty gorgeous. The food was excellent." Too bad she couldn't hold anything down.

Katherine paused. "Gorgeous cook, huh?"

"Yep."

"Mmm..." Her sister muttered. "Nah. Too many cooks in the kitchen, literally." She waved her hand dismissively. Katherine loved to cook and the thought of rivaling her skills with someone else didn't make a good match. "I consider nice human and good-looking cook a pro, so we have three." She continued pacing.

"You won't have to quit teaching ballet, which you love, so four. Anything else?"

Evangeline's expression went blank. She couldn't think of anything good about the situation, other than the four they came up with. Her shoulders sank. "I've got nothing, Kat, but thanks. This was helpful," she lied.

Katherine sat down again on the foot of the chaise. "One more question." She hesitated. "Is he handsome?"

Evangeline bit her bottom lip. "No...yes...he would be if he wasn't so controlling and vindictive." But Evangeline didn't care about looks. The one pro she wanted, the one thing that would make this entire situation okay, was if they were in love.

She was getting angry again, but this time, she let the fury claim her.

The hatred inside felt good just then and she made her decision; not that she had a choice.

Evangeline would marry Cyrus Stewart and be his wife. And after he drank from her, after they said their vows, and he placed a ring on her finger...she was going to make his life a living hell.

****

A glass shattered on the wall right by Evangeline's head. Cyrus had just flung his high ball at her. "Please, Cyrus, don't." She turned to flee, but the king grabbed her by the arm and held her to him.

She looked around his shoulder and saw her father sitting with his legs crossed at the king's dinner table in his study, sipping a drink. Her sister stood by the door shaking her head at her. "Eva, stop being such a baby and let him bite you. I don't know why you're being so selfish.

Good Lord, she was in the twilight zone. What was wrong with her family? How could they let him do this to her?

Cyrus slammed her against him and squeezed her body. He reached up and pushed her head to the side...

"Cyrus...please...please!"

Evangeline woke up to her body catapulting off the bed. The wind was knocked out of her stomach as it punched against something rock hard. Her face must have hit the same thing, but all she saw was black.

She screamed out, but the sound was stifled by cloth in her mouth. What the hell was happening? Was she still dreaming?

There was movement at her abdomen, a shoulder shifting back and forth, back and forth. She was being carried. All of a sudden, the movement stopped and she felt weightless, like she was flying in mid air, until a shoulder punched one more time into her stomach.

Okay, real or not, this was not cool. Evangeline began thrashing her arms and kicking her legs, hitting anything she could. A heavy, thick arm slid down from her back to her thighs as another hand reached up to the back of her neck. She felt a firm tug and froze when someone whispered.

"Quiet."

Oh Jesus. Oh Jesus. Oh Jesus.

Evangeline was fully awake now. This was too real. The movement at her stomach began again as she tried to get her bearings. She was no longer asleep in her bed, but outside now. She smelled fresh grass through the dark cloth over her face and felt cool air on her arms. Only then did she realize her wrists were bound together.

She tried to shake the cloth off her head, but it must have been tied around her neck.

This couldn't be happening. Who would do this to her?

This time, she screamed for real. Her screams came from the back of her throat and the cloth in her mouth couldn't do anything about it. The staccato hits on her stomach changed pace and she felt her body leaping along with her captor.

She was being kidnapped; actually kidnapped by someone she couldn't see. She knew it was a man because of the voice and the broad back she was flailing against. Her heart raced and she began to hyperventilate. It was too hard to breathe with the gag in her mouth, cloth over her face and the brutal hits to her stomach.

Fight damn it, Evangeline thought.

With all the energy she could muster, she thrashed like mad against her captor, for all the good it did. His vise-like grip held her tighter and they practically flew through the air.

He wasn't human. There was no way a human man could run at this pace and leap through the air the way they were flying right now.

Evangeline's stomach took another hit and she felt nauseous. She hoped she'd get sick all over the bastard's back, but before the dizziness could claim her, they stopped. When the man began walking at a normal pace, Evangeline stopped struggling to take in her surroundings. She could hear sticks and brush crunch under the monster's feet and the wind blowing the leaves on trees. They must be in the woods, but where?

Evangeline reached out all her other senses, but it

was no good. All she smelled now was the moldy wool cloth that began irritating her skin. She was trying to listen to everything around her, any useful information, should she happen to find a phone to call the police.

His footsteps changed abruptly. The sound was more rough and loud, as if he were walking on planks of wood. A door opened and creaked. He took more steps and then the door closed. She tried to judge if he turned left or right, but before she knew it, she was being tossed back. Evangeline landed on something soft, a bed.

Dear God, no!

The cloth was lifted off her face and she regained her sight. She blinked several times, trying to focus in the dimly lit room. She sat up too quickly and her head spun. It lolled on her neck and as her vision cleared, her eyes widened at the size thirteen's, two feet in front of her.

A deep rumble cut off the scream in the back of her throat.

"Relax. I'm not going to hurt you."

Chapter Six

This was a mistake.

The girl was scared out of her mind. What had he been thinking?

Adam stepped back from the bed and put his hands up to show her he didn't have any weapons. He hoped the gesture would calm her nerves, but she just shrank back, stumbling off the bed and to the corner of the room, her green eyes wide and trained on him.

"Try and relax. I promise I won't hurt you."

Her chest was heaving as she reached up and pulled off the gag he'd put on her. Not his finest moment, but he couldn't risk her screaming and alerting the rest of the house.

"What do you want?" She was trembling and her voice cracked as she stared at him. "Why are you doing this?"

Please don't cry.

Damn it, he was such a shit. "Look, I know you're not going to believe me, but this is just something I have to do. You're safe here—"

She charged him.

He was shoved back, more out of shock than from her strength. Evangeline pushed past him and ran toward the open door, but he caught her in one step. She wheeled around and started pounding his chest and arms. Her bound wrists hindered her efforts so she started kicking him.

"Shit!" Adam grabbed her by her arms and pushed her gently on the bed. "Stop it. You're going to hurt yourself. I told you, I'm not going to do anything to you," he yelled.

She was pissed now. Her dark hair was tousled, her skin flushed. "Fuck you!" she shouted. "You think I'm going to take the word of a kidnapper? Let me go!"

Jesus, she was beautiful.

Stepping back to give her some space, Adam put his hands on his hips. "I'm not...look...I'll explain everything when you've gotten some rest."

She gawked at him. "Rest? Are you crazy?"

Yeah. His sister was kidnapped, so *he* kidnaps someone. *Fucking hypocrite.*

Adam gestured toward her and said, "I can untie your wrists if you want."

"Don't touch me." She held her arms to her chest, glaring at him.

"Ok. Fine by me. Get some sleep." He turned around and stepped out, shutting the door behind him. As he reached up to click the pad lock, he heard her hit the door, trying to get out.

He stepped away and ran both hands through his hair, walking into the living room. He sat in an armchair giving him a view of the bedroom and the front door. He wasn't expecting company, but one could never be too sure.

Adam was glad there were a few members of his pack out patrolling tonight. By now, the others would know what he'd done. Jason was on rotation with Ramo and Alex and they must have sensed Jason's anxiety. It was radiating out of him before they'd parted ways.

He wasn't looking forward to listening to their objections, but he was damn glad they were out there. They needed to be extra alert now. He wasn't worried they would be found, but you could never be too careful. The Blacktail Fighters were the only ones who knew about this cabin in the woods. It had been used in the past for meetings, hearings and a few ceremonies even. The vampires sure didn't know it existed.

He shut his eyes tight. Evangeline was still pounding on the door. God, he was scaring the shit out of her. He wished she'd just trust him and try to relax, but he didn't blame her. He'd fight like a motherfucker too.

Adam told himself this would all be over soon. They were going to send a message to the vampire king, informing him he had his fiancé and if the king wanted to see her alive again, he would have to give up Serena.

Evangeline was in no danger. Adam would never kill a female, but the king didn't need to know that.

His head spun again with worry and insurmountable stress. It felt like Evangeline was banging inside of his head.

He hoped to God the king cooperated. Cyrus Stewart must have Serena. All the evidence pointed to him. His sister was taken at night, leaving work. One of her coworkers saw her talking with a man in a black leather jacket as she was getting into her car and then turn around and disappear with the stranger around the corner. It wasn't like Serena to take off with a stranger. A vampire must have compelled her.

There was a constant vendetta between werewolves and vampires and Adam had killed one of the king's kind, in his own town. *No, Adam's town*. He and his pack were here first.

Werewolves and vampires were always at each other's throats, but the vampires had gone too far taking out one of his Fighters. The king had to know his pack would retaliate. Before then, it had been years since the two species battled. Maxwell Jones and his partner tried their best to keep the peace. Sure there were fights here and there. Adam thought the past few years without a blood bath was pretty amazing, but Cyrus and Adam always had their issues. Two leaders in a small town was just asking for trouble.

The king took his sister; of this he was sure. It was just like the sneaky prick to take a defenseless young girl. When Adam got Serena back safe and sound, he was going to tear him to pieces. *Literally*. And if it started a war, so be it.

Evangeline Wolcott would just have to get back with the sorry-ass she'd dumped earlier today. Not that he cared. The fact it had bothered him when the human kissed her meant nothing. He was overprotective by nature and when the guy touched her while she was clearly blowing him off... simply touched a nerve.

So why didn't he let his beta handle the abduction? He was obviously pretty bad at it since he wasn't supposed to feel so awful for the one he was abducting.

He got up with a jerk, too wound up to sit still. Walking to the window, he pretended not to be affected by the woman's screaming. What he was doing sickened him. His great idea to kidnap Cyrus' fiancé was looking pretty stupid right now.

The woman must be scared out of her mind thinking he was going to hurt her and he couldn't think of anything to do or say that would calm her down, but he knew he had to do something.

The pounding on the door stopped. She was quiet now.

He hoped it was a sign she was beginning to cool down. He would go to her in an hour or so and explain or at least try to explain what was going on. He didn't want her to be frightened of him. Funny...when he first thought of this brilliant plan to take her he didn't plan on giving a shit about her feelings. But the minute he took off the sack over her head and looked into those damn eyes...

A wolf howled outside. It was Ramo. Definitely. He was pissed off about Adam's decision to kidnap a human and he was letting him know it.

"Shit," Adam muttered.

Ramo was coming this way. Reaching the door fast, he stepped out into the night. Adam did not want the guys in the house. The girl was scared enough. She didn't need to think there were more kidnappers and potential murderers in the cabin with her.

He saw Ramo leap over a large brush and burst into the clearing, hunched on all fours. When he saw Adam, he remained low to the ground, waiting for his alpha's acknowledgement.

Adam turned back to look at the window with the light on. Evangeline wasn't there, thank God. He turned to address his loud mouth cousin and Fighter.

"Phase back," Adam ordered Ramo.

Ramo stood to his full height. He was about six foot, five inches in his human form, but when he phased, he shot up another foot. Ramo was still morphing into his human form as he spoke. The hair was still receding on his face and body, as he opened his big fat mouth. "You mind telling me what the fuck is going on?"

****

Bars? Really? The maniac had actually put her in a room with bars on the window? She was living a freaking nightmare and she had no idea how to get out of it.

Evangeline paced the room as she struggled with the rope around her wrists. She almost had her right hand loose, but it was beginning to swell from all the pounding on the door.

Jesus! What did he want? Money? He was certainly barking up the wrong tree there. Her family didn't have any money. What was he going to do with her when he found out there was no cash incentive for abducting her? Would he kill her and bury her somewhere in the woods where she'd never be found? If he did kill her, would he do it fast or slowly torture her?

Her heart began pounding in her ears again. She had to sit down before she keeled over. It didn't do her any good to think the worst, but how could she not?

She closed her eyes with a sigh when her hand slipped free. Both hands and wrists were swollen and red. Rubbing them gently, she prayed no harm would come to her. Evangeline hoped he was telling the truth and would not hurt her.

There was movement outside the door and then two knocks. She froze on the bed, her wide eyes taking stock of the room, attempting to gather her wits. It was an ordinary bedroom with a queen-sized bed, two dressers, and a nightstand.

"I'm coming in. Step away from the door," his voice called out.

Something in her snapped. "I'm nowhere near the door!" she yelled.

He came in slowly and it took every ounce of self-control not to make a run for it. Going by his strength and speed he must be a werewolf. He was too tanned to be a vampire and werewolves were generally over six feet and this man was enormous.

Her captor shut the door and remained still. Heart hammering in her chest, she glowered at him. The man was so tall and built like a gladiator. It was hard not to be terrified of him. Her eyes shifted down to what he was holding, panicking as she thought of every possible thing he could do to her with…broccoli?

The guy was holding a small key in one hand and a bag of frozen broccoli in the other.

"I thought you might need this for your hand. Wasn't so smart, pounding like that, was it?" He jerked his head, indicating her red hands.

She flushed, her eyes narrowing at him. "You're not going to get away with this. As soon as my family finds out I'm gone, they'll call the police."

He stepped closer into the room. "No, they won't." Evangeline backed up against the headboard, unable to trust her legs to hold her up. He stopped when he saw her reaction and held up the broccoli before he tossed it on the bed in front of her.

"Of course they will," she said, not touching the bag of broccoli. She wanted answers.

"No, they won't," he said simply. "Your family will get a message early in the morning saying you're okay because you're going to call and tell them." Standing with his feet planted hip-length apart on the floor, he crossed his arms over his large chest. His forearms bulged in front of him, the rest of his arms threatening to rip the sleeves of his black t-shirt. "You're going to leave a message on your dad's voicemail telling him you and a friend decided to go to Chicago to celebrate your engagement. Tell him your catching a show, going clubbing, whatever. Then you'll tell him you'll be careful and will return in a few days."

She gaped at him, completely confused. "How did you know I was engaged?"

"Don't worry about it. Do you understand what you have to do?"

"My father's not going to buy it."

"Make him," he ordered.

"Wait a minute," Evangeline said pensively. Why would he have her lie to her father? "Does this mean you don't want anything from my family?"

He looked her over. To his credit his eyes stayed on her face. The man had strong features and an insane part of her brain thought how she might have been attracted to him if she'd seen him on the street or met him at a party.

His crystal blue eyes bore into her as he spoke, his face tight. "My problem is not with your family. It's with the bloodsucking dead guy you're about to marry."

"Cyrus?" she asked.

His nostrils flared at the mention of the king's name. "Yes. Your boyfriend took my little sister and the sooner I get her back, the sooner you can go home." He cocked his head in thought. "Answer this, have you noticed anything in the King's Coven that seems off?"

She stared at him confused. "You think the king kidnapped your sister?"

"I know he did. Now answer the question," he barked.

Evangeline shook her head and looked away. She had only been Cyrus' fiancé for one day and already she was in trouble.

What would this guy do when he learned the king hardly felt anything for her, but lust? If the king really did have his sister, he was not going to lose face and admit to it just for her release.

Her abductor cursed under his breath and turned toward the window. As he moved she caught the sight of a tattoo on the back of his neck. It was a full moon complete with the infant shadow and all. Her heart sank into her stomach.

Inhaling a sharp breath, she said, "You're Adam Perez, leader of the Blacktail pack." Her voice was soft and forlorn.

He turned, his eyes wide.

Evangeline lifted her hand slowly and pointed to the back of her neck. "I know the alpha of the Blacktails carries the moon tattoo on the back of the neck." The other Blacktail fighters had the same tattoo, but on the inside of their forearm.

He had the decency to look ashamed.

Evangeline felt a surge of regret run through her and bent her head to glower at the bed cover. She'd read books on the history of the Blacktail pack. They'd settled in Illinois in the seventeenth century. Adam Perez was the descendent of Xavier Perez who'd come from Mexico after the Civil War and married the Blacktail leader's daughter. She shook her head slowly, baffled. "What are you doing?" she pleaded. Her voice was strained. "You have a solid reputation in this town. Why would you do this?"

Settling his hands on his hips, he looked away and said, "You don't understand—"

"You could have gone to the police, the magister, Maxwell Jones." she began, looking around the room as if their surroundings could supply an answer for him.

"Don't be naïve. You have no idea what's going on here," he snapped.

She let out a breath and looked away, feeling utterly stupid for envying these creatures all her life. "My whole life I've wanted to meet a supernatural… today I meet two and I am completely disgusted."

"What?" he snapped. "Today?" His forehead creased as he stared at her. "What do you mean? You're engaged to a vampire." Adam stepped closer to the bed, but this time she didn't budge. She didn't think the alpha of the notorious Blacktail pack would do her physical harm, but to be sure, she'd taken stock of the room and the lamp just two feet away from her on the nightstand looked heavy enough to do some damage should he try anything.

"Perhaps you should have done better research, Blacktail." She didn't care her voice sounded mocking. "The king and I just met tonight. If you want your sister back, I suggest you kidnap someone else, because I doubt the king will give you one penny for me. So, either let me go or kill me and be done with it."

****

His phone rang loud and she jumped at the sound.

They were both staring at each other intensely, each one lost in their own thoughts. Without breaking his gaze, Adam reached into his jean pocket for his cell and pressed the send button on his smartphone.

"Yeah?"

Evangeline watched him closely. He tried to focus on what Jason was saying, but it was difficult when he was standing so close to her.

"A what? In these woods? What the…"

Jason's voice rambled on about a jackal. He must have been mistaken.

"Ignore it. I have no idea how it got here, but if it gives you trouble, kill it." He hung up.

He put his phone back in his pocket as he tried to absorb what Evangeline just revealed to him. He was feeling a mixture of confusion, shame and lust at the moment and it was wreaking havoc on his brain. She was disappointed in him. Why the hell did he care?

"You just met Cyrus Stewart tonight?"

She glanced at the clock on the nightstand. "Yesterday, yes." She was oddly composed now.

His face disgusted, he asked, "Why the hell are you marrying a vampire you just met?" He didn't know why this made him angry, but someone as beautiful as she was, who came from, apparently, a good upbringing should not be marrying a murdering stiff like Cyrus Stewart.

"That's none of your business." She looked away from him, her eyes growing moist.

"Did he threaten you? Is he forcing this on you?" He was closer to her now, his instincts telling him this woman needed protection.

Evangeline gave him a disparaging look. "What the hell do you care? You took me from my home in the middle of the night and locked me in a room in the woods."

He had no response and just stared at the broccoli bag on the bed.

"It doesn't matter why I'm marrying him. The fact is, your plan is not going to work, so you're going to have to think of some other way to get your sister back."

She was wrong. There was no way the king would let him get away with kidnapping her. Cyrus chose Evangeline to stand by his side as his wife. He was obviously affected by her. How could he not be?

Evangeline stroked her left wrist absently. The sight of two small puncture marks caught his eye. His reaction was instant.

Adam lurched forward and grabbed her arm with a growl. She shrieked, pulling back away from him as she stared, wild eyed. "HE BIT YOU?" Adam snarled, chest heaving with anger. He pictured the slimy fuck sinking his teeth into her porcelain skin and an uncontrollable rage engulfed him.

He barely noticed the look of fright in her eyes. She didn't move, too alarmed at his imposing height hovering over her and his vise-like grip on her arm.

"It's tradition," she whispered.

He looked down again at the marks on her wrist, just half an inch over her vein and his vision shifted. Adam felt his eyes turn yellow and his irises change shape.

Evangeline's quick intake of breath snapped him out of it. He felt her emotions seep through him. She was shaking, panicking for sure now. "If you're going to phase, please let me go."

Adam dropped her hand with a jerk and backed up.

He was so stupid. How could he not think the king would drink from his fiancé? "If he fed from you, he would have felt you were in trouble. He would have been here by now. You can't tell me he doesn't care. I know he does." Adam was standing with both fists clenched at his sides, his eyes still burning with rage.

Evangeline covered the marks with her hand. "He didn't drink from me. Not yet. He only broke the skin. I wasn't...ready..."

She was scared again, but not of him. Her fear stemmed from the bastard who was obviously forcing her into a marriage she did not want.

Anger spiked through his entire body and the need to kill was overwhelming.

He had to get out of the room before he broke something. "Go to bed. I'll wake you early to call your father." And without another glance, he stepped out of the room and slammed the door behind him.

Chapter Seven

She had to get out of here.

Clearly the Blacktail alpha was unstable. For an instant she'd believed he wouldn't hurt her and she'd actually been honest with him, but when he grabbed her... Why did he react that way? He must have been nervous Cyrus would come after her because of the blood bond. For a second she wanted to kick herself for not letting Cyrus drink from her, but she dropped the thought the instant it came. If the king had come after her, he would only hold her captive in his coven sooner rather than later.

Her life was no longer her own. She was trapped, no matter what happened.

Not knowing what was in store for her was driving her crazy. Sure, she wasn't in a rush to become his wife, but she still had...God...she had no idea when they were supposed to be married. All she knew was she needed to escape and return to some semblance of her life before she became Mrs. Stewart. *Ugh!*

Evangeline walked over to the window and examined the bars. She leaned down and opened the window slowly and as quietly as she could. There were six vertical bars screwed into two panels on the outside of the window. She guessed they were put in recently as there was no sign of rusting or dust of any kind.

Evangeline reached her slim arm through two of

them and felt around the bottom of the outside window. She was right. There were three screws on the bottom panel and another three at the top.

She jumped up, searching the room for anything thin and sharp. There was a corner dresser on the far side of the room and she ran toward it rummaging through the drawers. There was nothing but sheets, sweaters, a few t-shirts and... a small travel toiletry bag. She grabbed the bag and unzipped it.

"Yes!" she hissed, finding nail clippers along with creams and an array of other travel items.

She ran back to the window and reached her arm through. Her fingers found the tiny cross at the head of the screw and began working the file device on the clippers. It took some time, but she managed to unscrew the first one. When she was on the third screw, she jumped at a sound in the cabin and nearly dropped the clippers outside. It dangled between her index and middle finger and she had to slip her other arm through before it fell.

Frozen for a moment, she held her breath to listen to what the Blacktail might be doing. It was completely quiet. She hoped to God he was asleep and finished her work on the third screw at the bottom of the window.

Pulling the last one out, she dropped the screw on the ground with her free hand and brought her arms back in to test her work. Pushing slowly on the bars, now connected only on the base at the top of the windowsill, she moved it outward with ease.

She'd done it. She was free.

Evangeline slipped the clippers in the band of her yoga pants, thinking the sharp little blade may come in handy should she run into trouble, and as quietly as she could, angled both legs over the windowsill while still hanging on to the bars with one hand. The hard part was jumping off the sill while holding on to the bars so they didn't slam against the window. Leaping onto the ground, she managed, but not without banging her elbow. She bit down hard, trying desperately not to scream at the pain.

When her feet were planted on the grass outside, she gently let go of the bars and ran like hell.

Trees and brush of every kind filled the woods. Trying hard to muffle the sound of her footfalls, Evangeline focused ahead of her, straining to hear anyone or anything in the vicinity. She had no idea where she was going, but there was bound to be a road or path somewhere.

There was a shout behind her. "HEY!"

Evangeline made her legs move faster. Her feet were getting cut on the ground, but she ran on. There was no way she could out run a werewolf, but by God, she would try. Turning her head to determine how close he was, her foot caught in a tangle of weeds. She screamed in pain as she fell face first onto the ground.

Feeling utterly stupid, Evangeline placed both her aching hands on the ground to push herself up.

The growl in front of her froze her in place. Every single hair on her body stood on end as she slowly raised her head. Her eyes fixed on the long, gray snout first, then the slanted eyes up to the pointed ears that appeared to go on forever. Her body never convulsed so hard in her life.

This was no wolf, and no werewolf. Werewolves were man-shaped wolves. This gray creature was a freaking jackal, three feet away from her face and baring his teeth as it prepared to pounce.

Evangeline's last thought was of her parents and prayed it would be quick.

A heavy, burly hand pushed her chest back and the wind was knocked out of her as she flew, banging her head against a tree.

When her vision cleared, she saw a dark figure over seven feet easy, circling the jackal. The jackal attacked first, but the massive werewolf caught him with both hands and slammed him into the tree to his left and away from her. The jackal landed hard on its side and scrambled to its feet, ready to attack again.

Evangeline rose to her feet and reached for the nail clippers in her pants. Her movements distracted the werewolf. His eyes landed on her and she knew without a doubt this was the alpha of the Blacktail pack in all his glory.

"WATCH OUT!" she shouted.

Adam turned and caught the jackal, but not before it could sink his teeth into his shoulder. Adam howled in pain and wrenched the beast off him. It soared through the air, crashing on the ground mere feet from where she stood. The jackal found its footing, turned toward Evangeline, and let out a ferocious growl.

Her back hit the tree behind her and she held the nail clippers with the puny file out in front of her. When Adam reached out and grabbed the jackal by its neck, she let out a burst of air. Adam's massive, furry arm swung back and clawed the jackal, leaving three shiny red marks along its side.

The sound of heavy footfalls jerked Evangeline's head around and she watched as two other massive werewolves, one black streaked with gray, the other a deep brown, leapt into the fray.

The jackal whined when the brown one scratched it across the snout. Turning, it broke into a run, the two werewolves following right on its tail, kicking up dirt in their wake, and then they were gone.

Evangeline's heart was going a mile a minute.

Adam turned toward her and she shivered. He was quite a sight in his human form, but the animal she was gazing up at was like no other.

He stood, tall on his feet. Werewolves only crouched on all fours when they were about to pounce or run. They were half man and half wolf. He was shaped like his human form, times ten. Almost every inch of him was covered in black, coarse fur. The only parts of him not covered in hair were the palms of his hands, the bottom of his feet and his long torso encased in black, muscled, leathery skin. His shoulders stretched wide, about five feet. An image of big foot sprung to mind, but Adam's werewolf form was so much more…what? Scarier? Menacing? Beautiful? His face had morphed into a wolf's snout, but the shape of his eyes were all Adam. Only now they burned a bright golden bronze.

The sky was brightening all around them. As she stared, fixated, the sun began to cast him in a mystical glow. This glorious sight was more than she could ever hope for, ever imagine. For a moment they were the only two people on earth, Evangeline and the beast.

Adam took one step toward her and then fell to his knees. The rest of him hit the ground with a loud thud. He was on his side now, motionless.

Evangeline stared in disbelief. There was no way a jackal could seriously injure this mass of a man.

Werewolves must be allergic to a jackal's bite or something. She watched in amazement as he morphed back to his human form, shrinking to his normal size. In an instant he lay there, on his side, completely naked. His legs were the size of tree trunks, his arms as big as her thighs. She saw the terrible bite mark on his left shoulder. He was still breathing, but feebly. His eyes were closed and his forehead scrunched in pain.

She had two options: continue running and return home, leaving the alpha of the Blacktail pack to die in the woods or, and she shook her head as she thought, *heal him*.

Why was her initial reaction to help him? Adam Perez bound and gagged her, hurtled her out her second story window and locked her up in a cabin. She should despise him for what he'd done, but she couldn't. There were bigger things at work here. Things she couldn't explain, nor dare ponder. She couldn't help but be mesmerized by him and seeing him in pain tugged at her heart.

She was losing it.

There was no way she could ever leave him to die. Despite the fact he'd kidnapped her, the Blacktail alpha had just risked his life to save her. Sure, she wouldn't have needed saving if it weren't for him, but could she live with herself knowing she'd left the leader of the Blacktails to die?

No.

Her decision was made, regardless of the warning in the back of her mind reminding her of his treachery, something else, something stronger bound her to help him.

Evangeline knelt down beside him and put her

hands on his hot skin, covered in perspiration. His eyes flipped open, his lids heavy over blue, hypnotic orbs. His voice was a tense whisper. "What are you doing?"

She pushed him onto his back and fixed her eyes on his wound, fighting hard not to look down. Evangeline felt miniscule next to him. His chest was covered in a sheen of sweat and she had to push a crazy, inappropriate thought out of her head.

Evangeline took a moment to study his strained face. He had slightly sunken eyes, high cheekbones and a fierce jaw, but of all things, it was his nose that attracted her the most. It was long and straight, with a little bump at the top and every bit male. Suddenly she didn't see a kidnapper. She saw a beautiful leader who had gone through so much in his lifetime.

Evangeline knew the rumors about him, how he'd murdered his father. Some say it was to attain the alpha status, some say he'd just gone mad. Evangeline didn't believe any of those rumors. A man of his reputation could never kill in cold blood without a perfectly good reason. All she knew was Adam Perez had protected the Blacktail pack for years, and began the Blacktail Fighters to further defend their race from vampires, human extremists and other threatening packs.

"I'm returning the favor. You saved my life, now I'm saving yours."

She placed both hands on top of his bloodied shoulder. He jerked slightly, his eyes wide on her hers, but he was powerless to do anything else but grip her wrist lightly with his hand. "Stop." He must have thought she was nuts touching the deep gash on his shoulder.

She met his confused stare. "I think the jackal's bite was poisonous. You won't survive if I don't help you."

He gritted his teeth, fighting pain that surely ran through him.

She had to act fast. Her extreme healing side could sense the poison in his wound was slowly killing him. Her heart raced with anxiety. This sort of healing was going to do a number on her. "Do me a favor?" she said evenly.

His face was still in shock.

"After you're healed, bring me into the cabin. I'll be too weak to move." She focused her hands on his shoulder and felt the deep vibrations run from her chest, down her arms and into his flesh, before all went dark.

****

The sunset filled the cabin's only bedroom, lighting the room and its simple furnishings in an ethereal sort of way. Adam spent the last several hours in an antique chair in the corner, watching over Evangeline.

The chair moaned and his joints cracked as he sat up straight. His neck was stiff from angling it back for so long against the wall, but he ignored all the aches in his body as his eyes shot to the girl in his bed.

She lay on her side with her back to him. Evangeline clearly did not like the heavy quilt he'd covered her in, having kicked it off some time while he'd slept and made do with the thin white sheet instead.

His eyes were riveted on her sinuous form. The way the sheet hugged her hips and thighs made his blood boil and his morning chubby twitch.

God, he was such a shit. He tried to get the damn

thing down, but then he focused on the soft arch of her foot peeking out from under the sheet and his cock nearly busted through his fly.

Damn it!

She didn't deserve this, any of this. She didn't deserve to be ripped from her bed, forced to stay here with him and endure his lusting after her. He tried, but it was becoming increasingly hard to be around her and not want to touch her.

Evangeline let out a long breath and turned onto her back.

He could stare at her face forever. Even in sleep she was mesmerizing.

Stop it. Stop looking at her like that, you sick fuck. She saved your life and this is how you repay her?

Adam turned to gaze out the window. Why had she saved him? Why had he needed saving? Animals had bitten him before, but his body never reacted the way it did last night. What sort of poison was it?

The memory of her touching him sent tiny tremors down his back. Her hands were incredibly soft and small on him and her emotions were going haywire.

When she touched him, he could sense all she was feeling as if he'd felt it himself. She was a torrid mess of depression combined with panic, adoration, and attraction for him. The attraction part threw him, but more importantly, how the hell had she healed him?

As he'd lain there, he felt a soft vibration of some sort and then the pain was gone and it seemed as if his entire body was blanketed in a deep sense of tranquility.

The feeling was nothing he'd ever experienced in his life. Werewolves were fast healers, but the poison was spreading as fast as wild fire inside him. His whole body was numb and he was losing consciousness before Evangeline restored him back to health.

The wound on his shoulder had completely healed and when the gash had closed, the feeling lifted and he was back to normal, naked, with Evangeline slumped over his torso. Panic laced through him as he lifted her in his arms with ease, his eyes narrowed and fixated on her face as he carried her back to the cabin.

Her ability must have taken a lot out of her, which made him feel a million times worse than he already did.

He turned his head to check on her and froze.

Evangeline's entrancing olive eyes were trained on him.

His heart slammed in his chest. This woman was dangerous to him. He'd never reacted this way with any female, let alone a human.

She continued to stare, sad and dazedly at him. The sun made her eyes sparkle and her hair gleam a lighter shade of red.

He stood slowly, not wanting to alarm her, and remained near the window, a safe distance away from her.

She spoke softly, her voice scratchy as she did. "How long was I out for?" Her chest rose up and down as she breathed, her delicate breast straining underneath her white, flimsy top.

His mood was poignant now, because so was she. He couldn't believe how in tune he was to her emotions. It was almost as strong as his pack members. He glanced out the window at the descending sun. "You've been asleep for almost two days. It's about six in the evening, Friday."

Her eyebrows shot up. "Wow. I don't think I've ever been out that long. I guess I needed the rest."

"Yeah…uh…can I get you anything, food or something to drink? Are you in pain?"

She turned and it looked like she was contemplating the ceiling. "I am hungry, but I need something more than food right now."

Taking one step forward, he asked nervously, "What?"

"A shower."

Adam let out a shaky breath. "Of course. I'll go set up the bathroom for you. Just give me a minute." He turned and left the room, going across the hallway to the only bathroom in the cabin. The showerhead was worth shit as he'd tried it earlier while Evangeline slept. So he turned the faucet on in the old fashion claw foot, porcelain tub and checked the water four or five times before plugging the drain.

He made sure there was a clean towel for her and put it on the toilet so it was close to the tub, then picked it up and placed it on the hook on the door, thinking she might have to use the facilities.

When he came back to the room, she was sitting up at the edge of the bed, bracing both her hands on either side of her thighs, head hanging down. Adam moved to her quickly, kneeling down in front of her. "Are you going to be sick?" he asked in a worried tone, noticing the slight sheen of perspiration on her forehead.

"No. I just got dizzy trying to stand up."

"Oh. Just let me…"

Evangeline looked him straight in the eye and he froze. Her expression made his heart slam and then crumple to the pit of his stomach. At once, he felt an extraordinary emotion and he knew whatever happened here on out, she must be protected.

Evangeline Wolcott was the most beautiful woman he'd ever seen. Her eyes burned down to his very soul. Her head bent low, she stared at him, not with fear, but with determination and warning. She was silently telling him if he tried anything with her in her weakened state, she would rue the day she saved his life and so would he.

Adam raised both hands before reaching her and spoke gravely. "I promise I won't hurt you. I'm sorry I got you involved in all of this, but we can deal with that later. Right now, all I want is for you to get better, so please, let me help you," he finished, clenching his jaw as he waited, ignoring the fact he meant every word. He did not want to think about how much this girl's well being mattered to him.

Lowering her gaze, she nodded in resignation. Adam reached one arm around her back and the other under her knees. She must have been five foot seven inches with firm muscles from her years of dancing, but Adam was once again surprised how light she was in his arms as he lifted her off the bed.

She winced.

"Sorry, did I hurt you?" Adam paused, watching her.

"No, it's you. You're hot!" she said accusingly.

"Excuse me?" He was feeling even hotter around the ears right then.

"I forgot your body temperature runs hotter than a human's. It startled me, is all."

He smirked. "Sorry," he said, walking toward the bathroom.

"It's not your fault." She still smelled great and her scent was doing funny things to his head. Evangeline kept her head off his shoulder, but he knew she was struggling to hold it up. It made him move faster so she could rest her head in the tub.

Once they reached the bathroom, he set her down on the toilet with the lid down so he could turn off the faucet. He checked the water one more time and addressed her, awkwardly. "Showerhead's not working." He pointed stupidly to the showerhead. "Do you think you can take it from here?"

Her lips twitched in a slight smile. "I should be fine. I'll just take my time." She glanced over at the tiny round window. "And don't worry, I'm not going anywhere."

Adam looked at her shrewdly. "Just don't hurt yourself, okay? Yell if you need anything." He walked out and shut the door behind him.

He went into the kitchen to see if there was anything to eat. When he opened the fridge he saw the items Jason had provided for them. There were bottles of water, a gallon of milk, eggs, slices of cheese and a loaf of white bread. In the freezer, there were four frozen pizzas. Hell, it was more than what he had in his own fridge. Adam grabbed one of the pizzas, placed it on the counter and set the oven to preheat.

The cabin's small kitchen had been renovated only a few times since it was built in the nineteenth century. Adam had the light fixtures, counter tops and cabinets redone in the eighties and put in new insulation and drywall. He'd also repainted and updated the appliances in ninety-six. Everything was pretty much white except for the green counter top running along the back wall.

As he waited, he opened the cabinets to search for anything else. There were more bottles of water, cans of tuna and chili and four jars of peanut butter and four jars of grape jelly.

Adam shook his head. Fucking Jason and his peanut butter and jelly sandwiches. It was a good thing Adam took his place or else Evangeline might have starved to death.

He closed all the cupboards and threw the pizza in impatiently without waiting for the oven to preheat all the way. He walked into the living room, glancing only once at the bathroom door. He walked over to the sideboard and opened up the cabinet for something to do. There were two bottles of Johnny Walker Gold and about six bottles of Gran Patron Platinum. He was itching to open a bottle of tequila, but he wasn't about to imbibe with Evangeline here.

Adam knew how to hold his liquor, but these days with all the shit going on, he wasn't about to test his limits with a scared girl in the house. After all, he wasn't like his drunk of a father who didn't give a rat's ass who was nearby when he was on a drunken rampage.

Adam shut the cabinet door and paced the room, listening to the sounds coming from the bathroom. He could hear the water sloshing in the tub as she moved around. At least she hadn't fallen asleep.

His phone beeped, indicating he had a text message. Reaching in his pocket for his phone, he checked the message from Jason. It read: *Message was sent to the king. He should get it as soon as he wakes up. All the boys are on patrol.*

Adam nodded as he texted back. He wanted this

over and done with. Cyrus Stewart could retaliate all he liked. He just wanted his sister back at home, safe and sound. Adam would deal with the repercussions of his actions later.

Good. Send emissary at 5 AM. Stay out of sight and text me with updates.

He was stuffing the phone in his pocket when he heard Evangeline. He paused to listen and heard her groan and then curse. He was at the door in an instant, barging in without even a knock.

Evangeline jumped and shrieked as she covered her chest. The tub, except for her porcelain shoulders gleaming wet and silky, hid her entire body.

"What are you doing?" she yelled.

"I'm sorry. I heard you curse. I thought you hurt yourself. I'll go." Adam was shutting the door as he spoke, but she stopped him.

"Wait," she called out, distressed.

Adam held the door half open, but kept his eyes focused on the tiled floor. "What is it?"

Taking a deep breath, she said, "I can't get up. I think my muscles are too relaxed now or something. I'm sure I can handle it once I'm out of the tub, but I can't get up in this position..." Her voice broke off, frustrated.

Adam walked into the bathroom and shut the door to keep the warm air in. "I told you to call me if you needed anything," he said roughly as he grabbed the towel from the hook and threw it over his shoulder. He stepped to the tub, keeping his eyes leveled on her face and reached out to help her up.

She jerked away from him. "Wait." Her wide eyes met his. A flush filled her high cheekbones as she licked her succulent, wet lips. She had no idea how damn provocative her simple action was and he went hard instantly. Thank god he was hunched over. "Aren't you going to close your eyes?"

He snorted. "Then I won't see what I'm grabbing. Besides, it's nothing I haven't seen before."

"You haven't seen *me*!" she said angrily, her eyes blazing.

Yet, he thought.

He shook his head. What the hell was wrong with him? "Fine. I'll close my eyes and you lead my hands, but if I knock you into the sink, it's your own fault."

"Okay," she uttered meekly.

He closed his eyes and felt her pull his hands into the water and place them on her rib cage. She fit perfectly in his hands and he took his time lifting her out of the water, reluctant to let go of her sleek, soft skin.

When he set her down, he let go unwillingly and grabbed the towel from his shoulder, holding it out to her with his eyes still shut.

She took it from him. "Thank you. You can open your eyes now."

Evangeline stood before him with the beige towel wrapped around her torso, her hair dripping wet, sending droplets down her shoulders.

This woman would be the death of him.

Chapter Eight

Cyrus stepped out of the master bathroom and into his luxury suite in the King's Coven. He stood by the blazing fire as he dressed, pausing here and there to sip the espresso Girard had brought up.

With a smirk, Cyrus buttoned up his shirt as he thought how he must get used to warming up his body temperature on a daily basis now. His bride will not like him plundering her in the evening with a hard cold member. Vampires were as cold as ice in the evening when they awoke, unless they fed the day before and unfortunately, he hadn't.

He was going to remedy that today, however. Cyrus was going to pay his fiancé a visit and complete their betrothal contract. Confidence surging through him, Cyrus thought of the many different things they could do once she was in his arms, with her blood coursing through his body.

The little he'd tasted was enough to drive him wild. Never, in all his years, had he tasted anything like it. Evangeline was extraordinarily different from any woman he'd ever met. They hadn't known each other long and he was looking forward to discovering all her traits, but there was something about her that intrigued him to no end. To be sure, she was the prettiest girl he'd ever seen, but something else lurked beneath the surface. She was strong willed and resilient.

Advantageous qualities for a queen, he thought languorously.

Victor knocked on his door

"Come in." Cyrus was putting on his jacket as Victor came in and shut the door.

"Your Grace—" Victor's baritone started.

Cyrus cut him off. "Tell Florena to get everyone in the dining room in ten. I just have a few things to go over. Make sure the Mercedes is clean. We'll take it tonight." He paused by his valet as he slid his 1933 gold Patek Philipe round his wrists. "What is it?" Victor was just standing there, his face ashen.

"Your Grace, Florena received an email on the contact page of the home website. We don't have to trace it because it's pretty clear whom it's from." Victor held out a sheet of copy paper. "It was addressed to you."

Cyrus took the paper, curious as to why his manservant looked so on edge and read the short message in black ink:

I have your bride.

Release Serena Perez outside the gates at dawn or she dies. Leave the Wolcott's out of it. This is between you and me.

AP

Cyrus' face was motionless. He looked up at Victor. "Is this a joke?"

"I don't think so, Your Grace. Jane called her cell phone and no one picked up. She called the Wolcott's too and they just said she wasn't home. Didn't give any details."

Cyrus was reading the note again, his head beginning to pound. As he read it a third time, realization sank in. This was no joke.

"MOTHERFUCKER!" Cyrus crunched up the note and threw it across the room. His fangs bared. He stormed out of his room as he bellowed orders. "Get that piece of shit on the phone, right now. Send Florena and Girard to the Blacktail headquarters. I want Maxwell Jones here, like fucking yesterday. Do you hear me?" His shouts could be heard throughout the entire house. "Everyone in the dining room, NOW!"

The entire coven reached the dining room at almost the same time, some teleporting and others speeding through the house with cups of coffee in hand or a newspaper.

Jane ran in last, breathless as the king addressed them. Everyone was aware the Blacktail pack leader had taken Evangeline Wolcott. News traveled fast in the King's Coven. "Do we have any idea where he could have taken her?" Cyrus asked, his fangs still out.

Mary spoke up. "We can rule out Perez's round house." The octagonal house the alpha resided in was the Blacktail Fighter's headquarters. She was right. It would have been way too obvious and risky to take her there.

"Even if she was there, none of us would be able to step one foot on their grounds," Armando, his financial advisor, put in. Werewolves, like vampires, protected their grounds like Fort Knox. If a vampire came near the pack leader's home unannounced, they would find themselves facing a werewolf, a wooden stick through the heart or a laser aimed at their necks.

Florena was typing away on her laptop on the large table with an iPhone to her ear. She put the phone down and looked at him "The same message was left on the main voicemail. Sounds like Perez's beta, Linus."

Victor hung up on his cell. "I only get voicemail at their headquarters."

"Can we track Perez's cell?" Cyrus asked Florena.

"I'll try, but I doubt he took his own cell phone. He's probably using a burner phone. That's what we'd do." She typed away as she spoke.

"Why the fuck would we keep a stinking wolf here?" Girard asked as he lit a cigarette.

Cyrus was quiet for a moment, his mind going a mile a minute. There was no sense sending Florena and Girard to the pack headquarters. He knew the two could handle themselves, but who knew what kind of trap lay in wait for them.

Reeling, Cyrus paced the length of the table, hands on his hips. How the hell did Adam Perez know he was engaged to Evangeline? His coven wouldn't dare tell a soul and he doubted the Wolcott's were screaming it from the rooftops, and Evangeline only found out a few days ago... unless...

"The little bitch!" he said through clenched teeth, halting his stride.

They all turned to him in silence.

Cyrus looked at Victor. "You and Girard are going to pay Mrs. Vance a little visit." His voice was like ice.

"Your Grace..." Jane stepped forward, a worried look on her face.

"Jane, don't start with me! She was spying on all of us for the Blacktails."

"But—" Jane began until Mary shot her a warning look. Cyrus was relieved she backed down, but Jane continued to look nervously at him.

He concentrated on Victor and Girard. *Don't kill*

her, he told them both telepathically, *but be creative. Go.*

They nodded in assent and left the room. Jane stared after them, wringing her hands.

He pinched the bridge of his nose, furious. If he fucking touches Evangeline, it was going to be all out warfare in Wilmington. Where would the mutt take her? "This is ridiculous already. Florena, get that pussy beta's cell number. I want to talk to him, personally. Mary, get Maxwell Jones here. I'm settling this shit once and for all."

****

Starved, Evangeline ate in the cabin's tiny kitchen, feeling refreshed after her bath. To avoid staring at her companion, she took in the cozy kitchen's atmosphere. There was a window just over the sink showing a darkening sky, casting them in a dim glow at the little table for four under weak yellow lighting. Try as she might, her eyes kept wandering back to him.

Adam sat across from Evangeline, looking like an overgrown man seated at a kids table, watching her eat. His black shirt stretched wide over his huge pecks as he drummed the tabletop with his right hand.

She had four slices of the supreme pizza before he took a piece. "Are you going to have more?" she asked.

"Not hungry. It's all yours." He waved his hand over the pizza before placing it back on the table. His left hand rested on his knee, bouncing, picking up the drumming his hand had been doing seconds before.

Swallowing her last piece, she picked up the napkin on the table to wipe her hands. "Shouldn't I be the one with a nervous tick right now?" she asked, nodding at his knee and grabbed the bottle of water he'd given her.

His blue eyes met hers and his knee froze. "Bad habit."

Tilting her head speculatively, she crossed her arms under her breasts where his navy blue shirt read, *Bears,* in orange letters. Evangeline felt a million times better after her extremely long slumber, five slices of pizza and, although she was reluctant to admit, quite comfy in his double X t-shirt and blue scrubs.

Evangeline's cool attitude about her predicament was only slightly unsettling to her. She couldn't describe her calm demeanor after last night's events. She was resigned now for reasons that made no sense. Could it be because deep down she knew he would never hurt her? Was it the fact he'd saved her from the jackal, risking his life in the process, or her certainty he thought kidnapping her would save his sister?

She remembered waking up to his magnificent profile. Evangeline had felt a heavy feeling of sadness, not just for her messed up life, but for his too. This man was haunted and her heart went out to him.

She thought about his reasons for taking her. The sensible side of her was still peeved, but wouldn't she go to the ends of the earth for her own sister?

Katherine must be going out of her mind by now wondering what had happened to her. She was sure her family was going crazy with worry. And Cyrus...did he already know she was with the Blacktail alpha as his captive? For an instant, her stomach tightened, imagining what the king would do to Adam for taking his fiancé.

Again, her eyes fell on his. So much lurked behind those baby blues. Regardless of his rash decision, there was something about him, a peaceful aura that made her feel safe. Nonetheless, she would keep her guard up. Evangeline did not want to fall under this man's spell by feeling sorry for him.

"Feeling better?" he asked in a deep, smooth voice.

"Yes, thank you for the pizza."

He shook his head. "I can't believe you're thanking me."

She shrugged. "It's the polite thing to do."

He just stared, his eyes hooded.

Questioning her sanity again, Evangeline couldn't believe she was sitting at her captor's kitchen table feeling oddly relaxed. She didn't know why she trusted him, but her gut told her he was not the hard man he pretended to be.

It seemed as though they'd come to some unspoken understanding. It must have been their brush with death. They hadn't known each other for long and yet they'd been through quite a lot already. Hell, he'd almost seen her naked.

"Did your friends get the jackal?" she asked

"Yeah." His brow furrowed. "I'm sorry."

"It's not your fault."

One eyebrow rose, incredulously.

"Okay, it was, but I was foolish to think I could outrun a werewolf."

He pondered for a minute, pursing his lips. "You won't be here much longer. I promise."

She blinked. "May I ask what's going on?"

He stared at her thoughtfully before he spoke. His intense glare made her lightheaded. "We e-mailed your father from your account early yesterday morning. He's been calling your cell, but we let it go to voicemail."

"You have my cell phone?"

"Yes. It's dead though. The second e-mail told him the battery died and you left your charger at home. You told him you're safe and just need some time to clear your head." His eyes shifted down to her wrist. "And clearly you do," he said bitingly.

"I've never done anything like this. He's going to have a hard time believing it."

"I doubt you've ever been forced into an unwanted marriage before either," he said, his eyes darkening.

She shifted uncomfortably in her chair. "I don't want to talk about it."

Narrowing his eyes at her, he said calmly, "Fair enough. I just need to know one thing."

She looked at him, not wondering what he was going to ask, but because she couldn't look away.

He licked his lips and his Adam's apple popped up and down. "Has he hurt you?"

She gave him an incredulous look. "You mean done something worse than flinging me out of a window, suffocating me, or almost getting me killed by a jackal? No," she said sarcastically.

His face flushed and he took a deep breath, letting it out his nose. "I'm serious," Adam said menacingly.

"I said no." Evangeline glared at him. "I told you, we just met and other than biting me,"—she raised her wrist at him, the tiny marks were faint pink dots now— "and being arrogant, he hasn't done anything else. Can we drop it?"

He seemed satisfied with her answer and nodded.

Why did it matter so much to him how the king treated her? She found herself wondering what this enigmatic man would do to the North American King if he'd actually hurt her. They were almost identical in height, but Cyrus was slightly leaner, his build more like a swimmer. Adam's body was...perfect in her estimation and bigger than the king's.

He leaned forward and placed his elbows on the table, clasping his hands in front of his mouth as he spoke quietly. "You could have kept running, you know." His voice was calm and smooth again. "Why did you save me?"

They stared at each other for a moment. Evangeline had no explanation for why she'd done it. She shook her head and whispered, "I don't know."

His deep gaze was unwavering. "How did you heal me out there?"

Glancing down at her hands, she said, "I'm not sure. I've been able to do it for years."

He gave her an expectant look, telling her to go on.

Before she spoke, Evangeline questioned why on earth she felt comfortable enough to discuss this private part of her life with a complete stranger, a stranger who had just snapped at her minutes before no less. For some strange reason she felt he *cared*. She brushed the thought away and began speaking. Talking was way better than sitting alone with him in silence. "When I was younger, my sister almost died of Leukemia. Every doctor told us she only had a few months to live." She paused to swallow hard, looking over his shoulder, remembering those awful days. "We brought her home to be comfortable and one night I came into her room. I remember looking at her and seeing her stare up at the ceiling with tears in her eyes. She was so young. I remember feeling as though I would die without her. "

Adam's face was solemn as he listened.

"I felt a number of things. I was so unbearably sad, angry, and lost and started to tremble. At first it was a soft shudder, then I started to shake uncontrollably. I threw myself at my sister and the instant I touched her I felt this ball of energy leave me and shoot into her." Evangeline stared at her hands now in her lap. "I healed her." She spoke as if she still couldn't believe it. She met Adam's eyes. "I've never told anyone about my ability. The only ones who know are Katherine, my parents, and Katherine's doctor, Dr. Moros."

"The vampire doc?" Adam interrupted.

"Yes. Do you know him?"

"Of him."

Her eyes brightened when she thought of the man/vampire who had tried everything to save her sister. She'd heard he'd married a vampire a few years ago and turned himself. She hadn't seen him since he'd transitioned. "He's one of the nicest men I've ever known."

Adam bit the insides of his cheeks and frowned.

She ignored his glower. "Anyway, we don't know how it happens, but we've kept it a secret, so I'd appreciate it if you didn't tell anyone."

His frown deepened. "Of course not. In fact, I hope you never do it again."

Evangeline flinched. "What do you mean?"

"You were knocked out for almost two days and you're just barely recovering. You said it yourself; you've never been out that long. It's obviously taking a toll on you. Don't ever do it again," he demanded.

Shocked at his words, she stammered back, "Don't...tell me what to do. If it weren't for me, you'd be dead or dying right now. What would happen to your sister then, huh?"

His eyes blazed with fury.

Shit. His sister was a touchy subject, obviously. "I'm sorry. I know you're worried about her." She looked at him cautiously. "Mr...." She paused, feeling awkward addressing her captor formally.

He brushed his hand through his tousled hair edgily. "You know my name. Just call me Adam."

"Okay, Adam." She liked the way his name sounded out loud. "I believe you think the king has your sister, but I have to say, I'm not convinced he does."

He gave her a sharp look.

"Just hear me out before you jump down my throat," she said, exasperated.

He jerked his head to the side, but the scowl remained.

"It just doesn't make sense. The whole timing is off. Say he was plotting to take your sister. Why would he knowing it would cause trouble, perhaps even a war, when he was planning to marry me?" Rolling her eyes at herself, she went on. "I'm not exactly sure how long he's planned this, but according to my father, he's been watching me for some time. I find it hard to believe he was planning marriage, contributing to the Vampires in Transitions Facility and, as I read recently, signing a Vampire Treaty with the Asian King. Not to mention the attacks on your Fighters... it all just seems off base to me. Why would a king, albeit, a conniving one, who has struggled for control in these parts wreak havoc on his enemies now of all times?"

"I'm sure you think you know what you're talking about, but you have no idea the kind of filth Cyrus

Stewart is."

"I beg to differ." Evangeline's voice was laced with malice.

He clenched his teeth. "Then why the hell are you marrying him?" he hissed.

"I don't have a choice," she shot back.

His eyes fastened on hers, his expression unnerving.

Leaning back against her chair, she looked away. He was bent forward on the table, his arms bulging like he wanted to break something, fists clenched. "It's just something I have to do," she said more calmly. "It's fine. I've come to terms with it."

"No, you haven't. You tense up every time we talk about him and this overwhelming depression fills you up."

She sat up, stunned, remembering too late werewolves were emotional readers. *Great.*

Resting back against his chair, he nodded slowly at her. "Yeah, I can feel it. Depression is all around you. It never goes away."

They sat in silence for a while, eyes locked on one another. Evangeline was feeling something else at the moment and prayed to God he didn't sense it. His thick golden neck twitched as he spoke and Evangeline imagined herself kissing him all around his throat. She looked away.

Why did he care so much? Why did it matter to him who she married or how many people she healed? If she didn't know any better, she would think he actually felt something for her.

Evangeline stared at the countertop, but her mind and body were completely aware of the man in front of her and she shut her lids, fighting not to look into those intense eyes. Eyes that saw right through her, eyes that made her insides melt to pure mush.

Oh God! She was a freaking cliché'. Was she, like so many captives, suffering from Stockholm Syndrome? Yes. It had to be, because the sane part of her would not lust after her captor.

She looked at him reluctantly, and a huge knot formed in her stomach. "Look, I'll help you get your sister back."

"What?" he asked skeptically.

"If keeping me prisoner…"

He gave her a wry look.

"You know what I mean…if you think keeping me here will get your sister back, then I'm game. It's not like I'm in any rush to marry anyway."

Adam's nostrils flared.

"All I ask is you treat me with respect and let me walk around the house and not locked up in the bedroom the whole time. I'm not going anywhere after yesterday's debacle and I don't even know where I am." Shrugging, she added, "Are we agreed?"

Adam gave her a small smile and she found it hard not to look away from his lips. "Agreed." He leaned in close, his eyes darkening, not with anger, but what she could only describe as hunger. "But I suggest you get a reign on your hormones there."

She gasped in shock.

"Or *I'll* act on *your* emotions, Evangeline." Her name rolled off his tongue, low and sweet.

Her cheeks flushed as she stared at him. How in God's name could she control her emotions around this man?

Sitting back in his chair, he shook his head. "Sorry. You don't deserve that." He stood up. "I'm going out. I won't be far and I'll still be able to hear you. Don't worry, your safe, just call out if you need me."

Evangeline watched his broad back as he walked out of the cabin, barely noticing she gripped the sides of her chair. The craziest thought slipped through her befuddled mind and she pictured Adam Perez's large frame straining over her as he "acted on her emotions."

****

Peter Vance checked the time on his corner office wall. He'd be home late again tonight. As an Alderman and lawyer in Wilmington he often worked long hours. He didn't mind, though. It beat going home to be ignored by his wife.

Stretching at his desk, he wondered if he should pick up some Chinese food on the way home. There sure wasn't going to be a home cooked meal waiting for him.

Where had he gone wrong? Sure, he wasn't the same man he'd been years ago, fawning over Mona and buying anything and everything she ever wanted, but people change in a relationship. Peter wished his wife would see he was still here for her. He loved her still and wanted to make things work between them. He couldn't stand to have a wife who was never home, but whenever he brought up the subject, she'd jump down his throat.

He opened the left-hand drawer of his desk and took out his flask he'd gotten as a best man gift from his brother years ago. Twisting the cap off, he took a long swig of Jameson then placed it on the desk. Lord knows he'd just go fishing for it in a minute or two if he put it away.

Mona told him earlier she was going out to dinner with her friend, which meant she'd be gone as long as the wine held out at the restaurant bar.

Great.

His computer made a sound indicating he had a new email. He checked to see whom it was from and smirked.

His friend Seth sent him an e-mail and the subject read, *Open with Care ;)*.

Seth was a sixteen-year-old boy at heart. Shaking his head, Peter clicked the link and instantly a black and white image of a bathroom popped up. There were two stalls and two sinks along one side and near the adjacent wall were two men and a woman.

The woman was clearly drunk and servicing both men at the same time, loving every minute of it.

Squinting at the monitor, he recognized the ring she wore.

"Mona?" Peter said in disbelief.

He looked closer at the screen with wide, shocked eyes. It was her, his wife, fucking two guys in a bathroom like she'd done it a hundred times before. He checked the bottom of the screen to see this was streaming live. Just then, the two guys turned to look at the camera, and as if they knew he was watching, smiled, revealing fangs.

Chapter Nine

The annoying sound of birds chirping woke Adam at the crack of dawn. He lay sprawled on the sofa, one foot on the floor, the other dangling off the arm, his large body too big for the dainty thing.

He kept his eyes closed, his mind filled with images of Evangeline laying on her side in his bed, in the tub, wrapped in a towel and, he thought with a surge of possessiveness, draped in his oversized Bears t-shirt.

Adam remembered how her slick skin felt beneath his fingers and imagined what she looked like. His body was becoming overheated. He had no blanket and no shirt, but his chest gleamed with moisture. Draping his arm over his eyes, he refused to let the early morning light diffuse the hot images of her in his head. He fumbled with the buckle of his jeans, giving his hard on a little more room to breathe.

When it didn't help, he found himself slipping his hand in his briefs to shift his swollen sex, but the ache he felt for the girl in the other room made him grip himself hard. His face tightened and his jaws locked at his vice-like hold. Breathing a little heavily now, he began rubbing himself slowly, his chest heaving up and down, as he pictured Evangeline on top of him, gyrating her hips as he watched her.

A door creaked and his hand shot out of his pants at the same time he jumped up off the couch. Before

Evangeline could step out he zipped up and buckled his jeans.

She paused when she saw him, her hand coming up to tame her hair. She looked even more beautiful this morning in his shirt with her hair all tousled. When she looked him over, he didn't move, letting her get her fill of him, shirtless, and hard for her.

The energy between them seemed to swell to new heights. Her eyes lingered for a moment on his chest and her cheeks flushed. "I'm…just…" She stammered and pointed toward the bathroom.

He just nodded and she slipped in, closing the door behind her.

Sitting back down on the sofa, he placed his head in his hands and leaned on his knees. Cyrus better give up Serena and fast. There was no way in telling what he'd do if he was stuck with Evangeline for longer than necessary.

Maybe he should have left Jason to handle this part of the kidnapping. His stomach knotted, picturing Jason carrying her in his arms or taking her out of the tub.

And then it hit him.

It was absurd, but he wanted to be the only one to hold her, to see her wrapped in a towel, to watch her sleep peacefully. *Only him.*

Was he crazy? She was engaged to his immortal enemy. He couldn't think of her that way. After this was over, he would never see her again, so all his lustful thoughts had to be put aside.

His phoned vibrated in his pocket and he reached for it quickly. At 5:30 this morning Jason had called with news. The king left him a message stating he did not have Serena and demanded Evangeline be released.

Adam had expected this. It was only his first attempt. They were going to let the fucker sit on the knowledge his pack had his fiancé until he broke.

He read the message. *Maxwell Jones called me. I'm meeting him this afternoon once he gets some rest. Apparently he was with the king till early this morning. I'll call you with details.*

Fuck!

This was all getting out of hand. If Jones went to the cops, he and his pack were going to have to hit the road.

What the hell did this mean? Was Evangeline right? Did the king not have his sister? And if so, then where the hell was she?

His stomach lurched as he thought of the worst possible scenarios; raped, murdered, mutilated. She was thirty-two, but still a child by his standards.

Did Serena just split with some guy she was too afraid to bring around him and the Fighters? This seemed plausible since the guys all treated her like a little sister and were extremely overprotective. Perhaps she couldn't take it anymore.

No. If that were the case, then she would have called him. He hated the thought, but maybe he should go to the police. If Cyrus didn't have her, and he still wasn't completely convinced he didn't, then he would call the authorities. Although, he thought pitifully, if the pack hadn't found her, he doubted the cops could do better.

Until he found out more information, he was going to play this thing out. He'd managed to get control of Evangeline, or at least she wasn't trying to run or scared of him anymore and she'd left a message with her father last night when he got back. She told him she was visiting a friend in Chicago and she'd be back in a couple days. Evangeline had also left a message at the ballet studio apologizing for not showing up to work Thursday and Friday and she'd be back at work on Tuesday. The studio was closed on Sundays and Mondays.

Evangeline stepped out of the bathroom and walked into the sunlit living room. She looked around. "It looks different in here, more cheerful."

The sun caught her olive eyes and the worry he'd felt a moment before lessened slightly. Strangely, he was pleased she thought his cabin was cheerful. He wanted to make her feel comfortable and he was thankful for the room's cozy atmosphere.

Evangeline turned to look at him and caught him staring. She looked down at herself. "A little tip for your next kidnapping…grab some extra clothes for your captive."

He gave her a sardonic smirk. "I'll try to remember." He stood up and walked past her. "I'll throw your clothes in the wash before I take a shower, then I'll make us something to eat."

Evangeline's face brightened. "I'll make breakfast."

He paused in the hallway and regarded her.

"I'm no chef, but I can manage breakfast. Besides it'll give me something to do." She pointed at the coffee table. "You know the only reading material you have here is *Cigar Aficionado* and *Men's Health*. Considering my predicament, I was pretty bored last night."

Smothering the urge to laugh, he said, "Sorry,

those are my friend's magazines and I'm afraid we cancelled our *Cosmo* subscription."

"Darn. I guess you'll just have to suffer with my cooking then." She walked off into the kitchen and he turned to throw her clothes in the wash with a stupid grin on his face.

After he showered, he threw on a pair of jeans and a blue t-shirt and walked into the kitchen barefoot.

Evangeline was at the stove, flipping toast in a frying pan. "Can I help?" he asked.

She looked over at him. The image of her barefoot in his kitchen, wearing his clothes, and cooking was strange to him and oddly pleasant. "You had enough ingredients for French toast and I found syrup. Can you take out two plates?"

"Sure." He grabbed two plates and utensils and put them on the table, then grabbed two water bottles from the fridge.

Evangeline brought over a plate full of delicious smelling French toast and they sat down at the table to dig in.

"Not bad," he said through mouthfuls. "Thanks for cooking, by the way."

"You're welcome. It's nothing like my sister's French toast. I don't know what she does, but it's to die for." She shrugged at herself.

"So is this," he said quietly and an adorable flush colored her cheeks again.

They ate in silence for a while. She finished first and sipped her water, looking out the window. "Do you think we could go outside for awhile? I'd like to get some exercise and fresh air."

He paused, his trademark frown in place.

She looked at him pointedly, fiddling with the bottle in her hand. "I can't outrun you so you know I won't try and escape. Besides, I told you I'd stay if it gets your sister back."

Swallowing the rest of the food, he said simply, "Okay."

Her brow crinkled curiously. "Have you heard anything?"

Considering what to tell her, Adam decided on the truth. She wasn't the enemy here. Her bloodsucking fiancé was the enemy and the knowledge made him cringe inwardly again.

"A few hours ago Cyrus contacted my second…said he didn't have my sister and demanded we let you go. We didn't expect him to give her up so easily, even though we have you. He's testing us. I believe he knows I won't hurt you, but it still kills him to know you are under my care. He has also contacted Maxwell Jones." Evangeline's eyebrows shot up. "My beta is meeting him this afternoon," Adam finished, wiping his hands on a napkin.

"Max is a close personal friend of my family. He'll be honor bound to go to my father."

Adam leaned back in his chair. "I don't think he will just yet. Jones likes to settle things quietly. Alerting your family will start a ruckus."

She nodded at him thoughtfully, her gorgeous lips slightly parted.

After they cleaned up the kitchen, they stepped out into the sun for a walk. He didn't know how much exercise she would get, walking in his slippers, but she looked adorable anyway.

He led her along a narrow path he rarely used, and

took in the smells of the woods and the hot summer day.

Evangeline was back to wearing her black pants and white camisole. Although he loved it when she was in his shirt, she looked even better in her fitted clothes hugging her slender curves.

She walked in front of him and all he did was stare at her round bottom with the hot indent on the sides flexing as she moved. He could make a living studying her body.

Evangeline walked over to a large oak tree and turned around, leaning her back against it, taking a deep breath.

"Are you okay?" he asked worriedly, coming toward her.

She held out her hand. "I'm fine. I guess I'm still getting my energy back." Shrugging, she joked, "I must be getting old."

He sat down on a tree stump a few feet from her tree. "How old are you?"

"Twenty-two."

He cocked his head. "Wow. You're younger than my sister. Don't take this the wrong way, but you seem older."

She gave him a wry look. "Thanks. Unfortunately I get that a lot." Tilting her head curiously, she asked, "How old are you?"

He grinned. "Fifty-seven." Werewolves have a long life span of several hundred years.

"You don't look fifty-seven," she said.

"I'm actually considered young by our standards. Weres usually stop aging at twenty, some twenty-five, but I went through a lot in my twenties so the process didn't stop till I was thirty. Generally speaking, I look older than most werewolves."

She nodded at him. He had a feeling she knew a lot about his species. She already knew about their tattoos. He was wondering what she thought about him. The other night she said it was the first time meeting someone of the supernatural world. Was she interested in his world or repulsed?

"How old were you the first time you changed?" she asked with an adorable inquiring expression, the corner of her eyes squinting slightly.

Hey, maybe she was still interested. Adam kicked out his legs in front of him and crossed his arms. "I was ten when puberty hit. It's when we all phase for the first time. We get that along with all the other puberty crap."

"But, you knew what you were already, right?"

He nodded. "Yeah, I knew. I'm a pure blood so I'd watched my parents phase a bunch of times before it happened to me." He hesitated, an anxious knot building inside him. "How much do you know about me?"

The look on her face told him she knew enough. "I know the rumors," she uttered, looking uneasy. "You don't have to tell me anything, but I don't believe them."

He looked at her askance. "You what?"

She shifted against the tree uncomfortably. "I don't believe you murdered your father because you were crazy or to attain the alpha status. I mean… you have to go through a vote anyway."

He stared at her intently.

"I don't know why you did it, but you must have had your reasons. I've never killed anyone, but I can't imagine how it would feel. You've obviously had to live with anguish for some time now. It must be quite painful." She continued to stare at him apprehensively.

He couldn't believe what he was hearing. Any other woman would have been shocked to know she was standing in the woods with a man that had murdered his father. But here she was, almost consoling him.

"You've kept the peace in Wilmington, until now, and protected your pack. I believe deep down, you're a good man." Her voice lowered as she spoke.

Adam wanted to go to her, wrap his arms around her and claim her luscious mouth, but if he took one step, she would be on her back in a second.

He spoke up finally. "My father used to beat my mother." Evangeline's eyes widened. "When my sister was born, my father, in another drunken stupor, claimed she wasn't his child." He arched a brow. "Now, I don't know if she is or isn't. Still don't. Truth be told, I hope she's not my father's child. Thankfully, she looks like my mother.

"Anyway, I had been back and forth to Chicago and when my sister was born, I decided to stay close to home so I could watch over her. I knew how my father was and I worried over Serena and my mother. I went to work for my family's construction company." The Perez family owned a construction company and a lumberyard in Wilmington still thrived till this day. "I lived with Jason at the time, but I would pay my family a visit on my way home. One night, I came home and found my mother lying on the kitchen floor, dead." Adam saw Evangeline gasp and felt the pain course through her. She suffered for him.

"I'll spare you the details," he said, looking away.

Her voice leaden, she said, "Adam, I'm so sorry."

Shaking his head, he said, "What's done is done." He was thankful she looked away from him.

He didn't tell Evangeline his father was in the kitchen too. Xavier Perez sat at the kitchen table completely trashed, with his head in his hands. He had choked the life out of his wife in a jealous rage.

Adam shifted to his wolf form on the spot and attacked his father. His father fought back, futilely, too drunk to stand up straight or shift himself.

Before Adam broke his neck, his father had given him a brief nod, his tear stung eyes expressing their assent for his son to kill him.

Adam shook himself out of the past. He wasn't going to get swept up in agony again. His focus now was finding his sister.

Watching Evangeline closely, another notion came to mind. His focus was to find his sister *and* to save this woman from marrying a monster.

"Why are you marrying him?" His voice rumbled low.

She turned to him in surprise. "I told you," she whispered.

"No, you didn't. Tell me," he replied sternly.

Looking down at her feet, she took a deep breath. "My father stole funds from the king. I happen to believe the king compelled him into doing this, but I have no proof. Several of my father's investments had fallen through and my father resorted to gambling and lost terribly. The king was no doubt spying on my family and found out all this information. He compelled my father into taking money meant for the new

Transition Facility." She lifted her chin, attempting to look stronger than she actually felt, but she couldn't fool Adam. He listened with growing hatred for the bastard king. "In exchange for me, Cyrus is allowing my father to keep the money as a bride price and not go to the authorities."

"That son of a bitch," Adam growled, his forearms rippling as tremors ran through him.

"I tried to get out of it, but Cyrus threatens to do more to my family if I don't cooperate."

Adam sat forward on the stump, his elbows on his knees and fists clenched over his mouth. It was hard to get control right now. He wanted to kill Cyrus Stewart with a vengeance. "You can't marry him," he said with loathing.

She gave him a defeated look. "I have to."

"How could…" Adam stopped himself. How could her father let this happen? How could he simply hand her off to a fucking vampire? It was on the tip of his tongue to say this, but he didn't want to add to her pain. He was sure she was pissed at her father already.

"Can we talk about something else?" she asked miserably.

He nodded, still fuming over what she'd told him. He couldn't picture this sweet woman with a vampire, let alone the king.

"Does it hurt when you phase?" she asked tentatively. He had a feeling she was trying to distract him. Looking down, he noticed his clasped hands were red and his vision had altered. His eyes had shifted again.

He calmed his irises by pressing his thumb and forefinger over his eyes. "I'm used to it now. It did before, but after several full moons, your body gets accustomed to the pain." Dropping his hand from his face, he paused and looked at her with concern. Voice low, he asked, "Did I scare you the other night? When you saw me in my wolf form?"

She shook her head. "No, on the contrary, I thought you were beautiful."

He flinched slightly. *Beautiful?* She stared at him with her smoldering eyes and he felt his chest constrict. Jesus, the things she did to him…

Scrunching her brow in thought, she asked, "When is the next full moon?"

Adam remembered with a sense of foreboding what day it was. It was almost the full moon. Which meant, the moon heat, the day before the full moon was almost upon them. The day of mating or what Ramo called, Fuck Fest. He should have known she would wonder about this. "It's in a couple of days. Don't worry. You'll be gone before then," he assured her, clasping his hands again in front of him.

She looked at him uneasily. "What about…" she stammered.

Adam peered up at her through his lashes. "The moon heat?" he supplied for her.

She nodded. "Yes…what do you…I mean…do you have someone?" Her gaze was eager on him.

He stared for a moment then nodded.

She looked down, avoiding his eyes. "Is she your girlfriend?"

He shrugged. "Not really, just a heat mate. We're just there for each other during those days."

"And other days?" Her voice sounded cold.

"Truth be told, I haven't really had much time for a

relationship."

Her mouth was set in a thin line now and her chest heaved a little too rapidly. Surprised, he felt a feeling he hadn't sensed in another in a long time. "Are you going to be with her, then, in a few days?"

His eyes narrowed at her and he didn't need to read her emotions because she was showing them loud and clear.

Evangeline was amazingly *jealous*.

"Would it bother you?" he asked softly.

She shrugged and looked away. "What do I care?"

"A lot, apparently," he quipped.

She shot him a reproachful look.

Adam licked his lips, surveying her. "I won't go to her if it bothers you," he said smoothly, his eyes locked on hers, thrilling to the fact she was jealous. In all honesty, he only wanted to be with her and no woman, not even Reanna would satisfy him. And for some reason, he did not want to hurt Evangeline. Somehow, in their brief time together, she'd come to truly matter to him. "Tell me. Does it?"

Evangeline's soft voice was sweet and pulled at his heart. "Yes," she whispered as her eyes bore into his.

"Then I won't," he said matter of fact.

They were fixated on each other for a long while, this new revelation sinking in and wrapping them in a sheet of fascination.

The reality she did not want him to be with another woman made his chest swell and his entire body come to life. This new possessive side of hers was damn sexy and he wanted her.

In a raspy voice, she asked, "What will you do?"

Adam pushed himself off his elbows. "There are

ways we can cope without a companion. I'll be fine." He stood slowly and with long purposeful strides, came to her. Stopping only an inch or two away from her, he looked down at her lovely face. In a silky voice, he asked, "Do you want to be with me during the moon heat?" He reached up and brushed strands of hair out of her face. His eyes blazed as she shivered. "Do you want it to be you?"

****

Evangeline's heart was ready to burst out of her chest. She couldn't believe she was reacting this way, but the minute he revealed there was someone else, Evangeline had felt her insides freeze up and her heart leap into her throat.

Imagining him with some faceless woman, a werewolf, who shared this common bond, was enough to drive her insane.

What did she care he had someone else? She'd only met him a few days ago and he was her captor, no less. She shouldn't be having these feelings for him, but there they were. How it happened, she didn't know, but for some odd reason Evangeline wanted this beautiful, mysterious man all to herself.

His fingertips grazed her cheek, sending tiny tremors down her spine. "Do you?" Adam's husky voice murmured, his breath tickling her forehead. "Do you want it to be you, Evangeline?"

A tiny part of her wanted to tell him no, but she just nodded mutely as she stared at his perfectly sculpted lips.

His hand traveled from her hair to her neck and began massaging her throat gently. Silver blue eyes turned turquoise to midnight blue as he spanned his fingers around her jaw, arching her neck. Her heart quickened as he drew closer. The instant she felt his warm lips on hers, a fire lit inside of her.

Strong lips, gentle and yet firm, explored hers as his other arm came around her waist to the small of her back. When she felt his tongue glide along her mouth, seeking passage in, she welcomed him with a moan, their kiss becoming more heated and urgent. Pressing herself against him, she tugged him close, wrapping one arm around his neck, the other at his back, needing to feel every part of him. Her mind clouded at his touch, the smell of his skin, his warm body against hers and she pulled ever closer as their kiss turned crucial. She felt his arousal against her belly, his hips slowly rocking back and forth and her body reacted instantly.

Evangeline spread her legs and his thigh slid between hers, rubbing her tender sex roughly. She felt warm moisture ebb out of her and he groaned, squeezing her tightly to him, gripping the fabric at her back. He came up to stare at her and took a deep breath to smell how hot she was for him. Adam came down again and rained kisses down her neck, one arm still holding her, as he pushed himself more fiercely against her.

She felt her strap come down over her shoulder and then cool air as he bared one breast. Pulling slightly back to look at her, his eyelids heavy, he growled low and brought his mouth over her nipple.

She cried out in pure elation. Never in her life had she ever wanted a man more. She couldn't remember ever feeling such intensity, such yearning. It felt as though she would faint from the ecstasy they radiated.

He licked her nipple, sucking as he grinded her.

Evangeline lifted her leg around his waist and his ministrations on her breast got greedier. Her soft moans of pleasure urged him on and his breathing became loud and strained.

Adam came up, abruptly breathless. He leaned his forehead on hers, his hand still cupping her breast as his thumb played with her nipple. "We have to stop," he whispered and he sounded like a different man.

"No." She squeezed the back of his shirt as her other hand came down to grab his ass. "Don't stop." Her voice too, sounded like someone else, deeper and tense.

Adam and Evangeline were quite a sight. She imagined how they looked, pressed up against the tree, her leg around him, his thigh between hers with his hand on her breast.

Adam kissed her gently as he spoke. "If we don't stop now, I'm going to take you right here, up against this oak."

"Do it," she uttered, wanting him, needing him inside her right then. "I want you to."

Cursing, he pulled away, taking one lasting look at her exposed breast before covering it with her camisole.

Evangeline couldn't move. She rested her head on the tree as she tried to control her breathing. Adam stood in front of her, killing her with his deep gaze. "We should head back."

She looked away, slightly hurt he'd turned her down, but reality set in then, and she stood up straight. Her legs felt like Jell-O, but she forced them to cooperate, avoiding the aching pain in her chest.

Chapter Ten

The soft summer breeze was irritating. The woman standing on her third-story balcony contemplated starting a thunderstorm to emulate the anger coursing through her. Fury and rage were too miniscule words to describe the ferocity she felt, but she took it all with her usual calm, composed demeanor as she did everything else. Losing control was never an option.

She gazed at her view with wise eyes, eyes that had seen millions of things over several centuries. Things that would make the illustrious King of North America and Blacktail alpha cringe in agony.

The thought of the two supernatural species made her eyes flash and she felt them burn red. She'd allowed their growing races to run rampant for far too long.

Her jaw flexed before she spoke to her underling. "Our efforts, thus far, have been deplorable." She said, glancing back at her recruit.

The half naked man behind her bowed his head in subservience. "I understand mistress, but they are growing in population faster than we could imagine and with the King marrying—"

The woman turned to glare at him now, cutting him off, she said, "There will be no marriage, Leonardo, and you know it." She spoke to him as if he were a troublesome child and she a teacher.

"Of course, mistress. I miss-poke. I only meant—"

"Enough." She waved a hand at him. "Leave me. I believe Rosaline was looking for you earlier. Go and be of some service to at least one of us."

She watched as the young Leo hardened at the mention of her sister and turn to leave. Shaking her head, she thought of how frightened he'd been the first time he was brought to her and her sisters. The boy had screamed in agony as they had their way with him. Chaining his wrists and ankles were no longer necessary, but it certainly took most of the fun out of it.

They needed to work on their new toy down below…and soon.

****

They headed back to the cabin in total silence. Adam walked slowly, so as not to overexert Evangeline, but this time he kept up his strides with her. The last thing he wanted to see was her walking in front of him. Hell, it wasn't even the day of the moon heat, but he sure felt like he was going to explode.

He shook his head in disgust. How could he have taken advantage of her jealousy and put his filthy, murderous, wolf hands on such a woman? He was not worthy of someone like her.

Fuck!

Reading her emotions, he squeezed his eyes shut. She was feeling hurt, confused and horny. *Great*.

Just then, Adam felt a number of emotions near them. "Shit."

Evangeline turned to him. "What's wrong?"

Adam felt his Fighters as if they were shouting their sentiments for the entire woods. Jason and Alex felt embarrassed because they were about to encounter their alpha, all sexed up. Ramo was pissed and Nick was worried.

"We have company," he told Evangeline.

She looked at him in surprise.

"It's okay. They're my pack members." Instinctively, he grabbed her hand. "Do you want to meet them?"

Evangeline went from nervous to curious. He didn't know why, but he felt like he was about to introduce a girlfriend to his parents for some reason.

"Sure," was all she said.

They entered the clearing where his pack members were assembled in front of the cabin. Jason was sitting on the front steps, avoiding his gaze.

Alex stood next to Ramo, shifting his feet uncomfortably. Ramo's hands were on his hips, a look of impatience planted on his face as Nick stood next to him, fists clenched.

It was Nicholas who Adam addressed first with a palm in the air. His pack members could never physically do anything to him and they were subservient to him, but they sure didn't mind voicing their opinions and Nick looked like he was going to pitch a fit.

"She's fine," Adam told him.

Nick was worried he'd taken advantage of Evangeline. Good Old Nick, always a gentlemen. It was clear he was agitated and he flexed his hands, running them through his tawny hair. He nodded at Adam, but looked uncertainly over at Evangeline.

Adam watched Nick stare hard at her, studying her current state of emotion when he felt Nick become fucking smitten with her.

They stopped in front of his men and Ramo was

the first to approach them. He had short brown hair and brown eyes. He wore jeans and a t-shirt just like Adam and Jason, but he also sported a lip ring and several tattoos.

"Hello there. So you're the one we're starting a war over." Ramo smiled smoothly and reached out a hand to Evangeline, then froze as Adam snarled. "Easy there, cuz. I was just going to give her a customary shake of the hand." Ramo turned to Evangeline and cautiously took her hand. "Geez, you'd think I was stealing his bone or something." He winked at her and then stepped away.

Adam was still a little surprised how possessive he was over her and the knowledge of it scared him to death. She wasn't his, but he was acting as if she was.

"Evangeline, this is Ramo Perez, my cousin." Adam eyed her apprehensively.

Evangeline smiled at Ramo. It was hard not to smile at his cousin. The guy looked like he had a dirty joke on his mind all the time and it seemed to drive girls wild.

Adam finished the introductions. "This is my beta, Jason Linus." Evangeline looked at him in awe. She'd clearly read about his longhaired friend and that bothered him too.

What the hell! Get a grip. These men were like his brothers.

"And this is Nicholas Manning and Alex Suarez."

Evangeline shook all their hands and smiled politely. "It's nice to meet all of you."

Alex Suarez was the brain in his operation, and he always looked pissed. It didn't help he wore all black and his full mustache and beard gave people the impression he was about to hit them. Adam was afraid he might make Evangeline nervous, but she seemed fine.

"Aren't you a friendly hostage," Ramo joked and Alex punched him in the arm, hard. "Ow! Just kidding."

Nicholas spoke. "It's great to meet you, Ms. Wolcott, but do you mind if we talk with Adam privately for a moment?"

"Sure. No problem. I'll just go inside." Adam reluctantly let go of her hand. She gave Adam one last look before going in and this new sick, possessive side of his wanted her to stay with him. God, he was losing it.

As soon as the front door closed behind her Ramo and Nicholas started talking at the same time.

"Tell me you didn't sleep with the king's fiancé?"

"Are you out of your fucking mind?"

Adam bristled at his Fighters' tone. He turned first to Ramo, then Nick. "No and it's none of your damn business."

"This shit's gotta end, man." Ramo had gone from suave while Evangeline was around to pissed again. "I didn't like this plan from the beginning, but now you're getting involved with her? This is nuts."

Adam ignored the two of them and turned to Jason. "What happened with Jones?"

Jason stood up and shook his head solemnly. "He was with the king for several hours and was even allowed to attend the coven's meeting, but Maxwell is certain Serena isn't there. The coven thinks we want to start a war. They think we're making everything up to get total control over the area." Jason took a deep breath and looked away. "I'm sorry, man, but after hearing Jones out, I really don't think Cyrus has Serena."

Stunned, Adam stared at Jason. He wasn't the only one in turmoil over his sister. Jason Linus was giving off a profound sadness. You didn't need to possess the bond to know how in love Jason was with his sister. It was written all over his pain-stricken face.

He wasn't sure if Serena knew how Jason felt. He'd never actually come out and said it to her or Adam. Hell, Jason didn't like to talk at all, let alone tell his best friend he was in love with his sister, but Adam was not looking forward to the day he did.

Nick, Alex, and Ramo were looking at both of them, always uncomfortable when they felt Jason's soft side for Serena.

"Where the hell can she possibly be?" Nick asked.

Alex said, "I hate to say it, but I think we acted too swiftly on this one." He looked apologetically at Adam. "I mean…I would of done the same thing if it were my sister, but now we have to face the repercussions for taking the king's fiancé. He's going to want to retaliate."

Alex was right. He, Adam, had started a war for assuming his life-long enemy had taken his sister. Had he been thinking clearly, he might have thought of a better plan. He looked at his Fighters. They would stand by his side, fight with him and even die for him. He cringed inwardly at the thought.

Adam and Cyrus had kept the peace for so long, why the hell did he have to kill Tyson? How the hell did this whole mess start?

And where in God's name was Serena? He didn't believe she would take off of her own accord without telling Adam. She was smart and responsible. It just wasn't like her to up and bail.

Nicholas cut into his thoughts. "Adam?"

"What?" he said quickly, his eyes glued to the ground.

Nick stood with his hands on hips. He spoke carefully. "You have to take her back. The longer you keep her, makes it worse for all of us."

His sister was still missing, and he'd started a war with the vampires, and now he had to accept he was never going to see Evangeline again.

He had to take her back; back to her fiancé, the bloodsucking animal that was blackmailing her.

Jesus Christ. If ever he needed a stiff drink or better yet, a loaded gun to his head, it was right now.

****

Evangeline peered through the window at the five massive men gathered in front of the cabin. She didn't want to be nosey, but she couldn't help herself. They were huge and in their own chilling, gladiator way, quite beautiful.

She wondered which one was which the other night, fighting the jackal and kinda hoped they would all phase right before her eyes.

Was she insane? She was an unarmed woman surrounded by werewolves and she wanted them to phase. There was definitely something wrong with her.

Not for the first time, her gaze fell on Adam again. His stance was so powerful, so commanding and she remembered how it felt to be in his strong arms.

No part of her regretted their kiss. In truth, she was dying for him to kiss her again. She had never felt such rapture, such pure, exquisite passion. Evangeline felt her stomach lurch at the thought of his hands on her, his tongue laving at her nipple.

How could she feel such intense feelings for a man she just met, a man that had taken her hostage? As the thought came to her, she realized none of it mattered to her anymore. She certainly did not feel like a hostage. She wanted to be here…with him.

Evangeline watched as Adam shook hands with Nick and Alex and how Jason and Ramo both gave him a pat on the back. Whatever the pack members told him, it wasn't good news because Adam looked miserable.

He stepped slowly onto the porch and to the front door. Evangeline turned to him as he entered the small living room.

"What's happened?" she asked him apprehensively, her arms crossed tightly at her midriff.

His gaze on her was unwavering and utterly lost. "You were right," he said, slowly.

She raised an eyebrow.

"Cyrus doesn't have Serena. I don't know where she is." Walking over to the cabinet, he pulled out a bottle of tequila. He didn't open it, just stared at it with a lost anguish look, and then put it down. He turned to look at her. His shoulders slumped, he managed to rearrange his expression to the eerie calm that drove her crazy, and leaned against the wall. His voice heavy, he said, "You're free to go."

Pain shot through her chest at the thought of leaving him. She scrambled for some excuse as to why this hurt so much. She should be happy to go home, but how could she ever be happy? Her home wasn't hers much longer. She'd soon be with the coven and married to a vampire she despised.

"I'm so sorry I dragged you into all of this. Cyrus won't blame you. I'll make sure he knows it was all my doing. He won't...he can't...do anything to you...FUCK!" he shouted and reached for the bottle of Patron, flinging it across the room. The bottle smashed on the adjacent wall with a loud bang, debris falling along with its contents all over the floor.

Evangeline jumped at impact when glass hit drywall, but recovered fast. She turned to him and watched him cover his face with his hands. She hated to see him this way, so helpless and torn.

In a soft voice, he said through his hands, "I'm sorry. I didn't mean to scare you."

"It's all right. I'm fine." And she was fine. She was with him and as long as they were together she would never feel scared or alone. This realization didn't shock her. Hadn't she always known the Blacktail leader wouldn't hurt her? He was in pain now and all she wanted to do was comfort him.

There was an odd, yet delightful awakening building inside her and it mesmerized her. Evangeline couldn't take her eyes off him. It was as if an invisible force was pulling her heart toward this man. It pained her to see him this way and she wanted to take it all away. She wanted to be the one to relieve all the stress, all the grief in his life.

Adam spoke, his voice deep and strained. "I don't want you with him." His hands turned to fists and moved to press against his temples. Through clenched teeth, he growled, "The thought of him touching you drives me fucking insane."

Evangeline squeezed her eyes shut as the tears

came. Deep in her heart she'd hoped Adam's feelings toward her had begun to turn to something else, even as she denied her own because no good could come of it. The knowledge he cared so much, however, stirred her blood. He wanted her as much as she wanted him.

She didn't know how or why or when it happened, but somehow, during their brief and extraordinary time together, Evangeline had fallen in love with this tortured man, and his tortured soul.

When she raised her lids, she saw him up against the wall, leaning his head back with his eyes closed. There was no more thinking. She knew what she wanted and it was this beautiful, powerful, tormented man.

Barefoot, she walked to him and put her hand on his chest. Adam flinched and his eyes shot open. They stared at one another the way only they knew how, with intensity unlike any other and irrevocable love.

Adam's heated blue gaze moved to her hand on his chest. He covered it with his own, squeezing it gently to his heart.

Evangeline rose up on her toes and leaned in to place her lips on his and his breath caught before he broke contact.

"I can't. You're…I'm not…good. God, Evangeline, you deserve so much more." He reached up to cup her face in his hands. "You are truly the most beautiful woman I have ever seen and a shit like me shouldn't even be in the same room with you."

Evangeline shook her head slowly. "But we are in the same room and you, Adam, are the most beautiful man *I* have ever seen."

He gaped at her as her tears began to fall in earnest

now and she went on, her throat tight, her voice heavy.

"I know I have to leave…"

Adam's face contorted again and his jaw flexed.

"But, I can't leave without telling you…I'm in love with you."

"*Jesus*." Adam groaned and pulled her to him. His lips crushed hers painfully, tasting her salty tears as they moved wildly together, clutching anything they could get their hands on. The kiss became feverish, consumed in passion, hurt, love, pain…

They both felt the instant the kiss turned into something else. Evangeline moaned against his mouth and reached down to his jeans, unbuckling, unzipping…

He pulled back again, gripping her wrists. "Oh God, baby, don't." Adam was panting hard, his breath caressing her skin.

Evangeline freed her wrist and nodded at him. Taking his hands, she pulled them around her waist, then slipped her hand down his briefs and grasped his arousal. Her mouth found a perfect crevice at his throat and her lips moved hungrily over his skin.

Adam shuddered and cried out. "Baby, please." He begged, lax under her ministrations. "Are you sure about this?"

Evangeline's hand pumped slowly up and down in his pants, loving the way his face strained with intensity. She reached up to kiss his mouth. "I've never been more certain about anything else in my entire life."

Adam trembled again at her touch. "If we don't stop now, I won't be able to later."

Evangeline looked at him. "Good." And then she

stepped back and pulled her camisole over her head, revealing her breasts.

Adam's eyes flashed yellow and he pounced with a growl.

****

His body was on fire.

Evangeline stood before him, topless. He could stare at her perfect breasts forever.

They were impeccably round, with the sweetest nipples pointed straight at him.

He didn't waste any time, but made his move.

She was his and he was going to have every inch of her.

Adam kissed her roughly, molding her lips to his as he picked her up and carried her to the couch. He sat her down with her back to the cushions and knelt down in between her legs on the old sheepskin.

Evangeline moved her hands all over him as she kissed him back. She reached down to lift his shirt off and he leaned back for half a second to get rid of the damn thing before coming back to her. This time he reached for her breasts. He held one in his right hand, rubbing his thumb over the nipple as he flicked the other with his tongue. Her raspy moans did crazy things to him.

He couldn't believe he was right here, with Evangeline, kissing her, touching her, licking her…

He had to have more. Suddenly, Adam felt the greed of a possessed man. He reached down to the waist of her pants and without losing the grip of his mouth on her nipple, he eased her flimsy pants off.

His woman was going commando.

"Jesus Christ." Adam looked up at her. She must

have seen something in his gaze, because her eyes widened briefly and then she smiled. Evangeline reached for him and kissed him fiercely, arching her back off the cushions, grabbing his hips, pulling him further between her thighs. She grinded against his jeans and even through the denim, Adam felt how hot and wet she was.

Coming up, he captured her tiny waist with his hands, and watched her face, breasts, and torso writhe before him as he pushed himself on her.

"Adam, please." Evangeline's sweet voice moaned. "I need you inside me." She grabbed at his forearms now, her head thrown back above the cushions.

"I know, babe. Soon." Adam didn't know where to look. Her head was back, but she was staring at him from beneath her lowered lids. It was sexy as hell. If he slipped inside her now, he was going to come in half a second. He had to make this last.

Adam leaned over her and kissed her full lips softly now before making his tour down her luscious body. He made sure to pay homage to her two beautiful orbs before traveling down to her flat stomach. As he worked his way down, he wrapped both arms around her two toned thighs, positioning her just the way he wanted.

He sat down on his haunches and gazed at his delicious prize.

"Oh, baby." He moaned.

Adam tried to control himself as he lowered himself between her legs, but it was no use. He went in like a madman, tongue out and slipping through her folds to penetrate as deep as he could.

Evangeline cried out and jerked her shoulders

back, lifting her hips to him. Her nails dug into his skin on his arms where they remained securely fastened around her thighs, moving them in the direction he needed them to go.

He continued on, roaming his tongue along her slick sex until he found what he was looking for. Once his mouth discovered her perfect jewel, it didn't let go. He sucked it and Evangeline shuddered, her moans growing louder, then Adam flicked his tongue rapidly, making her scream. He felt her body spasm as she climaxed.

Adam savored every taste of her before coming back up. He came down and fastened his mouth on her breast as he unbuttoned his jeans.

A tiny sense of reality crept into his mind as he released himself right against her sweet sex and he paused. Adam laid his head to the side on her chest, hugging her hips to him.

"Adam?"

He was silent for a long time before he spoke. She felt so perfect in his arms. "Evangeline, are you sure—"

She cut him off and brought his head up an inch before hers. "Yes. Adam, I love you." Evangeline's voice is what killed him. He felt how much she loved him in the way she spoke. "I don't want to think about anything else tonight. I just want it to be you and me."

His heart swelled and he kissed her gently. When he pulled back, his eyes seared hers. "I love you, Evangeline. God, I love you more than anything in this world."

As he kissed her with all the love he possessed, he slipped himself inside her, stretching her, filling her up with all of him. Her eyes closed as she moaned, "Oh

God, Adam."

It was all he needed. He began to move slowly, and then his body overcame him, his movements becoming faster.

Evangeline was tight and wet around him. It took every ounce of control he had not to find release. He'd waited so long to have her, he wasn't going to finish yet.

Adam kept moving inside her, his thighs working hard as they slammed against the couch. He leaned back slightly to watch their body's union as he pumped in and out of her sweet flesh. Lifting his head to look at her, a low growl escaped him. Her olive eyes were half closed and her lips were swollen and moist from their kissing. Her head pulled back against the cushion and she gasped through short breaths, "I'm coming! I'm—"

He lost it.

Wrapping her legs around his waist, Adam reached up to grab the back of the sofa and drove into her with increasing force, finding his own release. He heard his deep moans mingle with hers. His hips slowed as he spilled himself in her hot core, his body shuddering as he came down.

It was a good thing they were in the middle of the woods because their moans would have startled any neighbor.

Adam slumped on top of her, trying to ease the pounding in his chest. Evangeline's hands came up to massage his head softly, sending chills down his spine.

He didn't want to let her go. Fuck, he was still inside her. How in God's name could he live without…

A thought came to him just then, and he sat up. "Are you on something?" he asked.

She looked at him. "What do you mean, like birth control?" Evangeline was still lying back, looking sated and gorgeous. "I take the pill."

"Ah. Ok." Adam nodded, breathlessly. "You know I'm safe, right? Weres don't get diseases."

"I know." Caressing his face now, she gazed at him with such love he felt his chest constrict.

Another fucking thought crept into his wheel-turning head. "Why are you on the pill?" His face was serious now as he thought about Hot Pants on the bridge by her house.

She smiled at his frown and smoothed the crease between his brows with her thumb. "To prevent pregnancy…"

"Who the—" Adam's furious tone began, but she cut him off.

"In the event I actually have sex," she soothed.

Before he could stop himself, he blurted, "What about your guy on the bridge?"

Evangeline looked at him for a moment. "That was you? In the woods?"

Adam clamped his mouth shut sheepishly.

Smirking, she shook her head at him. "I didn't sleep with Richard, if that's what you're thinking, but it's always good to be prepared."

The fact she hadn't slept with the guy only slightly eased his anxiety. He came up and zipped his pants. Evangeline gave him a worried look, but then he lay down on the couch and brought her on top of him. He reached over behind him to grab a knitted throw and wrapped it around her.

"You were with someone once." It wasn't a question. She obviously was not a virgin. It didn't matter to him, but his sick jealous side had to know who he or they were.

Evangeline looked down at his chest. "Yes, but do you really want—"

"Yes," he said simply.

She nodded and thought for a moment, then shrugged. "It was about two years ago, when I was in college. We dated for a few months. I thought I was in love and so…we did."

Adam was watching her carefully. "What happened?"

Evangeline shook her head and her soft hair tickled his chest. "I don't know. He disappeared."

Adam looked incredulous. "He ditched you?"

Casting him an exasperated look, she answered, "Yes, and thanks for putting it lightly. He ditched me. There."

"I'm sorry. It's just hard to believe. Were you hurt?"

Evangeline thought for a moment as if she were solving a math problem in her head. "You know, I wasn't as upset as everyone thought I should be. I guess I really wasn't in love with him. It was probably just a crush."

The thought of Evangeline with some faceless man set his blood to boiling. He wasn't stupid. He knew women didn't always wait till they were married to seal the deal. Hell, he lived through the seventies, but times were even faster now. He just had to remember Evangeline loved him.

But, she wasn't exactly his.

Adam played with a tendril of her hair, avoiding eye contact. There was something about the night he'd taken her from her room bugging the hell out of him. "You said you just met Cyrus the other night, right."

She looked at him. "Yeah."

Cautiously, he went on. "If something happened between the two of you…you could tell me."

"Adam!"

Looking her straight in the face, he said in an even tone. "You called out his name."

Evangeline stiffened in his arms. "What?"

Adam remembered the night he'd slipped into her bedroom. There was a moment he'd just stood there, mesmerized by her and then, she'd called out Cyrus' name.

That's when he'd pulled her out of the bed, roughly. It had bugged him she was dreaming about him. "The night I took you, you were asleep…dreaming about him." The words coming out of his mouth felt like venom on his tongue. "You were moaning and you kept calling out his name."

Adam watched as it all came back to her. He couldn't believe he was getting all riled up over a dream, but he couldn't help himself.

"It wasn't a good dream, Adam. It was more like a nightmare."

He watched her carefully.

Evangeline kissed his chest and looked him in the eye. "I could never feel that way about him."

Adam continued playing with her hair as he mulled it over.

"Um…Adam, unless you grabbed my pills before you flung me out the window, I really don't think Cyrus or my past relationships matter at the moment."

Looking at her, he could tell she was trying to

lighten the mood by changing the subject.

She smiled. "Don't worry. I'll double up when I get home. Besides, werewolves are only fertile during the moon heat, so it doesn't matter anyway."

Nodding, he said nothing. Stupid reality was bursting in on their sweet moment and he knew where the conversation was headed.

"What can I do?" Adam's calm voice moments before disappeared. He was all business now.

Evangeline frowned at his chest, wringing her hands between his pectorals. She knew what he was asking and she didn't want to talk about it, but it was inevitable. She took a deep breath. "There's nothing you can do. He won't—"

"Beg him!"

She looked up and their eyes locked.

"Please, Evangeline. I can't take you back knowing I'll be taking you to him." Adam's hands were holding her tightly to him. "I can pay him back every cent. He can't…"

Evangeline was shaking her head. "The money doesn't matter to him. He wants me and God knows what he'll do to my family."

"Then I'll kill him." Something in his voice shocked Evangeline.

"No." Her eyes were wide on his. "You wouldn't do that to your pack and you know it. I know you love me and I know how much you hate him, but your pack will have to face the consequences if Cyrus is killed."

She was right and he knew it. They only had this moment to share and he did not want to spend it arguing with her about some motherfucker.

He came up and lifted her off the couch with him,

carrying her to the bedroom.

He had to take her back, but Adam wasn't going to let her go until he had to.

She was his, body and soul, and he was going to savor every moment.

Chapter Eleven

Evangeline woke with a start. It was still dark outside and the cabin was as silent as a grave. The only light was the soft, low glow of the waxing moon.

She felt strong arms around her and Adam's chest at her back. As secure as she was just then she'd never felt more alone in her life.

This is not going to last, she thought.

This sweet moment they were sharing would soon end. He was returning her around three in the morning so she could slip inside her house unnoticed.

She was returning to her family and to her mess of a life, or what was left of her life as it was no longer her own.

Evangeline tried to imagine living the rest of her life with Cyrus Stewart as her husband and the empty feeling growing inside her became painful. A tear slipped down her cheek and disappeared in her hair. She couldn't picture it at all. Adam's face always replaced Cyrus'. How on earth was she going to live without Adam?

Now she understood the sappy *my heart is breaking* quote. Her heart felt like it had shattered into a million pieces. If she was depressed before, it did not compare to the despair she now felt over losing Adam.

They had become so unbelievably close in such a short amount of time, but it felt as though they had loved a lifetime's worth.

She felt Adam stiffen behind her and knew he was feeling the terrible pain she was silently going through. His arms squeezed tighter around her and he buried his face in her hair.

"Please don't cry, babe." Adam's soft whisper made her cry harder.

Evangeline turned into his arms and hugged him fiercely to her. "I don't know if I can do this," she sobbed. "I know I have to, but the thought of never seeing you again kills me."

Adam held her, not saying a word. She knew he was fighting to control himself.

There was no solution for them; no solution would bring them any happiness or contentment. It was out of their control. It was as if they were puppets and the Vampire King of North America held the strings.

Evangeline looked up and their gazes met. There were so many unspoken words between them.

"We should go," she said suddenly. "The longer I stay, the harder this is going to be."

They got up and dressed in silence. Neither one of them made eye contact as they readied themselves for the journey home.

They made their way out the door and Evangeline was startled as Adam lifted her in his arms. He smiled boyishly at her and her heart tightened, cutting off the ability to breathe. "Next time, I'll grab shoes for you too," he joked in a small voice and nodded at her bare feet.

She held on to him tightly as he took off at a steady run and she managed to take a last glance at the cabin, which, at first, had been her prison and had quickly become their sanctuary.

They didn't break the silence until they were close to her home. The trip back was longer than it had been a few days ago. He wasn't running at a fast pace, but more of a jog. She didn't know where exactly they were, but she knew they had to be close and anxiety laced through her once more.

Evangeline's head had been tucked in the crook of his neck, but their impending end made her panic and she had to look at him.

She didn't need supernatural powers to sense Adam's nervousness. His face was set in stone and the pain in his eyes made her shatter and she began to tremble.

Adam finally looked at her and his face softened somewhat.

"*Please*," she whispered as the tremors ran through her body and the tears spilled from her eyes, knowing he felt exactly what she needed.

He slowed to a walk and then finally stopped. Without a word he brought her over to a tree, and set her down gently on her feet.

There was no reason to speak. They both knew what would happen. The urgency was all around them.

Adam's hands never left her. He put his hand at her back to protect her from being scratched by the bark of the tree. Their gazes locked, he slid her pants down smoothly and freed one of her legs. Her skin tingled at the cool, early morning air as he released himself, lifted her thighs to wrap around his waist and slipped himself slowly inside her.

She was whole again.

Shuddering at their union, Evangeline watched as

he slid himself in and out of her in an agonizingly slow rhythm. She met each thrust with passion and aching force.

One arm was locked around her as he held onto the tree behind her with the other. They didn't kiss. If he kissed her now she would surely die. They just stared at the torture in their eyes as they tried to fill the void for a bittersweet moment. Her face was drenched in tears and his eyes, once again yellow, were building moisture. All too soon, he broke contact and squeezed his lids shut as they came together, panting heavily.

Adam rested his head on her shoulder and embraced her, crushing the life out of her. When he came up, he righted their clothes and picked her up once more and took off.

When her home came into view a few minutes later he slowed his pace and then stopped just before the bridge, setting her down under the cover of the trees.

Adam straightened and sniffed the air. He hadn't said a word since they'd left, but now he spoke and sounded like someone else. "There are vampires patrolling around your home. They were just here a few minutes ago." He met her frightened stare. "Don't worry. The guys are not far. Besides…" Adam's look became grave again. "As long as you're returned and I agree to a summit with the coven, they won't do anything."

She stiffened. He must have had contact with his pack and Maxwell while she'd been asleep. She hoped the coven would stick to their word. If anything should happen to him…

"Can you get in alone?"

She looked at the distance from the house to where

they were.

His jaw flexed. "I'm not allowed on your grounds." His lips curled and he hissed, "Part of the deal."

Her face grew tense.

"No vampire or werewolf is allowed in or around your grounds after tonight, at least not until after the summit, according to Maxwell Jones."

Nodding numbly, she thought there might be a key in the flowerpot on the side of the back door.

"Go." Adam was trembling now, violently. She turned to him and he shook his head at her. His yellow irises burned and right before her eyes, he began to grow in height. Skin was stretching over his muscles and she heard the cracking of bones and tendons. "Go." He growled more loudly and without another word, she turned and ran toward her home.

Behind her came the howl of a wolf, a wolf she would never forget.

****

"Eva!"

She jumped up, her sister's shrill cry startling her out of a deep sleep. Evangeline had cried herself to sleep around five o'clock in the morning. Her head was pounding now and her sister's shouting did not help.

"Holy shit!" Katherine yelled, slamming the door behind her as if it would muffle her voice. "What the hell happened to you? And don't give me any shit about going to the city. I called you a hundred times. Why didn't you answer me?"

"Calm down," Evangeline said groggily as she slowly got out of bed. She felt the soreness between her legs and an ache stabbed through her chest. Images of Adam thrusting into her on the couch, the bed and

149

against the tree flooded her mind and her knees gave out. She sat down hard on the bed. Horrible reality was sinking in and sucking the energy right out of her. "I'll tell you everything, just give me a minute."

Looking up at her sister, she noticed Katherine wore an expression of pure fury. She still had on her pajamas, a Victoria's Secret T-shirt falling down to her knees and cozy socks. Evangeline could not help but wonder and envy how lucky her sister was to have her whole life in front of her. She could do whatever she wanted. Suddenly, Katherine's impulsive and sometimes-reckless behavior didn't seem so bad. At least she had choices, choices she, Evangeline, didn't have.

Katherine's face softened and her eyes widened. "What's wrong?" Her voice was soothing now.

Evangeline realized a tear had slipped down her cheek and she wiped it away.

Katherine came to sit next her, giving Evangeline her undivided attention.

She knew she could be honest with her sister. She trusted her with her life and Evangeline needed to let it all out at the moment.

"I was kidnapped, Katherine." Evangeline's tone was low and calm, but she giggled a little when she said *kidnapped*. God, she would love to be kidnapped by Adam again.

"What?" her sister whispered, clearly confused.

Evangeline went on to tell her sister everything. She told her about Adam, the Blacktail pack, the jackal, the pizza he made her… everything, except she didn't go into detail about them making love. She simply told her it happened, but of course, her sister could not be deterred.

"You slept with him?" she asked, wide-eyed with shock and curiosity.

"Yes," she said, sadly.

"Oh, my God."

They sat silently for a moment, both lost in their own thoughts. She felt as though her life were at a standstill now. The fact she was supposed to marry the king didn't override the pain of losing Adam. What was she going to do? How could she ever be with anyone else when deep inside her soul she knew she would always be completely devoted to him?

"You love him, don't you?" Evangeline looked up to find her sister staring.

Nodding pitifully, she said, "I never in a million years thought I could feel this way. It's awful."

"Don't say that!" Her sister got up and stood in front of her. "This is...this is so...wow..." Katherine stared out the very window Adam used to take her. She could tell her sister was finding it all terribly romantic. Funny, Evangeline had been terrified when she realized she was being kidnapped, but it seemed like a long time ago now.

A sudden thought occurred to her. "Has Maxwell Jones been here to see Dad while I was gone?" she asked her sister worriedly.

"No. At least, I haven't seen him."

"Do you think Dad believed my message?"

Katherine shrugged. "They've been worried, of course, but I covered for you. I lied and said I talked to you and you were doing fine. I'm not sure they bought it because I was worried too. You know I'm a bad liar."

Evangeline was now nervous to see her parents. It

was one thing to confide in her sister, but she did not want to see her father's face when he found out she had been kidnapped by the Blacktail alpha. And her father would definitely find out, either from Maxwell or Cyrus. Her father would blame himself for this too and she hated to see him so worried over her.

She got up and headed for the bathroom. "I better go talk to Mom and Dad."

"Wait!" Her sister stopped her before she could close the bathroom door. "How was it? Making love? To the alpha?" Katherine's gorgeous dark eyes sparkled with delight.

For one brief moment she felt the rush of excitement she had felt in Adam's arms and she gave her sister a small smile. "Let's just say, I hope your first time is with a man as wonderful as Adam."

****

When Evangeline finally dressed and came downstairs it was almost noon and Maxwell Jones had beaten her to the punch. Geoffrey had been livid to find out she had been kidnapped by the Blacktail pack. She assured both her parents she was all right and she was not hurt in any way. At least not in any way they could tell.

They spoke for an hour in the living room and she told them everything she could, leaving out falling in love and having mind-blowing sex with a werewolf.

After what seemed like forever, Maxwell stood up and said he was leaving. "Before I go, can I speak to you privately, Evangeline?"

She started. "Sure—"

"Hang on, Max. What can't you say in front of us?" Her father had stood too, looking suspiciously at his friend.

Maxwell was never one to beat around the bush. "If Evangeline wants to share this with you after we're done, she can, but let her decide." He looked her father dead in the face. "Geoff, please."

Her father gave her a worried look and she could see the tension in his face.

"It's all right, Dad." Giving him her sweetest smile, she hugged him and her mother who looked worse than her father. "Kat's making lunch. I'll join you guys in the kitchen in a minute."

When they left the room, Evangeline turned to face Maxwell, wishing her father hadn't gotten rid of the double doors that once hung in the doorframe during the house's third renovation. She didn't want her family to overhear their conversation.

"How upset is he?" She knew he wanted to talk to her about Cyrus and give her warning.

Maxwell's somber expression made her stomach bunch up in knots. "I'm not going to lie; he's in quite a state. I have never seen him like this. His reaction to your abduction worries me. I was able to talk him out of retaliating, but who knows how long before he changes his mind. I made them both agree to stay off your property. If you see any vampire or werewolf here, you call me right away. They need to stay far away from each other until the summit. Cyrus understands the repercussions should he ignore this." He paused and gave her a strange look. "He's really into you, Evangeline, which brings me to what I wanted to speak to you about."

She sat up straighter on the couch.

"I already know he did not complete the vampire

betrothal contract, otherwise he would have immediately realized you were in trouble and been able to find you. Unfortunately, he is still seething at the fact you were trapped with a werewolf for several days." Maxwell looked at her and flushed. "By the way...you don't have to confide in me, but if something happened with Perez, you better take it to your grave."

Damn! How could he tell? She must have given it away somehow during their conversation earlier. She kept her mouth shut, not wanting to deny or confirm Maxwell's suspicions. Evangeline struggled to keep her expression straight.

"He's going to ask you if something happened between you two and you have to learn to calm your breathing so your heart doesn't race. Don't shift your eyes either. He is a master at reading people."

Evangeline started to panic. Jesus, what if Cyrus found out? What would he do to her? What would he do to Adam?

"Now," he went on and sat down next to her, "the king wants you at his coven as soon as possible. I'm here to take you there. I insisted on coming along for your protection." He made a rough sound.

Definitely panicking now, she asked, "Why do I need protection?"

"Cyrus is going to complete the contract."

Her heart dropped straight to her toes.

"I can't exactly do anything, except bring him up on charges should he get carried away."

Stunned, she uttered, "I see..."

"I'm certain he won't hurt you, but I know you have never been bitten before and the temper he is in might make him more aggressive."

Evangeline sat staring at the floor. Didn't she know Cyrus would have to bite her eventually? Why was she more nervous now than she was when they had met?

She knew.

It was because she was in love with Adam and she didn't want Cyrus' hands or mouth on her. She didn't want any of this.

Getting up from the couch and trying desperately to sound calm, she said, "Let's eat first, then we'll leave." She wanted to spend time with her family for a while before heading to the coven.

Why did it feel like she was about to have her last meal?

Chapter Twelve

They followed the huge, scary vampire, Victor down the hall to the king's office where they had dined a few days ago. Try as she might, Evangeline's tough exterior was waning. Even Maxwell's presence didn't give her any comfort.

When they reached the door, Victor only cracked it open and blocked their view inside. It was quiet and Evangeline just knew they were communicating telepathically.

After a minute, he turned and shut the door. "Go on in." His deep baritone was unnerving. He looked at Maxwell. "You can wait in the dining room."

"No. I'm going with her."

Victor glared. "Either you walk to the dining room, or I drag you."

Evangeline blanched.

Maxwell turned to her. "Evangeline—"

"It's okay." She tried to smile. "Really, I'll be fine."

He grabbed her arm and pulled her close. Speaking low, he said, "If he hurts you, scream."

Her heart leapt. Why did lawyers have to be so blunt?

"I'm sure he won't hurt me," she lied.

Maxwell turned and she saw Victor take his arm and lead him down the hall toward the dining room.

Evangeline summoned up the last of her courage and entered the lion's den.

A single lamp on the desk dimly lit the room. It was still light out, but the thick curtains were drawn to keep the sun's rays from coming in. Cyrus sat in the corner of his office on a leather armchair, a drink in hand.

It was two in the afternoon so it was the middle of the night to him. He looked pale and disheveled in black slacks and a black shirtwaist, unbuttoned at the top. His hair was tousled as if he had just gotten out of bed and he had a day's growth of beard.

Stepping forward, she lifted her chin. "You wanted to see me."

He smirked, but said nothing.

Evangeline stood ramrod straight as he stared. She had no idea what he was thinking, but she was getting irritated. Were they going to just stand there all day?

She took a deep breath. "I appreciate you not going to the authorities or retaliating against the Blacktails. It would have been stupid to start a fight over me."

Cyrus still said nothing. His eyes slowly assessed her from the top of her head to the tips of her toes.

"I wasn't hurt, in case you were wondering. I was treated kindly, considering..." She was rambling.

Cyrus finally spoke. "Are you defending the animals who abducted you?" He sounded calm, but his face was tense.

"No. I mean...I...I don't blame them. They're worried for one of their pack members. I don't appreciate being physically taken from my home, but I understand why they did it." She hesitated, her face softening slightly. "I'm glad you didn't have Serena

Perez."

He raised a brow. "Did you doubt me?"

"Actually, no, I didn't." She really hadn't doubted him. Hadn't she told Adam she didn't believe Cyrus had taken his sister?

He straightened up in his chair, leaning forward with his elbows on his knees. His eyes were black on hers. "Other than physically taking you from your home..." He began and his jaw flexed. He asked, "Did he touch you?"

And there it was.

She debated telling him the truth. Would he be so disgusted a werewolf had touched her and turn her away, forgetting all about this marriage business? What if he got so angry he hit her or worse? Maxwell's warnings resounded in her head. Cyrus might forgo the deal and retaliate against the Blacktails if he knew she and Adam had been together. She couldn't have that on her conscious.

Evangeline stared him straight in the eye. "No. I told you. I was treated well." She didn't move, hoping her poised stance and devil-may-care expression was a good front.

He scrutinized her for what seemed like forever.

Taking slow breaths in and out, she watched him closely.

"You'll stay here for the rest of the day. You can return tomorrow morning. The wedding will be next weekend. My coven is taking care of everything. All you have to do is show up on Saturday night. You're family is more than welcome to attend."

Evangeline didn't say a word. It was all too depressing. They were really going through with this joke of a wedding and there was nothing she or anyone could do about it.

Cyrus placed his drink on the floor and gripped the arms of his chair. "You realize had we completed the contract, this would not have happened." He was seething. Her mere presence was making him angrier than he'd been before.

Evangeline nodded and before she could say a word, he sped toward her and she was slammed up against the door, wrapped tightly in his arms. She cried out as one hand gripped her hair, painfully at the base of her neck. Evangeline could hardly breathe with his heavy weight pressing on her. "You're hurting me!" Gasping at the sting his grip inflicted, she tried to push him away, but it was useless.

He was livid. Cyrus' eyes were silver now, fangs out. "A fucking werewolf had his hands on my future wife. I want to fucking kill him, but I can't. Do you realize how this makes me feel?"

Staring at his fangs, she dreaded the pain they would cause. He had promised it wouldn't hurt, but he obviously didn't care about being gentle. "I hate you!" she whispered, a treacherous tear falling.

Cyrus held her tighter. "Good!"

He struck.

Pain seared the skin at her neck and she let out an uncontrollable scream as she felt his fangs dig deeper into her flesh. Squeezing her eyes tight, she forced herself to shut up and bit down the urge to wail.

Evangeline tried to calm herself, but it was no use. She was too frantic. The pain was unbearable. She whimpered softly as he sucked roughly at her throat. Then she felt his arousal against her thigh and she wanted to vomit.

Struggling against him, she lost track of time and didn't know how much he drank. Her vision blurred and she was getting dizzy.

"Please!" She was pushing at him again. "Stop, please!"

Evangeline felt him stiffen and slowly he came up. Eyes closed, his head hung back, Cyrus' fangs were still out and she could see her blood around his lips. "*Fuck*!" He groaned, opening his eyes to look at her.

"Let go of me." She felt weak and tired and her neck throbbed as if she'd been stabbed with a pitchfork.

"I've never tasted anyone quite like you." He was breathing heavily.

Glaring at him through hazy eyes, she muttered, "I don't give a shit. Let me go!"

Slowly, he pushed himself off her, letting his hands slide over her back and waist before he took a step back.

With all the energy she could muster, she pulled her arm back and smacked him across the face.

The last thing she remembered before she fainted was the pain in her hand and hoped to God she at least hurt him a little.

****

"How is he?"

Jason shut the door to Adam's round house, pausing to listen for any activity over the blaring music. He heard a drill buzzing in one of the upstairs rooms. Led Zeppelin was blasting on the iPod, which indicated his friend wanted to drown out the heavy thoughts in his head, otherwise the old man usually had on the Beatles.

Ramo was eating a sandwich, clearly having come from the kitchen to answer the door. It was the day before the full moon, and tonight they would all be enduring the moon heat. The hours leading up to it made them very hungry. Jason brought along a prescription of Klonopin for Adam, which helped Jason during these nights without a heat mate. It didn't do much, just dulled the mind so they didn't have to think too much about how badly they needed to have sex and it tricked the brain into thinking they weren't actually in pain. Hopefully it would let Adam sleep through the moon heat.

"He's being an idiot, ignoring me and shit." Ramo rolled his eyes and continued eating.

Jason looked at Ramo. He had no idea what it felt like to fall in love with a woman. It was wonderful and painful, beautiful and heartbreaking. Ramo only lusted after women. He'd never let a girl get too close. Ramo was married to a werewolf in Chicago, but he hadn't seen her in years.

"I'm going to talk to him." He checked his watch. "You should probably get a move on." You didn't want to run into a werewolf during these nights. Years ago during the moon heat, Ramo had been working long hours. When he finally headed off to meet his heat mate, it was too late. He passed a bar and two girls stumbled out, drunk. They started flirting, crazy style with Ramo and he lost it. Thank God, they were willing. They ended up going at it in the bathroom of the bar for an hour and the owner called the cops. They were all arrested.

Ramo checked his watch too. "Right, good thinking." Ramo's heat mate lived about thirty minutes out of town.

As his pack member left, Jason headed up the stairs, following the noise of the drill.

He knew his friend was hurting badly and couldn't blame him. Evangeline Wolcott was quite a woman. He only wished his friend didn't have to suffer over losing her the way Jason suffered over Serena.

Yeah, Jason knew exactly what Adam was going through.

When he reached the second floor, he could see Adam through his bedroom's open door. He was in the bathroom he'd added to the master bedroom ten years ago. Looked like he was in a remodeling kind of mood. Adam was taking out the counter surrounding the sink. Jason saw the tub leaning against the wall next to his dresser. There were bags from a hardware store and boxes off to the side and he knew by the end of the day, Adam was going to have a brand new bathroom.

Adam switched off the drill when he saw Jason and cocked his head.

Jason held up the plastic container with the Klonopin pills. "I brought you these."

Nodding, Adam hit the pause button on the iPod and stepped out of the bathroom. "Thanks."

"You might want to take two now and then three or four at sun down." For a human it would equal an overdose. For a werewolf it was just enough.

Jason watched Adam take two and put the rest in his pocket. They stood looking everywhere, but at each other.

"Need any help?" Jason asked.

Adam shook his head, mopping the sweat off his brow. "I'm good."

They lapsed into silence again. They were the two saddest motherfuckers on the planet.

Adam cleared his throat, still not looking at Jason. He walked over to a box and started cutting it open with his Swiss army knife. "Is it always like this?"

Jason started. "What?"

Adam still avoided his gaze, keeping his voice down. "Is it always like this...for you? This horrible fucking feeling?"

Jason understood. "Yeah, pretty much."

He nodded, clenching his jaw.

Jason added pathetically, "We love like madmen."

Adam finally looked at him. "I've heard of this, but fuck."

A werewolf's love for another was seriously intense. If their kind was misfortunate enough to fall in love, it was for life. They became protectors, living solely to please their mate. Adam and Jason now suffered the same loss of their soul mate. Looking closely at his friend, he thought he was looking in a mirror. They had the same dark circles and perpetual grimace.

Adam massaged his chest and Jason knew he felt the stabbing pain that never went away.

"Wish I could say it gets better," Jason said.

Adam looked at him intently. "I haven't given up on her."

Jason knew he referred to his sister.

"We're going to find her."

"I know," Jason said dismissively. He was going to lose it if they went on talking about Serena. He walked over to the bathroom, inspecting what else needed to be done. "Hand me the tape measure."

163

"You don't have to—" Adam began.

"I know, but I'm gonna." Jason was determined to help his friend. They could both use a big distraction right now. They would put all their effort in this bathroom and when they were done, they'd pop a few more pills and hit the Patron till last man standing.

****

He wanted to tell Jason he didn't have to stay, but he knew his beta needed to keep busy as much as he did. Besides, having Jason around was the equivalent of being alone. He knew Jason wouldn't ramble on.

Adam rubbed the ache in his chest again. He wondered what was happening with Evangeline. He wanted to know if she was all right. Had she met with the king yet? Adam felt his stomach drop for the umpteenth time since he'd left her. What would Cyrus do to her? If he hurt her...agreement or no agreement, he'd kill the son of bitch and worry about the consequences later.

What the hell was wrong with him? How could he just sit back and let Cyrus have his girl? The thought of her being in the same room with him fucked with his head. A slimy bastard like Cyrus Stewart had no right to one so lovely. And he, Adam, had basically handed her over.

Adam wasn't himself. He didn't think he'd ever be the same again. Evangeline had turned his world upside down. How was he going to live without seeing her face everyday...hearing her voice...

He thought of what his father would say to him about all this. Xavier Perez would have knocked him over the head and told him to man up and fight for his woman. The thought of what his father would have said to him shouldn't have bothered him, but it did.

Adam wondered how his father could still torment him from the grave and he remembered the repentant look he'd given him as he let his own son murder him.

Had his father really loved his mother? Did he go through the same turmoil Adam was now going through when he thought his mother had cheated on him? There were no excuses for what his father had done, but Adam couldn't help but wonder. Could he flip out the same way?

No!

The thought of Evangeline getting a paper cut killed him. There was no way he was like his father. His love for Evangeline was pure and real.

The ache in his heart was proof enough.

He shut his eyes. The image of her tearstained face as he'd slowly made love to her against the tree haunted his dreams. He could still feel her hands squeezing his shoulders and pulling on him. He had never made love to a woman with such aching passion. She'd sent tremors down his entire body. He was beginning to feel the moon's affect on him. It was going to be a rough night.

Not for the first time, he prayed she was all right. His arch nemesis was an evil prick, but even Cyrus wouldn't hurt a woman like Evangeline. Would he?

He had to see her.

Somehow, he had to see her to make sure she was okay. Ramo was ragging on him to go to the city and throw himself in his work. Perez Construction was working on a block of town houses on the North side of Chicago, but Adam had instantly vetoed the suggestion.

He could not be so far away from Evangeline. He wasn't kidding himself. He knew the king was going to marry her. Cue stomach drop. But, as long as he still breathed, he would make sure she was all right. Until they put his cold, dead body into the earth, he would be her bodyguard. Married or not, Adam would watch over her. He might be digging himself an early grave if he continued on this path, but he didn't care.

Evangeline Wolcott had a protector for life.

Chapter Thirteen

Jane was fuming.

The meeting had been tense enough with everything going on, but when the king came in looking disgruntled, to discuss the summit, Jane had nearly lost it.

Everyone present this time of year in the King's Coven would be at the summit...everyone but her.

Even Maxwell Jones, a human would be there.

Mary spoke behind her. "But, my love, we've been over this. No, please don't give me one of your looks." Jane half turned to glare at her as they crossed the threshold into their room on the second floor.

Jane walked over to the window, staring off into the night.

Mary and Jane had the day off today, but with everything going on, everyone was on duty. Usually on these days they would cuddle up in their bed and watch a movie or read together. Sometimes they would spend the day drinking wine and talking for hours. Mary always had a good story for her. She'd lived through so much as she'd been born in England in the nineteenth century. Jane was fascinated with her tales.

She felt as if she had her own personal history novel. All she had to do was ask a question about nineteenth century London and the *Ton*, and Mary would regale her with a time her cousin had gotten drunk at a ball for an Earl and spilled a drink on his wife.

Jane clenched her teeth, fighting the urge not to yell at her wife now.

Was she going to be stuck in this body forever?

Was Mary ever going to turn *her?*

"Jane…" Mary's husky voice sent chills down her spine.

"I hate you're going to the summit to meet with werewolves without me. I'm going to go crazy with worry. If you turned—"

"Please don't start," Mary cut in.

"No! Listen! If you turned me, I could help. I am the only damn human in a vampire coven. How do you think it makes me feel? Do you think I like the way Victor and everyone else stares at me like I'm fresh meat? Oh, stop!" Jane said exasperatedly when Mary's fangs came out. "All I'm saying is, we agreed you would turn me before we got married. Why won't you do it now?"

Mary's fangs retracted and her shoulders slumped. "Darling, we've been over this. I want you to enjoy the life you have right now for just a little while longer. You're still young. You don't know if you will still want this in another few years. Please," she added.

Jane turned to look at her, knowing she was the only one who ever saw the vulnerable look Mary gave her now. Only Jane could bring out this soft side in Mary. She knew Mary thought Jane would someday leave her for some human male or female.

Jane was young, but the love she felt for Mary was insurmountable. She could not imagine her life without her.

"What if I don't want to wait any longer? I know, despite what you think, I want to be with you, *forever*." Jane leaned forward, emphasizing the word forever. Her hands were crossed under her breasts and the low cut dress she wore gave Mary an eyeful.

A shadow cast light out from the hallway where Mary hadn't shut the door.

"Hi, Evangeline." Jane's expression changed dramatically, erasing the scowl into a cheerful smile.

From the corner of her eye, she saw Mary tense and turn toward the door. Jane would bet the entire coven Mary was doing the whole *if looks could kill* thing on the poor girl.

She watched Evangeline ignore Mary and turn toward her.

"I'm sorry. I didn't mean to interrupt. I was just wondering if I could speak to you for a minute?"

"Sure," Jane said politely. "Go on up to your room. I'll be there in just a minute."

Evangeline turned and walked off to the right. The door slammed shut by itself just as she was out of sight.

Jane looked at Mary reproachfully. "That was rude."

"I don't care."

Jane lifted her chin and stalked past her wife. "Will you for once think about what I said?"

"Where are you going?" Mary's voice rose louder than usual.

Jane stopped and turned. "I'm going to Evangeline's room."

"You're not going to her bedroom when you are angry with me." Mary stood, hands on her hips.

"Geez. Thanks for the trust, honey." Jane turned to

open the door. Before she could take a single step, she felt a gust of air as Mary sped to her in a blink of an eye, slamming Jane back against her chest.

Jane felt Mary's breasts heave up and down at her back as Mary's arms came around her. Jane closed her eyes. It wasn't fair. Jane had no control over her mind when her wife touched her.

Mary kissed her gently on the shoulder, and whispered heatedly, "You have ten minutes."

Jane shuddered as she left the room.

It was one of the hardest things Jane ever did, but she would make it up to Mary.

****

The view of the sunset from the gaping windows was picturesque, but Evangeline could not appreciate its beauty. She sat in the expansive room in a comfy purple chaise by the window, feeling like a prisoner. A large bed with a floral duvet took up most of the right side of the room, a massive dresser with a flat screen was on the adjacent wall, and an antique desk nestled near the window.

He bit her.

She knew he would, but the whole scene kept replaying in her head. She rubbed her neck again.

Cyrus was so angry. She had never been the cause of such fury in a man. When men were not avoiding her, they always treated her with the upmost respect.

"Knock, knock." Jane poked her head in with a smile.

"Hi. Come on in." Evangeline sat up straighter and eyed her visitor. Jane was flushed and her hair was a bit more out of place than it was a moment ago.

Instead of feeling uncomfortable, for obviously

she'd just fooled around with her wife, Evangeline once again felt envious. Why couldn't she find happiness like Jane's? Why couldn't she be with the one she loved?

Jane sat down in the chair by the desk, her dress hiking up a bit to reveal smooth, tanned legs. She gave Evangeline a nervous smile. "Is everything all right?"

Evangeline looked at her.

"I'm sorry, of course not. Ignore the question." Jane rolled her eyes. "You must be going through a lot right now. Is there anything I can do?"

"Convince the king to marry someone else."

Jane's small smile fell and she looked away.

"I'm only joking, Jane," she said lamely.

Jane took a deep breath. "I can only imagine what you're going through and I doubt anything I say will change that, but..." Jane hesitated as if she were searching for the right words to say. "He really isn't so bad."

"Not so bad?" Evangeline was incredulous. "Look at what he did to me." She pulled her hair back to reveal the bite marks on her neck. "He all but ripped my neck apart and drained me of enough blood to make me pass out."

Jane shook her head. "I'm not defending what he did to you. In fact, we're all pretty shocked how upset he's been since he found out you were kidnapped and what he did to you earlier. This may seem really insensitive, but he clearly has great feelings for you to have lost control."

"He doesn't even know me."

Jane tilted her head and scrutinized her. "Evangeline, he knows you more than I do, and even

I'm crushing on you."

Evangeline flushed.

Jane smiled at her. "Don't worry, I'm very much in love with my wife. I'm simply proving a point. You're so unbelievably beautiful it's hard not to stare at you like an idiot. Just looking at you makes me happy. Can you imagine what it does to His Grace? Add to the fact you're adoringly graceful, educated, and independent. You work even though you don't have to. God, what man wouldn't want you?"

Evangeline rubbed her temples. "Jane, he hurt me…"

"I know. I'm truly sorry he did." She leaned forward, her eyes serious. "This is not comforting given the circumstances, but, it really does feel quite amazing when you're relaxed and willing." Jane turned her head slightly and Evangeline saw two tiny puncture marks on her neck.

"You seem happy here." It wasn't a question, but Evangeline knew it sounded like one.

"I am." Smiling softly, she settled back in her chair, looking out the window. "I love when Mary and I can get away for a few months, but I grew up here and I just wish…"

Evangeline sensed something was troubling Jane. Giving anything to change the subject, she asked, "Are you all right?" She'd definitely walked in on an argument earlier, and wondered if she'd said something to drudge up Jane's distress.

Jane shook her head. "It's nothing." She looked down and smoothed imaginary wrinkles from her dress. Shrugging, she said, "I love it here, but it'd be easier if I was…" She paused.

Evangeline knew what she was about to say. "If you were a vampire?"

Jane looked up. "Yes."

Evangeline didn't know what to say. At one point she thought they might have a few things in common since they were both human and about the same age, but clearly she'd been mistaken. Evangeline wouldn't know how it was to grow up amongst vampires and she never thought of becoming one. Jane was very sweet, but she was beginning to wonder if it had been pointless to talk to her about her troubles.

There was a hard knock on the door and it swung open. Cyrus stood next to Maxwell who looked as bad as she felt.

"Janey, my dear, will you excuse us please?" Cyrus entered the room in the same clothes he'd had on earlier.

"Of course." Jane jumped up and crossed to Evangeline. She bent over and kissed her on the cheek. "Dial 101 on the phone if you want to talk. I'm here for you."

"Aren't you sweet, Jane. Let's go." Cyrus gave Jane a bored look and opened the door wider, then closed it after her.

Evangeline stared hard at him. She wanted to believe he was a stand up guy, vampire, whatever, but every time she was near him she wanted to scream.

Maxwell came over to her. He bent down and felt her forehead, then turned her head to the side to inspect her neck. "Are you all right?"

"I'm fine, Max."

A vampire named Florena had been there when Evangeline woke up. Apparently she'd worked as a nurse before she came to work for the king. Florena examined her and aside from telling her she had a slow heart beat, which could be from the loss of blood, she said she was fine.

After checking her vitals she'd made Evangeline eat a chicken sandwich, five chocolate chip cookies, and two glasses of cranberry juice. Florena had sat the entire time watching her, not saying a word. When she'd finished, she'd grabbed the tray, told her to relax and left.

Maxwell looked at her closely, then nodded. "Ok. I'm staying the night too and I will take you home in the morning. I've called your father, but he still wants to speak to you."

She nodded vaguely. Evangeline felt Cyrus' eyes on her and she turned. He simply stared at her with his hands in his pockets. "Is there something you wanted?" she asked him coldly.

He smirked and trailed his eyes over her. "Are you offering?"

"You pig—"

"Evangeline—" Maxwell started before the king cut him off.

"Not to worry, Max, I've grown used to her insults." His eyes seared hers. "I've been advised to issue an apology and swear to you I will never hurt you or take anything from you by force ever again." He sounded as if he'd rehearsed the words for Max's benefit.

"Apology not accepted." Evangeline glared now.

Maxwell took her elbow. "Evangeline, please don't make this harder for yourself. You're going to have to look on the bright side here. Yes, I know there isn't one, but find something, because this is the course we are on and it's not going to change."

Evangeline froze. He was right. Hell, she'd known it all along. Why was she still fighting it all?

She just looked away, her teeth clenched.

"Gives us a minute, will you, Jones?"

She felt Max stiffen next to her.

"Trust me, Jones. I've gotten it out of my system, or *in* as it were."

"Your Grace, this is not a joke. She is a human being and my best friend's daughter. You had your chance today and you blew it."

Cyrus' brows drew down and his shoulder's tensed. "Watch yourself, Jones."

"I won't apologize for this. I consider myself responsible for her and I will return her to her father in one piece. So you will have to physically throw me out, but I'm not leaving you alone with her tonight. Not when…"

Cyrus waved a hand at him. "Fine then." He snapped. "Just quit your whining."

Evangeline felt the king's eyes on her again. "I can seal those for you, if you like?" He referred to the puncture wounds at her neck.

She glared at him. "I don't need anything from you."

"Eva," Max warned.

Cyrus went on, ignoring her rude remark. "Then, you'll have a nice reprieve before we meet again. We are meeting the dogs on Wednesday for a summit."

Evangeline jerked, her expression changed swiftly, stunned. She'd almost forgotten about the summit.

He continued. "As my future wife and queen, you

will be there. It is necessary for you to learn our ways. I don't think keeping my bride in the dark is very wise considering all that's happened."

Nodding, Evangeline fought a sense of gratitude toward him for including her.

He paused, his eyes somber on hers. The way he was looking at her gave her an odd feeling. "I will never hurt you again, Evangeline." His voice was stern. "I swear it on my coven."

And for a fleeting moment, she believed him.

Chapter Fourteen

The next day passed with very little excitement and it felt as though her life had gone back to normal. She had breakfast with her sister in the kitchen then helped Katherine pack her things for school.

After a year at the University of Illinois, Katherine said she'd had enough and wasn't returning. She was now going into culinary arts at Le Cordon Bleu culinary school in Chicago. This perfectly suited her sister, who was very talented in the kitchen and heaven knew she'd gotten herself into some questionable situations the previous year. The family only hoped she focused her ever-wavering attention on food, not trouble.

As she helped Katherine fold her laundry, she was thankful her sister did not mention Cyrus or Adam or any part of the supernatural world. Instead, her sister rambled on about the apartment she was renting and how she hoped classes didn't last too long so she could go out and meet new people.

It felt nice to just complete a simple task like folding clothes in her home. It was comforting to know their mother was in the next room on the telephone with a friend, while their father was at work.

It hit her so suddenly. One moment she was feeling okay and then it was as if grief came and punched her in the stomach.

She was going to miss this. She was going to miss

the normalcy of her life. God, she hadn't even begun to think about marriage until the king dropped this bomb on her. Was she even old enough to marry? Twenty-two was beginning to feel like twelve to her.

Evangeline shook her head and forced herself to come out of her reverie.

It was going to happen. This was life. She didn't get to choose what hand she was dealt, so she'd better suck it up and roll with the punches.

Later Evangeline took a long hot bath soaking up the chance to just be. As she toweled off, she felt the hairs on her nape raise as if someone were watching her.

Grabbing the white cotton nightgown she rarely wore, she threw it on, afraid there was something or someone waiting for her in the bedroom. As she stepped out, she realized she was just being paranoid. Her room was completely dark, except for the glow of the...

Moon.

Evangeline's entire body froze as she glanced toward the window, a shudder running down her spine. Slowly, she turned and walked in a complete trance toward the blessed window Adam had taken her through. Her legs felt as heavy as tree trunks as she moved. When she reached the glass panes, she inhaled sharply.

The great orb consumed the night sky with its yellow glow. It was as if Adam had made the moon full for her alone and placed it low in the sky for her viewing pleasure.

Memories swam through her mind. There were so few, but she found herself thinking of his sexy disheveled jaw and the gorgeous muscle on his shoulder she'd clung to as he moved inside her.

Her eyes were fixated on the bright sphere that transformed her man into a wolf, and recounted every single conversation they'd had, dissecting everything he'd said to her in a new perspective, not as a prisoner now, but as his companion or *babe* as he liked to call her.

Before her mind reached the inevitable question *Where was he now*? Instinct told her she already knew.

She felt the pull of the moon and cast her eyes down to the thicket of trees near the bridge.

He was there.

"Adam." Her whisper was strained and she pressed her hands to the glass.

Adam stood in full wolf form, his eyes glowing in the dark as he stared up at her, his chest heaving as though he'd run a marathon to get there.

She took off.

Evangeline sprinted toward her bedroom door without hesitation. She only wished she had on running shoes to get her there faster and was only dimly aware her nightgown was a bit too short and flimsy to wear outside.

She didn't care. Adam was there and nothing in this crazy, hectic, manipulated world was going to stop her.

She flung the back door open and sprang out into the summer night. Her hair fell loose from the bun she'd put it in before her bath. Her feet hit the stone walkway hard, then the grass as she ran toward the bridge.

Adam paced on all fours, watching her with searing

yellow eyes, his back arched. As she came over the bridge, he paused and stood to his full, impressive height.

Evangeline slowed and came to an abrupt stop on the other side of the bridge. She had seen him in his wolfman form before, but somehow he appeared different to her now. He stood magnificently among the trees. He was over seven feet tall with imposing wide shoulders, blanketed in dark black hair. He was absolutely and incredibly, beautiful.

She gazed at him, nonplussed. Why didn't he reach for her?

Adam broke eye contact and stared at the ground. He seemed to be hesitating and began breathing harder than before.

"No." Evangeline spoke and shook her head at him. "Look at me." He couldn't phase back tonight, not during the full moon and she knew he worried he might frighten her. When he complied, she said, "I'm not afraid."

She took a step toward him and he tensed.

With a sad smile, she whispered again, "I'm not afraid," and closed the distance between them at a run. Before she could leap on him, Adam bent low and scooped her in his massive arms. Holding her close to him, he turned and headed into the woods, walking on his hind legs, his snout clamped shut as his eyes focused far off in the distance.

Evangeline didn't know where they were going, and she didn't care. She was in his arms and nothing else mattered. She knew he just wanted to get away from her house where her family could see them through a window or God forbid, anyone else who might be lurking about. Although, Adam would sense if anyone else were around.

Slowing, he walked her over to a fallen tree trunk. Adam looked at her for confirmation and she nodded. He brought them down on the ground and sat with his back against the bark. She felt his thick legs under hers as she sat cradled in one enormous arm.

The warmth from his body was soothing. Evangeline curled up closer into the crook of his arm and fixed her eyes on his powerful wolf face watching her so closely. Lifting her hand, she rubbed his chest, fascinated. "You're beautiful."

Adam took a long deep breath and then shook his head slowly, his yellow eyes never leaving hers.

"Yes, you are." She rested her head on his arm and smiled up at him. "I think it's a good thing one of us can't speak. Not just because it will make saying goodbye harder, but now you can't argue with me." She gave a short laugh and then her voice became tense. "God, I've missed you so much."

His thick, dark chest seemed to swell in accord. Adam reached up with his free hand and froze. He looked as though he was about to caress her cheek or hair and stopped himself, looking from her to his hand, now a sharp claw. Quickly, he moved it away, settling it on the ground.

"Give me your hand."

Adam gave a low rumble, but she ignored him, reaching for his arm and pulling it toward her. She took his claw, delighted at the feel of his other cupped around her waist beneath her and held it in her hands for a moment, studying it carefully. His palm alone had become larger than her face and long, pointed claws had sprouted from each finger. The palm was black leather and smooth while the top was covered in dark fur.

"You can touch me," she said and put his paw over her cheek.

Closing his eyes briefly, Adam gave a soft guttural groan.

They sat together quietly. Evangeline could not quite describe the feeling of being in love with a wolf. It did not seem odd to her on any level. In fact, it felt like they had done this a million times before. It was as if she'd seen him phase into a wolf a hundred times and this was the normal way they spent their moonlit evenings.

She could do this every day and feel completely content with her life. She was in love with the man and the wolf. It was who he was and she was proud of him.

Evangeline had closed her eyes, loving the way his warm paw felt against her cheek, when she heard him groan again. He felt where her thoughts had gone.

She opened her eyes and smiled warmly at him. Good. She wanted him to know she loved him no matter what.

His eyes moved to her hand, holding his. He let go of her face and gently turned her wrist.

Oh no!

After checking her right arm he moved to the left and inspected the inside of her wrist.

Please don't, she thought and instantly became nervous.

He looked at her. Damn it. Adam could feel her panicking and a low growl began to rumble deep in his chest.

Evangeline shook her head. "No, I'm fine. Don't worry..." Too late, she gave it away by tilting her head slightly to cover the marks on the left side of her neck.

Adam's fur stood on end and his growl grew louder as he pushed her hair back and carefully turned her face with the back of his paw.

"Adam..."

The puncture marks were faint, but were clearly visible in the moonlit night, as once again, Cyrus had not healed her wounds and she'd refused his late offer. Her ability to mend completely hadn't stood a chance when he'd clamped down as hard as he did and it was taking longer than usual to heal.

"I'm okay, Adam."

His big burly chest pumped up and down and his breathing grew shorter and shorter. His lips curled up to reveal sharp, glistening fangs.

She put her hands on his chest in an attempt to calm him, but his entire body was vibrating beneath her and she was afraid he might explode.

Adam grabbed her and squeezed her tight against him. She was pressed hard against his chest as his neck angled back. The shudders and growling instantly stopped and an agonizing howl ripped through the air.

Evangeline felt the sound tear through her heart and tears stung her eyes, spilling down her cheeks. The tortured sound seemed to last forever. She didn't want him to hurt, and she wished he had never seen the marks.

When it was over, she felt his head lower and his chest relax. He bent low and nudged her cheek with his snout. Turning her head slightly, she felt velvety wet strokes on her neck. Adam lapped at the puncture marks and Evangeline could not remember if werewolves had healing capabilities.

He came up and their eyes met. This time she put her hand on his elongated, anguished face.

"It doesn't matter." She felt the ripple of remorse run through him. "Please. Just hold me."

And he did. Adam held her in the comfort of his arms all night. She woke up some hours later in the same position, at the feel of fur running over her skin. It was still dark out and clearly Adam had not fallen asleep. Instead, he seemed to study her every curve. He ran the back of his paw down her neck and shoulder, over her arm and further down. It carried over her belly and onto the tops of her thighs, to the tips of her toes and back again.

Evangeline felt goose bumps rise over her skin. He carefully avoided any private area, undoubtedly afraid she might become uncomfortable. On the contrary, however, Evangeline stirred in his arms and found herself becoming heated at his touch.

He froze in mid stroke and looked at her. Dropping his hand, Adam pushed himself back against the tree behind him, attempting to break closer contact.

"I'm sorry." She snuggled into dark fur and patted his chest. "It felt so nice...I couldn't help myself."

Adam simply sat ramrod straight, gazing at her.

She sighed. "I want to be with you again."

He stiffened, impossibly more.

"I know we can't, but it's the truth. I hate to think the last time I'll see you will be with *him.*"

He shifted under her and she looked up, his gaze intent.

She hesitated, "He invited me to the summit on

Wednesday."

Adam snarled and cut the earth with his claw.

"Please, calm down. I know what you want to say. You don't think I should be there because it might be dangerous, but listen…you and your pack won't hurt me, right?"

He gave a quick nod.

"Okay, and neither will his coven so I don't think there is any danger. At least I get to see you, even though I'll be with…you know."

Adam calmed down, but looked away.

"Adam." The foolish thought suddenly popped in her head and she couldn't believe she was about to blurt it out. "This may sound completely insane and the more I think about it, the more I think you're going to hate it, but,"—she took a deep breath—"after I'm married…" She closed her eyes at the sound he made. "Will you let me come to you?" She left it to him to fill in the blanks. Referring to what they had as an affair didn't seem right.

Adam stared and she knew he understood.

"Ok, well, clearly you can't give me an answer and the more I think about it the more insane it sounds. What we have is so much more and I couldn't leave you every time. You know what? Forget I asked."

****

He couldn't believe his ears.

Evangeline wanted to step out on the king after she was married?

The instant she said it a part of him wanted to say *hell yes*, but the logical and more rational side of him thought this was nuts. There were a hundred factors against them.

If the king found out his queen was having an affair with a werewolf, he would go ballistic and start a war with his pack, not to mention he would undoubtedly kill Evangeline for betraying him.

Adam's chest stung at the thought of Evangeline being hurt or worse killed because of him.

No. Absolutely fucking *no*.

He'd rather die of blue balls at a late age than live without her in this world.

Adam looked her up and down for the thousandth time tonight. She was the most amazing creature on the face of the planet. The love emanating from her set his body on fire. There was no way he could be with her once in a while and then send her back. He wasn't built that way.

Evangeline leaned her head further back on his arm. They couldn't seem to take their eyes off each other. They simply sat quietly, listening to the wind rustle the leaves on a nearby tree.

Evangeline let out a long breath before she spoke. "Being with you was the most incredible experience of my life."

Adam felt his groin tighten, but made sure nothing moved. He knew she was talking about the amazing sex they'd shared. His eyes pierced hers, reading her like a book.

"I want you to know he will never have all of me."

Adam closed his eyes in a tormented scowl. He needed to hear it, but didn't want to. It nearly killed him to think about the king putting his hands on her.

"I love you, and nothing will ever change that." Evangeline's long, lithe body arched in front of him. Her breasts stretching the little nightgown she wore.

"This,"—her arms hugged her chest and stomach—"is yours. It will always be yours." Her eyes were heated and moist with unshed tears.

God, he loved her.

Once again he shifted slightly to hide any feel of him. He was thankful the amount of fur down there hid his erection, although, he wasn't entirely sure. He didn't exactly get aroused when he was hunting or racing with his pack during the full moon. In fact, this might be the first time this happened while in full wolf form. The moon heat was enough to tire him out for the full moon. *Jesus.* The things this woman did to him.

The emerging growl startled him. Evangeline cocked her head to the side and inspected him through heavy lidded eyes. "If this is the last time I'll be in your arms…"

He knew where she was headed and his hair lifted, a low rumble began from his core.

No. Stop her. He couldn't let her…

"Then I want it to be something you can truly remember." Evangeline's delicate hand came up and brushed the wire-thin strap off her shoulder. Before his hideous paw could stop her, she brought the thin white material down and exposed one luscious, exquisite tit.

He stayed completely still, but could not help the deep drone coming from him.

"Put your hands on me." She stretched back, her long, smooth, muscled thighs spreading slightly.

Adam still didn't move. If he did, he would fucking rip her apart. He was strong in his human state, but like this he could really hurt her. His ability to stay still when she was so alluring was a testament of how much he loved her.

He cursed in his head, but for fuck sake, he wanted to see more.

Evangeline seemed to read his mind. The hand holding the material down below her breast moved.

His gut jerked.

Reaching up with her slender fingers, she circled the tiny bud of her nipple. Her other hand journeyed down those glorious thighs and lifted the hem, causing Adam to come close to losing it. He felt completely lightheaded as he watched her every move.

Evangeline's lips parted, her breathing becoming enticingly heavy as she uncovered her luscious sex and lower belly. He felt her bottom move over his thigh as she writhed in his arms. His chest was pumping and the pants coming out of his nostrils sounded like he was about to give birth.

Long lashes closed over olive eyes as she rubbed her thighs together, straining with desire and he...was...loving...it. It killed him not to touch her, but he didn't care. Her body was so wonderful, he could gaze at it for the rest of his life.

Her breathing changed and he felt her arousal coursing through her. She arched her back, hair spilling over his arm as her breast came achingly closer to his face.

"Is this too much for you?" Evangeline whispered headily, bringing her hands up to caress his chest.

The whole damn situation was so erotic, a jolt so powerful ran through his entire body at her touch and he bit down hard to control the spasms bursting to get free.

Her eyes met his, undoubtedly gruesome glare. "I'm sorry. I couldn't help myself." She relaxed in his arms, lying tantalizingly bare before him.

He wanted to remember every part of her, the texture of her hair, her smooth skin, the tiny beauty mark between her breasts…everything.

Stirring in his arms with eyes glossed over, she turned to him and smiled her sweet, sexy smile.

"Something about you brings out the wild side of me." She laughed softly and closed her eyes.

Adam covered her up, reaching with his claw to carefully lift a strap over her shoulder. Evangeline was breathing deeply and he could tell she was drifting off again.

He should take her back now, but he remained where they were, completely captivated by her.

I'll take her back in a minute. I just need to be with her for just a few more…

****

Evangeline awoke three hours later in her bed. She was snuggled comfortably under her quilt. She turned over onto her back, feeling utterly despondent and alone.

Was that it? The last time she would be in Adam's arms?

She swiped at the silent tears and a bright color next to her head caught her eye. Turning, she saw a red rose lying on the pillow next to hers.

Evangeline sat up instantly and grabbed for it. Where had he found a rose last night? Her parent's garden didn't grow roses. She stared hard at the deep, velvety lapels, then noticed something wrapped at the bottom of the stem.

A thick, coarse locket of black fur was tied to the stem. It was held tight by what looked to be a few strands of her own hair. The deep red knotted around the black looked so right, yet so sad. At least a part of them would remain together forever, but it wasn't enough, not nearly enough.

Lying back down, she clutched the rose to her chest. As she lay, unseeing eyes staring at the ceiling, she pictured Adam in his human form now doing the same thing with a thick locket of *her* hair.

Chapter Fifteen

"See you next week, Miss Evangeline."

"Take care, Tasha." Evangeline waved goodbye to the rest of her students as she swept up the rosin powder off the hardwood floors.

"I'm taking off too." Natalie Valentino, the owner of Valentino's Dance Studio, gave Evangeline a speculative look before going.

Upon returning to work, Evangeline had thrown herself into her lessons, avoiding any and all conversation with the other instructors or her boss. The dead giveaway was her evasive demeanor. Evangeline was hardly quiet in the work place. She got along fine with her coworkers and engaged them in conversation during breaks, sometimes going out after work for dinner or drinks.

"See you tomorrow, Natalie." She gave her boss a smile that didn't reach her eyes.

She knew they were wondering what was going on but Evangeline did not have the energy or the desire to discuss her predicament. They'd find out soon enough she was married to the Vampire King of North America. Saturday, in fact. No doubt, awful Mary would put a piece in the paper as soon as they said, *I do*.

As she stepped into one of the offices in the back where they kept the lockers, she rubbed the stiff muscles at her neck, anticipating and yet dreading the night's events. She couldn't help but wonder whether or not the vampires would forgive the werewolves for kidnapping their future queen, doubtful, or more likely a fight would ensue.

She switched her ballet slippers she wore in the studio for her black Prada ballet flats. After two sleepless nights, she debated bringing a change of clothes, but who knew what was appropriate for a vampire/werewolf summit. Deciding she didn't care, Evangeline left on her black leggings and threw a loose white yoga shirt over her black camisole. If the king didn't approve, then he could just kiss her ass.

"Miss Wolcott."

Evangeline jumped at the sound of her name. "Jesus!" She looked angrily at the king's henchmen. "Victor, you scared the crap out of me."

"Sorry." He didn't look the least bit sorry as he stood, taking up the entire frame of the office doorway. "His Grace is waiting in the car."

Clutching her hand to her chest, she asked blankly, "For what?"

No emotion showed on Victor's hard face. Evangeline thought, if he stood still for longer than two seconds, someone might mistake him for a statue, a really scary statue. "He's here to take you to the summit. Are you ready?"

Having no strength to put up an argument Evangeline shrugged. "Yeah, let's go." She grabbed her Mark Jacobs satchel and the keys to lock up the studio.

Outside, Cyrus sat in a black Jaguar. She slipped in the back with him and shut the door, giving him only a brief glance. "Hey." She sounded like he was picking her up in a car pool.

The interior was wide and cool with beige leather. There was silence as Victor started the car, then, "Are you all right?"

"I'm fine," she said, not looking his way.

"No, really. You look pale."

Cyrus grabbed her hand and she was forced to look at him. "Just tired."

The look he gave her confused the hell out of her. Did he actually care how she felt? There was no mistaking the concern in his eyes and the instant she saw it she remembered how she'd thought it would have been great had they met under different circumstances. How wonderful it would have been just to be friends with someone like him, even though he was as arrogant as they come.

Evangeline turned away from his speculative gaze. "I'll be fine."

Cyrus let go of her hand and adjusted in his seat. The car lurched as they took off into dusk. There was a deafening silence in the car as they headed to wherever they were going and Evangeline had the strangest urge to break it. Before she could ask where they were going, Cyrus spoke up.

"This is a standard summit. I don't want you to worry. Maxwell Jones will be there to mediate of course, but with me and,"—Cyrus' nose flared as he paused—"the Blacktail alpha, we will be able to control our subordinates."

Staring at him pensively, she asked, "What is the purpose of this meeting? I thought it was understood by all parties that your coven doesn't have Serena Perez."

He looked her over before he spoke. "Evangeline,

as you know, you're to become my wife, as such, future queen to North America. It is an extreme insult to me, my coven and my realm to attack what is mine."

Evangeline stared.

"Right...women's cursed liberation." He rolled his eyes. "You know what I mean when I say *mine*. You are already considered a part of my coven, so any offense against it, is a direct offense to me."

Her brow furrowed at this. "I don't want an argument between your coven and the Blacktails over me. It's ludicrous. I'm fine. Can't we forget all about it?"

Cyrus gave her an exasperated look. "That's not exactly how we work, my dear."

He turned from her, leaving her to her thoughts. They made a left somewhere and the town's decadent little lampposts fell behind them.

"Can you promise me something?" Evangeline looked at him.

"No."

She waited quietly for an explanation.

Cyrus let out a frustrated breath. "Evangeline, I don't make promises I cannot keep and by the sound of it, you're revving up for a long one about peace and forgiveness."

"I thought you wanted me to learn your ways. How can I learn if I don't ask questions?"

He looked at her pointedly. "Ah, but you are not asking a question, Evangeline, you are making a demand. I don't know what will become of this meeting, but I can assure you will not be in danger. As for the dogs...it is still to be determined."

Evangeline's stomach lurched. If anything

happened to Adam or any of the Blacktails, she would never forgive Cyrus, but what power did a human have over two powerful supernatural forces?

They drove on and as they did, Evangeline tried to soothe her nerves. Initially, she'd been thankful to be invited to a summit, but now she was wondering what had she been thinking? She had no idea what would happen, but she needed to save her anxiety till they arrived. Fighting the urge to vomit, she turned her head toward her window and closed her eyes, taking in long pulls of air.

Collecting her composure, she opened her eyes and stared out into the night, completely aware of the man next to her and thought how many times would she sit next to him like this as husband and wife, king and queen.

"Cyrus?"

"Mm?" He seemed to be lost in thought too and did not look at her.

She hesitated, staring at his profile. "Why?" Evangeline whispered. It was a vague question, but she knew he understood.

He turned to her and they stared for a while. Amazingly, she saw his eyes soften for the very first time. It was unnerving. "I want you. Isn't that enough?"

She answered stoically, "You don't even know me."

"I know plenty."

Evangeline continued to hold his gaze.

He took a deep breath and spoke evenly. "You studied at the Joffrey Academy of Dance since you were eight years old and received a BA in Liberal Arts and Science at DePaul University in Chicago. You love to dance and do so beautifully, but in the past you faint whenever you overexert yourself. After years of training, you gave up becoming one of the greatest dancers in the business to teach ballet to children, here, in Wilmington.

"You go out with friends on occasion, but for the most part, you're a homebody. Your first boyfriend was in high school, but you grew apart after you graduated. You dated one Leonardo Russo, giving him your virginity in college. He disappeared without a trace shortly after." Cyrus gave her a pointed look. "I've looked, the man is nowhere to be found."

Evangeline couldn't speak, and she certainly didn't want to know how he knew so much about her.

He went on. "Your mother is Rachelle Wolcott, formerly, Rachelle Smith, adopted by Hannah and Walter Smith. Your father is one of Wilmington's oldest families and you know I know him." He spoke to her in a low tone, his eyes never leaving hers. "You're sister, Katherine, almost died of Leukemia as a child, but is now healthy and quite a handful."

Cyrus paused for a moment, his gaze moving down to stare at her lips. "I know you are probably one of the most beautiful women I have ever seen." His eyes roamed over her face. "I sense strength and fire in you you're not even aware of."

His cool hand caressed her cheek, and slowly, tilted her chin to inspect her neck.

Her puncture marks were healed, but she froze, not knowing what he was going to do.

Shaking his head, he let go of her face. "I'm barbaric, and I'm afraid I can't help it," Cyrus said a matter fact. "I promise you though, the next time I

196

touch you, you will enjoy it."

Evangeline wanted to tell him she would never enjoy it. She would never enjoy being in his arms when she was in love with another man, but she'd lost the ability to speak.

"When you stop fighting me, you will realize I can make you very happy. You will want for nothing as my wife."

Except for Adam, she thought. She turned from him to stare out her window again.

The car fell silent once more as they pulled into a deserted lot of an abandoned warehouse just outside of Wilmington.

Victor parked the Jaguar and got out to open the door for her. He shut it behind her and she came around to stand next to Cyrus. He looked down at her and there was no smirk or smolder in his stare. He was all business now, unsmiling and sober. "I want you to stay right next to me at all times, understood?"

Her stomach dropped again, but she nodded.

"All right." Cyrus put a hand at the small of her back and guided her to the windowless door at the side of the building.

Heart pounding, Evangeline waited for Victor to open it for them and stepped through into a desolate room bigger than her house. The one room warehouse was surrounded by gray stone about eight feet from the concrete floor, then towering windowpanes up to the ceiling about thirty feet from their heads. It looked to be an old abandon warehouse store, left empty and in a dreary state. The night's sky was black now, the only light from within was the bright fluorescent fixtures scattered around the stone walls that did little to brighten up the place.

As they entered the ominous room, Evangeline realized they were the last to arrive. Two groups of people stood facing each other in the middle of the room.

The King's Coven took up the highest point of the warehouse on a high platform closest to the back wall. There was a long table where seven vampires sat spaced out in a line, with a vacant chair in the middle. She imagined this set up was Cyrus' idea to intimidate the Blacktails. Evangeline recognized Mary, Girard, the good-looking cook, and the somber Florena, who had helped her after Cyrus fed from her. There were four other fierce-looking vampires she did not know glaring down at the werewolves.

Evangeline looked in their direction and froze. Adam was standing in front of his Fighters. His incredible blue eyes met hers and for a moment she was transported to their last night. It was heartbreaking to see him in his wolf form, but more so to see him now as himself. He was as striking as ever in jeans and a black t-shirt.

Their eyes held for a mere two seconds before he broke contact, but she saw the warning in his eyes. He did not want them to give away their feelings in front of the king and his coven. Instead, he cast a sardonic glance at her body, giving any onlookers the impression he only saw her as a piece of meat, but she knew he was taking the opportunity to assess for any injuries and to reach out and feel the mood she was in. In fact, if her instincts were correct, she would bet Nick, Jason, Alex and Ramo were doing the exact same thing and she felt a great amount of tenderness toward the Blacktails. She hoped they could sense her gratitude.

Adam looked at Cyrus then and the tension in the room increased by a hundred. His gorgeous jaw twitched and his chest heaved slightly. Jason looked like he wanted to put a restraining hand on his shoulder, but thought better of it.

"Are we all nice and cozy, then?" Cyrus' sarcastic voice broke the icy silence and he moved forward toward the platform. "We are sorry we're late, but we've had a lot of catching up to do." Cyrus' meaning was clear. She tensed at his words and his possessive hand at her back as they moved toward the empty seat between Florena and a male vampire.

Evangeline fought the urge not to look Adam's way, but she saw through the corner of her eye Jason step up to stand right next to him and she knew it was his way of calming Adam down. She wanted to smack Cyrus' hand away, but didn't dare.

Play along and hopefully nothing bad will happen, she thought and prayed it would be over soon.

"Good to see you, Magistrate."

As Cyrus shook hands with a bald, pale man, Evangeline chanced a look at Adam. He was glaring at the king, but glanced her way. The instant his eyes met hers, she melted. This was complete torture. She was standing on the wrong side. She should be next to him. Adam's controlled mask broke slightly, and the longing filling his eyes spoke volumes.

"Shall we begin?" Evangeline jumped slightly at the Magistrate's voice and turned to see him better. He was thin and gaunt with crooked teeth and very little hair on the sides of his head.

Cyrus inclined his head at the Magistrate then

turned to her. "Would you like to sit, my love?"

Shaking her head, Evangeline insisted he take the empty chair. Cyrus sat in front of her and refusing to let her go, took her right hand and held it over his left shoulder, reclining and looking as though he'd just entered a dinner party. He played with Evangeline's fingers and smirked at the werewolves like the cat who caught the canary.

Evangeline took a deep breath. If she took her hand back, it would draw attention to them and the last thing she wanted to do was irritate Cyrus while they questioned the Blacktails, but she hated doing this in front of Adam.

The magistrate spoke just as Maxwell Jones entered. "We have called this summit to discuss the kidnapping of Evangeline Wolcott, member of the King's Coven and fiancé of the King of North America."

Maxwell took up position between the King's Coven and the Blacktails on the main floor, placing his briefcase down on the platform next to him.

The Magistrate addressed Adam. "His Grace has called this summit, which is why I am here, but I see you did not bring your adjudicator. It's not required, but you are within your rights to do so."

"It won't be necessary," Adam said simply without expression.

The bald vampire turned to Cyrus then. "Will Miss Wolcott be giving testimony tonight, Your Grace?"

Cyrus stared ahead, his eyes now glaring at Adam. "No, she will not."

The Magistrate hesitated.

What? Why wouldn't Cyrus let her testify? She

was afraid to, of course. There was every chance she'd say something and give away her feelings for Adam, but it seemed odd they would bring her here and not allow her to speak. She wanted to disagree. What if she could save Adam from whatever Cyrus had planned?

Cyrus felt her tense and squeezed her hand, warning her to keep her mouth shut. "Montague, Miss Wolcott has already given me the details of her abduction and therefore, I can testify on her behalf."

Evangeline saw Adam shift slightly.

"Very well," Magistrate Montague drawled. "Adam Perez, on the night of August second, you, in full awareness of your actions, abducted Evangeline Wolcott from her home with intent to harm her if the king did not meet your demands. Do you deny these charges?"

Adam's deep tenor sent chills down her spine and she realized she had missed his gruff voice. "No, but I do deny any intent to harm Miss Wolcott. It was a ruse to get what I wanted."

"Is this true, Your Grace?"

Cyrus took his time to answer. "Evangeline was fine when she came to me. I examined her myself." He continued to play with her fingers.

Evangeline groaned in her head and briefly closed her eyes. God, did he have to make it sound like he'd stripped her naked?

Adam's nostril's flared and she had a sinking feeling Cyrus caught his little tell tale sign.

As all vampire eyes were on the werewolves Evangeline stared at Adam now. With the tiniest of movements, she shook her head a fraction of a millimeter to indicate to him Cyrus was lying and not to

201

go off the handle.

He stared at Cyrus, but she knew he caught her movement and turned his gaze to Montague.

Too late, Evangeline realized Cyrus' man, Victor stood behind her.

Damn. She prayed he had not seen, but she felt Cyrus' hand become still on hers.

"Mr. Perez, were you aware Miss Wolcott was engaged to Cyrus Stewart, on the night of the abduction?"

Adam looked lethal. "Yes."

"Ah, and are you aware the penalty for kidnapping a member of the King's Coven is five years in SPONA, and twenty-five to life for kidnapping a member of the realm?"

Evangeline's heart sunk. SPONA was the supernatural prison. Most did not come out alive, as their security system seriously differed from human prisons.

Before Adam could speak, Maxwell raised his hand. "Magistrate, may I interject? Evangeline is not yet a member of the realm and was not quite affianced to His Grace as the vampire betrothal contract was not completed at the time."

She could kiss Maxwell Jones.

"Therefore, in my opinion this is a hearing to discuss the kidnapping of a civilian and nothing more."

Montague turned to Cyrus. "Is this true, Your Grace? Was the betrothal contract not complete?"

Cyrus continued to stare ahead. "We were in the midst of the betrothal when Perez kidnapped Evangeline. I assure you, the contract has been *thoroughly*, completed."

This time, all the Blacktail Fighters tensed.

"Right," Montague said. "However, I'm afraid Mr. Jones is correct. She was a civilian at the time of the kidnapping."

Cyrus glared at Montague now. "She was under my protection."

"I understand Your Grace, but it still stands to reason, she was not yet a part of your coven, not yet your fiancé and far from Queen of North America."

Cyrus' pale face looked at Montague with murder in his eyes. "I'll marry her right now then."

****

Evangeline's hand flew out of his. Cyrus gave a quick glance at her wide-eyed expression before looking back at Montague.

First order of business when Evangeline and he returned from their honeymoon was to appoint a new magister.

Fucking technicality.

He should have known, but his anger at the mutt in front of him made him call for the summit. He'd actually gone through the appropriate channels and it was blowing up in his face. He needed to keep his nose clean while he negotiated with the Asian king. Otherwise, he would have never gone by the books.

Montague looked momentarily dumbfounded, then, "You have every right to marry her now if you wish. I can perform the ceremony, but I'm afraid it won't change the circumstances—"

"Cyrus!" Evangeline's sing song voice unruffled his nerves. He loved when she used his name. Turning to her, he saw pleading in her expression.

She shook her head slowly at him, her green eyes

penetrating his. "Don't do this. Please. Not like this."

What was it about her that turned him into a sap? He looked her over. It was a sign she hadn't fought him today. In fact, he believed she was warming up to him. If he showed a little compassion now, he may even get the chance to go a little further.

After the summit, he intended on taking her back to his coven for a late dinner. After which, he hoped to show her just how gentle he could be when he fed from her. Once he showed her how wonderful it could be, she'd be putty in his hands.

Tearing his gaze from her hypnotic eyes, Cyrus addressed the Magistrate. "Alas, my fiancé has been looking forward to a ceremony under more attractive conditions." He put his hand around her waist and brought her closer to his side. Her lovely tits were now at his eye level.

"Very well," the Magistrate said. "Does Miss Wolcott want to press charges against Mr. Perez for kidnapping? I can bring her case to the police on her behalf."

He would love to see the alpha dog sent to SPONA now, but it would take much longer if he went through human channels. Before he could answer, though, Evangeline spoke loudly.

"No."

Cyrus whipped his head around at Evangeline. All eyes were on her.

She gave Cyrus a nervous smile before addressing the Magistrate. "Mr. Montague, Mr. Perez took me out of desperation to find his sister. I don't want to press charges against him for doing something I would have done myself for my own sister."

Montague looked confused and turned to Cyrus. "What is this?"

Cyrus glowered at Evangeline. "Are you absolutely certain you don't want to press charges?"

"Yes. I told you," she spoke softly to him now, "I don't want any trouble brought upon by me."

He was curious. Something was up.

Cyrus spoke to Montague, "Mr. Perez was under the impression *I* took his pup of a sister."

Maxwell cut in. "Serena Perez, a Blacktail werewolf and sister to the alpha male, Adam Perez, has been missing for several weeks and Mr. Perez had reason to believe the King's Coven had taken her due to recent events."

"Because these bloodsuckers killed Tyson Maury!" the werewolf, Ramo shouted at them.

"Yeah? Did Patrick Ford chew off his own head then, motherfucker?" Girard yelled back.

"Your Grace, please," Montague urged, gesturing at both sides as the tension in the room spiked.

Cyrus would like nothing more than to go head to head with this filthy pack, but unfortunately they needed answers first and his fiancé was present. He gave Girard a look to back off.

Reluctantly, he took his arm from around Evangeline to fold his hands on the table. "We have not brought these matters to your attention, Magistrate, but it seems unavoidable."

Maxwell stepped closer to him, but remained below. "Your Grace, this is a summit to discuss Evangeline's abduction. I can't allow her to stay here if you're going to debate about other threatening issues. Please, for her safety, let me take her out."

"She is not leaving my sight, Max."

On the floor, Jason Linus stepped up, ever his master's beta and eyeing Victor who had moved around stealthily to the end of the table. He cocked his head at Victor. "Tell your boy to relax."

"*I* don't take orders from dogs," Cyrus jeered, but in his head he spoke to Victor. *Don't make any move unless I say. Got it?*

You're the boss, Victor replied back.

Maxwell spoke to the Magistrate about the attacks on both the werewolves and vampires as the testosterone level continued to rise. Cyrus glared at the alpha, his coven baring fangs, hissing at the Fighters who'd hunched slightly. All but Adam growled low as they glared back.

Maxwell stood directly between them. "So you see, it has escalated to this."

"You're lucky to be a-fucking-live after Tyson," Ramo uttered fiercely.

"We never touched Tyson Maury, you idiots," Zach heckled back.

Cyrus felt Evangeline grab his shoulder. It was a mistake to bring her. This was why summits were dreaded. None of the supernatural could keep a level head. He wanted to rip Adam Perez apart, limb from limb.

He was becoming sole vampire now, the urge to attack clouding his judgment. The cool façade was for show, but hell if he could forget Adam had taken his future wife. With a sinking feeling, he realized the alpha felt something for Evangeline. It was written all over his face.

And what had Victor meant when he telepathically

told him Evangeline was signaling Perez?

The room resounded with hissing and growls as insults were thrown back and forth.

"Could there be other supernatural forces behind these attacks?" Evangeline raised her voice.

The warehouse went silent.

Evangeline looked from Cyrus to Adam to Montague. "I mean...are there any witches in the area? Aren't they the sworn enemy of werewolves?"

Cyrus stared at Evangeline, trying to put meaning to her words. He knew if he was thinking logically they would have made sense, but with anger obscuring all reason, she might have asked, *"Where is the bathroom?"*

Maxwell cleared his throat. "I think it's something to consider, don't you, Magistrate?"

"Yes, she makes a valid point."

A goateed werewolf called out, "I can tell you it was no witch that got your little friend in the woods though."

Perez growled at his man. "Stand the fuck down!"

Too late, Florena had stood up, eyes shining. "You little shit!"

Easy, Flo! They may be lying to start a fight, Cyrus said to her quietly.

Then find out if they are or not, cuz I'm ready!

Cyrus spoke to Adam now, privately, his eyes boring into his. *You want this to get messy while she's standing right here?*

He leered as Adam jerked, obviously taken aback by Cyrus' silent communication. The other Fighters felt it too. They looked from Adam to Cyrus now.

I know you have feelings for her. Call off your dogs

and we can continue this another day. We'll be happy to kill you when Evangeline is out of the vicinity.

He watched Adam's chest rapidly rise and fall. His pack moved now like the wolves they were, crisscrossing behind their leader, just waiting for an attack. He shouted to Montague, "Are you sentencing me or not?"

Montague had gone quiet, watching both sides nervously. "You will not be held accountable for the kidnapping of Miss. Wolcott, but I'm afraid we will have to reconvene on other matters Mr. Perez."

"Can't...Fucking...Wait!" Ramo shouted.

Smart man. Cyrus continued to communicate telepathically with Adam.

Both masters knew they would settle this without the Magistrate or Jones.

Cyrus stared at the dark alpha, hating every fucking part of him. He couldn't help himself. *Did you fuck her?*

Cyrus swore Adam's eyes widened slightly, but he could have imagined it. The man shook his head.

He had believed Evangeline the other day, but he needed to hear it from him. A shake of the head wasn't going to do it though. Cyrus reached out his senses, trying to hone in on the alpha's pulse.

Evangeline was standing so close to him though and her weird staccato of a heartbeat caught his attention, then...

What the fuck was that?

Forgetting to listen to Adam's pulse, Cyrus froze. Coming from his left, he heard a distinct flutter of beats. He turned his head slowly. The entire room disappeared before his eyes and became utterly silent as he listened. Evangeline's stomach was right in front of his face and the rapid pace of an infant's pulse beat in his ears.

He felt Evangeline look down at him.

Pain and fury like no other pierced through him and he reacted without even thinking.

Cyrus put his hands on her roughly, one around her back and the other on her stomach. He needed to be sure.

"What are doing?" she yelled.

He heard and felt the infant's heartbeat more clearly now. Cyrus' felt his eyes turn and his fangs punch out. In the back of his mind he heard the Fighters growling at him and didn't care. He got up, hovering over her, their noses, tip to tip. Trembling, he spoke through clenched teeth. "You're fucking pregnant?"

Evangeline lurched back and stared at him, horrified. "What? No. Of cour—" Before she could finish a glazed expression swept across her face and his black beat-less heart exploded as she grabbed her stomach and turned to look at the fucking werewolf.

He turned as Adam's face faltered and then pure astonishment washed over him.

It was his. He fucking knew it.

Vaguely he noticed everyone had watched and understood their exchange, but Cyrus had grown cold, shuddering as he became dizzy with grief. He hissed through fangs at Adam, "You bastard!"

Cyrus heard Evangeline's heart pound in her chest as she trembled in front of him. He grabbed her by the arms, feeling completely drunk with rage, he shook her hard. "FUCKING WHORE!"

The room exploded.

He turned and saw the Fighters phase into seven feet tall wolfmen. Debris of clothing went flying as they changed. Adam's black form came hurling at him, but Victor got there first, knocking him back. When Adam got his footing, he lurched at Victor, picking him up off the floor with one hand and flinging him at Florena and Gabe. They went down like bowling pins, but jumped back up and leaped into the fight.

It was chaos all around them. The sound of growls and the pounding of fist and paw echoed in the warehouse. Both sides were putting up a good fight, holding their own.

Montague ran to the nearest exit, while Jones was herded toward the far wall by the onslaught unfolding, shouting at Evangeline to run. Cyrus' target was Adam. As he was about to leap from the platform, Jason pounced on him, knocking Cyrus onto the table, and cracking it down to the floor.

Cyrus heard a scream. He watched as a chair flew through the air and hit Evangeline, knocking her down.

Cyrus and Jason both scrambled to get to her, as Mary and Anthony fought Alex and Ramo precariously close to where Evangeline lay. Blood splashed as they came forward when Ramo slashed Anthony across the face with his claw.

Evangeline was on the floor, trying to get up, when they got to her. Jason pushed him out of the way, clipping his arm with his muzzle before leaping over her. The werewolf turned, hovering over Evangeline, to snarl at Cyrus. He was protecting her from him like a lion protecting his cub.

He continued to growl at Cyrus as Evangeline got to her feet, clinging to the wolf for support. She turned frantically around at the ensuing chaos and found Adam fighting relentlessly with Girard.

Adam sought her out at the wrong moment and was blasted into the stone wall by Girard's fist.

Cyrus was about to take over for Girard when Evangeline screamed.

"ADAM!" Evangeline's earsplitting cry ripped through the warehouse, and she ran out of Jason's arms and into his.

"Cyrus, please! Stop this!"

He gave her an agonized look, dizzied by hatred for this pack, by her betrayal.

"If you ever cared at all for me, please! Don't let your coven die for what I did. Please, Cyrus. Stop this!" She held onto his arms with a death grip.

He looked at his would be queen in complete defeat and through gritted teeth, he told her miserably, "You have no idea what you've done."

She looked like she was ready to pass out. Breathing hard, she barely heard him as she looked around to find Adam.

Christ, she fucking *loves* the bastard. It was too much.

Cyrus sought out the alpha. *I'll call off mine if you call off yours?*

Adam immediately turned to him, and then howled at his Fighters. At the same time, Cyrus called out, "Halt!"

Vampire and werewolf froze in mid fight, the room becoming instantly silent as each side waited for further instructions.

Cyrus had become someone else. Never in his entire life had he felt such agony and the bitter taste of defeat.

Fine. You've won her. Take her now. Cyrus' head rolled on his neck. *Get her out of my sight.* He turned to Evangeline and pushed her away from him.

Jason caught her. Evangeline's sweet lips he would never taste mouthed to him, *thank you.*

He told his coven to stand down. Evangeline jumped off the platform and landed flawlessly on the floor, dashing toward Adam as he four-footed it toward her.

She jumped into Adam's burly arms, hugging him tightly. Cyrus bit down hard in disgust.

Adam cradled her like a baby and turned toward the door, his pack falling back and following their alpha backwards in the same direction.

His coven watched them retreat, panting heavily.

"Get out!"

They looked to him, but he ignored them, glaring at the place Evangeline had just disappeared from.

They scattered and teleported with quickness.

Good.

Cyrus arched back and let out a yell heard across five towns. The windows of the warehouse shattered at the same time, raining shiny debris in and outside.

****

Outside, the pack froze at the piercing scream and turned to look at the explosion of glass from the building.

Evangeline gripped the fur at Adam's arms and squeezed her eyes shut.

She whispered to him, "*God, what have I done?*"

Chapter Sixteen

Adam placed Evangeline down gently by the SUV and stepped away a few feet to phase back. It took a considerable amount of energy to do so when his testosterone level was through the roof and the image of the prick's hands on Evangeline still seared his mind. Completely naked now, he stormed toward Evangeline who looked pale and terrified. Adam reached out and cupped her face in his hands, bending his head to place his forehead on hers.

Closing his eyes, he calmed his breathing, taking in her scent and warmth and dazedly thrilled to be touching her right now. "Are you all right?"

She nodded mutely.

He let her go, abruptly. "Let's get the hell out of here."

Adam opened the passenger door and slipped her inside.

"Put your belt on."

She nodded and did so.

He came around and sat in the driver's seat, shaking his head as they took off. He couldn't believe how things had turned out. The last thing he thought would happen was to end up sitting next to Evangeline on his way home.

He scanned the area for the Fighters. He knew Nick and Alex were still lingering around the warehouse, waiting until he and Evangeline were out of sight, while Ramo and Jason had taken off to patrol around the round house.

Evangeline let out a long breath.

She was with him.

Evangeline was sitting beside him with his baby inside her. *God. A baby!*

He reached out his keen senses as he'd done back at the warehouse when Cyrus announced she was pregnant. There it was, his baby's heart beating fast as hell.

Nervous now, he turned to check on her. "How are you feeling?" Shit, it was like he knocked up his high school girlfriend or something.

Evangeline was clutching her stomach. "Is it true?" She turned to him.

Adam nodded.

"It's so early though. How…"

"I'm a wolf," he said tersely, and glanced uncertainly at her. "You won't carry like humans. Our fetuses grow at a rapid rate." He inhaled sharply. "That's if you choose to…" God, he couldn't say it, didn't want to think it.

Her eyes widened at him. "You think…why would you even say…?"

Adam stared straight ahead as he drove. "Evangeline, I don't know how this happened." He scoffed at himself. "Okay, I do, but it has to be the moon heat for us to conceive, but you're human." He hesitated. "It must not matter to humans, but I don't know how this is going to be on your body. We're going to have to research previous cases like this—"

"Adam, I'm keeping our baby no matter what."

His chest constricted as he looked at her and grabbed for her hand, twining their fingers together and holding her knuckles to his mouth.

They drove in silence. The closer they got to the round house, the faster he drove. When they arrived, he put the SUV in park and jumped out. Coming around, he picked her up and carried her to the door.

"Adam, I'm fine. I can walk."

"Just let me, okay?" he said tautly.

Evangeline kissed his cheek and placed her head in the crook of his neck.

He punched the code on the panel by the door with one hand and slipped inside the house, shutting the door with his bare foot.

Evangeline giggled. "How many times have you come home naked?"

"Too many times to count."

"The neighbors don't complain?" She smirked at him.

"As you saw, my house is at the end of the street. I have the Midewin meadow on one side and on the other the houses are spaced out. My nearest neighbor is an old widow and the little lady actually enjoys it. I also think her mind's slipping, but nevertheless, she gets a show every now and then."

Adam brought her to the kitchen and set her down on the granite counter top. They were almost eyelevel now. "How do you feel?" he asked again as she hadn't answered him in the car.

"I felt tired all day and a little nauseous on the way to the warehouse, but I'm feeling fine now." She reached up and held his face in her hands. "I can't believe I'm here."

He turned his face and kissed the palm of her hand, savoring the feel of her touch. "I'm never letting you out of my sight again." His lips continued on, kissing her wrist, then trailing up her arm to her neck. "Are you sure you're all right?" His voice was low and heavy now.

She was breathing hard, eyes closed. "Yes," she whispered.

His hands went down to her waist and pulled her closer to him as hers came around his back and up his neck. He went hard instantly and it pushed up against her thigh. "I need you, baby." He moaned as she turned her face to his and kissed him hard, her sweet tongue sweeping over his lips, searching his. He kissed her greedily. Adrenaline from the fight ran rampant through his veins and it was all he could do not to rip her clothes off. Adam's hands came down and squeezed her backside, pulling her up against his arousal as their tongues fused together. He slowed their fierce pace and sucked gently on her lower lip, grazing it with his teeth before pulling away.

Tilting his head back, he stared down at her through heavy lidded eyes. "Stop me if I'm going too fast or too rough. I can't seem to get a grip on myself."

The sound of shoes falling on hardwood was her response. Evangeline pulled away from him to lie flat on the counter top, giving him easy access to slide her pants off and toss them on the floor.

Her long legs slid around him, and pulling her shirt down to expose a succulent breast, she took his left hand to mold it over her nipple, encouraging him. Adam didn't need any more encouragement. He played with her nipple with his forefinger and thumb, pinching it slightly. Her nipple hardened under his touch and she writhed beneath him.

Evangeline moaned as he rubbed the tip of his cock over her hot core, teasing her, and she whispered, "Adam, please."

"I seem to recall a little vixen torturing me the other night." Adam's other hand moved to his mouth, licking two fingers as he hungrily watched her panting for him, and brought them down to rub the jewel she'd flaunted the other night. It had taken an insane amount of self-control not to fuck her in his wolf form and for days he thought of how he wished to touch her again.

Evangeline's head rolled back and her torso shot up. "Adam."

Jesus, her voice was sexy.

She grabbed his left arm at her nipple, squeezing it hard. "You're killing me."

His thumb took over her spot, moving it around in quick circles and slipped two long fingers inside her. She was wet and ready and about to come. As soon as the first spasm closed around his fingers, he slipped them out and slammed into her.

"AH!" they moaned in unison.

Gripping her waist, he began to pump hard, beating his swollen sex into her, never missing a beat. Evangeline hung onto the edge of the counter with one hand and his forearm with the other, her head turned to one side, eyes shut, jaw clenched.

A very small part of him said to take it easy, but he couldn't do it. The selfish bastard in him had to stake his claim, mark his territory. She was his mind, body and soul, completely and utterly his.

He knew he was gonna come fast at this rate and

sure enough, Adam cocked his head back and screwed his eyes shut as a powerful orgasm rocked through him. He moaned deep, slowing his hips as beads of sweat poured down his body.

"Holy shit," he hissed, gasping for air. Shoulders pumping up and down, he bent over to brace himself on the counter. "I'm sorry." He shook his head, his breath shaky. "Did I hurt you?"

She looked spent, but the gorgeous smile she gave him told him she was just fine. "Of course not and don't ever apologize for *that.*"

He helped her up and kissed her softly. "I should have been gentler. The baby—"

"Is fine." She kissed him again. "The baby is thrilled we're together. Don't worry."

He let out a huff. "You're carrying my child. I'm afraid I'm going to worry for the rest of my life."

Adam lifted her off the counter top and carried her up the stairs to the newly renovated bathroom off the master bedroom.

He set her down near the sink. "I need a shower and uh,"—he looked uncomfortably at her—"you smell a little like *him.*"

She nodded silently and looking around at all the gray marble, she said, "It smells like fresh paint."

Adam lifted her arms to take off her shirt. "I just redid the whole bathroom, me and Jason."

She looked around again and he could swear understanding washed over her face, but she left it alone.

Adam opened the shower doors and turned on the faucet. "I'd love to try out the new whirlpool with you, but it's late and I think you should rest."

She smiled dreamily at him. "A shower is fine."

They showered together, taking turns to lather each other up, pausing several times for heated kisses.

When they were dry and snuggled in his California king-sized bed and down comforter, neither of them felt the least bit tired.

Evangeline lay in the crook of his arm, rubbing his chest. Adam could not describe in words how it felt to have her here with him. He had the woman he loved in his arms and the baby they had made together. No man in the world could be as happy as he was right now.

His heart skipped suddenly. First thing in the morning, he was researching werewolf and human mating. They couldn't be the first people to have done it, but if it were dangerous he would have heard something by now.

"Adam."

"Yeah, babe? Are you comfortable?" he asked, shifting her closer to his side.

"Yes, very." Raising her head to look at him, she rested her chin on his chest.

"I forgot to take my pill when I got home." Her expression was worried. "It honestly slipped my mind. As soon as I got up, my sister was there, yelling at me, and then Max came and told my father everything and took me to the King's Coven. It was irresponsible of me—"

"Shhh. I'm not blaming you, Evangeline." He smoothed her hair with his free hand. "God, I'm thrilled you're carrying my baby. We just need to be smart about this now." He looked at her sternly. "The baby is growing fast. That's why you're feeling nauseous and tired so soon, because you're carrying a werewolf." He waited for her eyes to widen or for some sign carrying a wolf inside her disgusted her, but none came.

Evangeline simply stared thoughtfully.

"Which,"—he took a deep breath—"is why I mentioned options earlier. It's your body, Evangeline, and completely up to you if you want to carry the child to term or not."

"I told you, I'm not terminating this pregnancy."

"I know what you said, but it's a lot to ask of you. You're still young and have no knowledge of raising our breed. I would understand if you didn't want to."

She thought for a moment and his insides froze. Shaking her head suddenly, she said, "I've been studying the supernatural for years. I know humans have bred with werewolves successfully." Evangeline stared at him hard. "You have no idea how happy I am I'm carrying your baby. We're going to get through this and be proud parents of a little boy or girl."

Adam's throat stung as he listened to her and gulped hard before he spoke. "You know, babe, it may just be both. Werewolves tend to breed like any other animal." God, she could be carrying a litter. The thought made his heart quicken. He'd love to have a whole mess of kids with her, but he just didn't know how her body would handle it.

She smiled brightly at the prospect then sensed his nervousness. "We're going to be fine. I know it."

He prayed to God she was right. If anything should happen to her, it would be his fault. If he lost her, he'd jump off the damn Willis Tower, no, he'd burn his fucking house down with him in it. Yeah, he'd need to suffer.

Adam chased away his crazy thoughts. It was no

use thinking about it now. He had to focus on Evangeline and their baby. They were his life now, his family.

"Wait a minute. Did you say Max told your father about my taking you?"

Evangeline lifted her head sharply off his chest. "Um, yeah."

"Fuuuuuck." He shut his eyes and pinched the bridge his nose with his fingers. "Your dad's going to shoot me, isn't he? First I kidnap you and then impregnate you in the space of a few days. Jesus, if I were him, I'd shoot me and feed me to the vampires."

"No, we're going to work this out. In fact, I think he is going to be pleased I'm not marrying—" She froze in midsentence, her face paling. "Oh, God, what's Cyrus going to do to my father?" She sat up in bed, holding the comforter to her chest. "How could I have been so stupid? He's going to kill him for what I did!"

He sat up too, leaning his back against the headboard. "Calm down, babe. I really don't think he's going to do anything to your father."

She stared at him wide-eyed. "Why? What happened? I know he was communicating with you telepathically. What did he say?"

Her knowing their vampire ways bugged him slightly. "He said I'd won you and to get you out of there."

She jerked her head. "And?"

Adam watched her carefully now. "He said to get you out of his sight." Just as he thought, she looked troubled by this. She stared at the headboard in thought, her eyes unfocused. "Does that bother you?"

Evangeline turned to him as if she just realized he

221

was there. "Of course not, I mean, my feelings aren't hurt or anything, but he…he…didn't look good."

Adam felt the ugly sense of jealousy run through him. He leaned his head back as he watched her with a scowl. "He realized how we felt about each other and it killed him. We all felt it." He was referring to his Fighters now. The intensity of the king's feelings toward Evangeline made him sick to his stomach.

"Why do you think he won't hurt my father?"

Adam tamped down on his bitter feelings. Evangeline was here now, in his bed with him. "Several reasons. One, he gave you up. Forcing this marriage on you was a game to him and he lost. He's feeling defeated and humiliated, and I don't think his wounded pride will want to bother with your father now. He'll want to show both of us he doesn't care. Second, and I think you already know this, you and I are mated under werewolf law as you're carrying my baby." His eyes softened at her as he said this. "Therefore, any threat against your father and he'll have the entire Blacktail pack to deal with, even more so than he did already." He played with the ends of her hair. "Despite our temper toward each other, we really do want peace…eventually."

Evangeline lay back down and hugged him hard. "I hope you're right."

"I don't want you worrying about a single thing, okay? Let me deal with everything, even your father."

Evangeline laughed nervously.

This time it was Adam who lay in the crook of her arm, with his hand protectively covering her belly.

****

"Mom? Did you hear what I said?" Evangeline

stood facing her mother in her parent's master bedroom. Rachelle was at the edge of the bed where Evangeline had told her to sit before revealing the big news.

They had decided to wait till after Evangeline got off work the next day so they could be together when she told her parents. As the baby was growing fast, they couldn't exactly wait to make the announcement. Adam told her she would be showing in two weeks.

Adam had had the foresight to call Maxwell last night and let him know Evangeline was safe and with him. He assured Max he was going to relay to Geoffrey everything that had taken place.

After the incredibly uncomfortable introduction to her father, Adam told her he needed to speak to Geoffrey alone. The look on Adam's face told her not to argue, this was going to be a heated discussion and he didn't want her getting upset. Anxious, but eager to get this over with, she'd gone upstairs to find her mother, leaving Adam to break the news to Geoffrey about last night's events and her condition.

Rachelle's face was pale as she stared mutely at her daughter now. Her mother was a woman of few words, always melancholy or worried about something, the complete opposite of Evangeline and Katherine.

Evangeline sometimes wondered if her mother was actually happy being married with two daughters. It seemed she loved her family from afar, never actually expressing her love and affection.

"You're pregnant?" her mother asked quietly.

"Yes." She smiled encouragingly.

Rachelle replied calmly, her expression bland. "With your kidnapper's baby?"

"Okay." Evangeline rolled her eyes. "The whole "kidnapper" thing needs to stop. I told you, I offered to stay with Adam to help him get his sister back. Mom, he's really a great guy and I'm so happy when I'm with him. We're in love. Trust me when I tell you this is good news."

Her mother continued to stare blankly at her.

Evangeline waited and when her mother still said nothing, she said irritably, "Mom, please say something. I can't read you. Is this shock, anger, what?"

Suddenly her mother buried her face in her hands and began to wail.

Evangeline looked up at the ceiling and let out a long breath. "Mom, please stop. There's no need to cry. I'm happy. You should be happy too. You're going to be a grandmother." She sat next to her and put a reassuring arm around her.

Rachelle continued to cry for a while as Evangeline comforted her. When she calmed some she took her hands away from her face and looked at her daughter.

Evangeline gave her a warm smile to let her know she was fine.

Her mother stared at her awkwardly, her eyes shimmering. "It's all my fault."

"What? Of course not—"

"No!" Rachelle cut her off, shaking her head wildly. "I should have told you a long time ago, but now…"

Rachelle let out another wail and Evangeline waited quietly, no longer smiling, but listening anxiously, her heart beating quickly now. "What are you talking about?

Her mother inhaled sharply. "It's too late. God! Please, don't hurt her. It wasn't her fault."

Evangeline shot up from the bed and rounded on her mother. "Mom, what the hell are you talking about? What's wrong?" she shouted.

Rachelle stared at her now as if she were a stranger. Evangeline had the craziest urge to shake her mother.

"Mom!" Her mother looked like she was about to pass out before she spoke and when she did, Evangeline's world came crashing down.

Rachelle stared miserably. "You were never supposed to have a baby, Evangeline."

Evangeline winced and jerked away from her mother. "What? Why would you say that?"

Rachelle shook her head numbly and whispered, "What have you done?"

Chapter Seventeen

The following weeks after their announcement were the happiest and saddest Evangeline had ever experienced. Her life had completely changed so rapidly, she had to stop and wonder if she were living a dream.

Upon leaving her parent's house, Adam had insisted she move in with him. His reasoning was only he could take care of her in her condition and he simply needed her close to him. She knew how he felt because her feelings mirrored his, but she also knew he was trying to protect her from her parents.

Adam had told her about the fight he'd had with her father. The fifty-four-year-old man had actually rolled up his sleeves and shoved Adam several times in an attempt to get him to fight, even punching him in the face, but Adam didn't budge. He'd even told a shocked Evangeline he respected her father for hitting him, for he would have done exactly the same thing had it been his own daughter.

To her utter dismay, Geoffrey was not speaking to her now. When Evangeline had come down to his office after her bone-chilling conversation with her mother, he'd walked out without looking at her.

The next day, she'd gone back to pack a few things, but no one had been home. Katherine was in Chicago already, and was ecstatic to become an aunt to a wolf, as she'd put it, when Evangeline called her with the news.

"They'll come around, babe. Grandparents can't resist holding their grandchildren in their arms," Adam told her one night as they lay on his overstuffed couch in the living room watching television.

She smiled at him as she flipped through one of her many books on motherhood. Evangeline knew he worried all the time. He was constantly fussing over her and making jokes to make her feel better. Truth was, as hurt as she was her parents weren't speaking to her, she was so happy to be with Adam he really didn't have to worry. He made her feel like the luckiest woman in the world.

They slipped into this life together so easily it almost astounded her. She barely had time to think how fast things were going because it came so easily to them. It seemed as though they'd been together for years. He made love to her every night. They showered together in the morning and talked over dinner they'd prepared together in the kitchen. Evangeline could not remember feeling so happy and at ease.

Adam lay with his head in her lap, watching the flat screen over the fireplace. He changed the channel and a rerun of the day's soap opera came on.

Evangeline looked at him, raising an eyebrow.

He grinned at her sheepishly. "What? My sister used to watch this show, so I had to. I check every now and then to see what's going on. I swear it's my one and only guilty pleasure." He winked.

Evangeline tensed slightly. The subject of his sister was always stressful, but Adam seemed okay as he continued to flick through the channels.

The Fighters continued to search for her on a daily basis. Adam sent Alex and Nick to Chicago to talk to another pack, but so far they had not learned anything new. Whenever Evangeline was at work, she knew Adam was out searching for Serena. She prayed the girl was okay and they'd find her soon. She hated seeing him stressed.

"What does your pack think about your secret soap opera fascination?" Evangeline teased in an effort to distract him.

He gave a short laugh, his boyish grin making her breath catch. "You're going to sell me out, aren't you, babe?"

Three weeks into her pregnancy, Evangeline was showing like a woman six months pregnant. Her swollen belly amazed her. She was feeling the bond mothers share with their unborn babies, talking to her belly and poking back whenever the baby kicked.

One morning Adam woke her up excitedly, his eyes wide and shining. He'd been staring at her naked belly and saw a tiny foot push outward under her skin. The look on his face had brought tears to her eyes.

The following day, Evangeline and Adam went to the doctor for a checkup and discovered they were having twins. Thrilled beyond belief, Adam called the Fighters over to the house to celebrate.

They all sat in the dining room eating pepperoni pizza, what Evangeline craved, along with nachos, bananas, and Ramen noodle soup.

"I hope it's two boys," Ramo said, sitting beside Evangeline, fisting a lager. "We need little punching bags around here."

"Hey!" Evangeline scolded him playfully.

"What? You know any kid of his,"—he pointed at Adam—"is going to drive us all nuts."

Adam looked at her. "He's joking, babe. I was an angel."

"Fuck that. He was a little monster."

Nick gave Ramo a look. "If he was a monster, then I don't even want to know how you were."

Ramo laughed. "No, you don't." He took a swig from his beer. "Of course, Alex wants you guys to have two girls so he can teach them to braid hair."

Alex flipped him off.

Evangeline watched the Fighters round on each other with a smile. They were closer than any family she'd ever known. Even Adam was happier than she'd ever seen him with his Fighters all around him talking about his impending fatherhood, even chiming in to abuse Ramo or Alex, as was the habit around the Fighters.

"Damn, Eva, when are you coming up for air?" Ramo teased her as she took another slice.

Adam came to her defense instantly when Evangeline couldn't with a mouth full of pizza and giggling simultaneously. "Leave her alone, she can eat the whole pizza if she wants."

Ramo was staring at her comically. "I'm pretty sure she did. Next time I'll bring seven pizzas instead of four." He looked around the table. "The twins are gonna be born with pepperoni-shaped birth marks."

They all laughed.

Ramo continued on. "But really, I hope they look like you, Eva. Just think if it were *our* babies, they'd have my stellar good looks. Alas," he said mournfully.

"We seriously need to find his mute button." Alex

told Adam then looked back at Ramo. "Don't you get tired of your own voice?"

"Hell no. My voice is hot. Anyway, the babies like my voice. They're jumping all over in there." Ramo reached a hand over Evangeline's belly.

Adam growled low.

Evangeline looked over. "Adam, stop. I don't mind."

Ramo spoke for his cousin. "We can't help it, honey. I'm touching his mate and his cubs, it's in our nature to be protective." Yet, Ramo continued to lay his hand over her stomach, waiting for a kick. "Relax, bro, I'm family so get used it. Hey! That was a strong one!" he announced as one of the babies kicked into his hand.

"Okay, you felt them kick. Now get your hand off my mate," Adam barked.

In the fifth week of her pregnancy, the doctor put her on bed rest to Evangeline's disappointment. Adam, however, loved she would have to stay put. From then on, her doctor referred her to Dr. Moros, the very man who nursed Katherine as a child. Since turning into a vampire, Dr. Moros began studying the anatomy of vampires and werewolves. He had become extremely popular in the East Coast for curing physical ailments of the supernatural *and* humans. His ability to multi-task at lightning speed elevated his status over the last few years.

Adam had been a bit hesitant to call the good-looking vampire doctor down from Boston, but Evangeline reminded him Dr. Moros was one of the few who knew about her healing powers and could be very helpful should something unforeseen happen.

"Wow, you've grown into a beautiful woman,

Eva," Dr. Moros expressed when he first visited Adam's round house. "Look at you! You could be a model."

Evangeline blushed helplessly then suppressed a laugh at the expression on Adam's face. Dr. Moros had a Clark Kent thing going on, an older Clark Kent with graying hair at his temples. He was tall and handsome with glasses and adorable dimples. "Thank you, Dr. Moros. It's great to see you again. How's married life?"

An odd look flickered over the doctor's face before answering. "Fine, fine." He sat next to her on the living room couch and Adam came closer to hover over them. "And how is Katherine? Is she still living at home?" His face softened somewhat as he spoke about her sister.

"Not at the moment. She's in Chicago now, studying to be a chef." Sensing Adam was becoming annoyed as they chatted on, she changed the subject to the purpose of the doctor's visit. "Dr. Moros, have you ever delivered baby werewolves from a human before?" she asked lightly and they began to discuss her delivery, which would occur in the next week or two.

The doctor assured them everything was going to be fine. He, personally never delivered cubs from a human, but he'd read up on it and said it wasn't much different from delivering humans at all.

The following week was filled with deliveries from Pottery Barn and Baby's R Us. Adam turned the guest room next to the master bedroom into a beautiful baby's room. He worked endlessly, painting, putting up shelves and assembling two cribs. All Evangeline could do was shop online.

On the morning of September twenty-second, as

Adam stood at the stove flipping pancakes for breakfast, Evangeline felt her first contraction. She froze from turning a page in a Land of Nod catalogue at the kitchen table. "Adam," she uttered, as the pain grew stronger.

Dr. Moros had warned them her labor would spring on her quickly and not last very long, just like her pregnancy.

Adam turned to look at her and paled.

"It's happening," she breathed, then winced at the blinding pain slashing through her. "Call—call—" But before she could finish her sentence, she fainted.

****

"She's coming around. I don't want to risk moving her to a hospital. Like I said, at the rate the labor is going, we won't make it in time anyway."

Adam listened numbly to Dr. Moros. The doctor seemed to be speaking to him from the far end of a tunnel as he sat on the bed next to Evangeline, his heart pounding in his ears.

The moment he'd realized the babies were coming, he'd rushed to Evangeline's side, barely making it to catch her as she slid off the chair. "Why...why did she faint? Is it normal under these circumstances?" He meant, of course, a human bearing two werewolves. He shivered and ran his hands over his face.

The doctor was disinfecting a bunch of odd-looking tools that made Adam's head spin and his stomach churn. "I'm sure it was just from the pain. It hit her pretty fast." He was moving at lightning speed. *Thank God!* He sped from the bed to the makeshift table preparing for the delivery. Dr. Moros moved back to the edge of the bed in a flash, laying something down. "Contractions usually begin subtly, then progress, but things are happening much faster for her."

Vampires might be his sworn enemy, but they could move at an unbelievable pace. It had taken Dr. Moros one minute to get dressed and teleport to the house from his hotel. Adam had to keep telling himself this doctor was cool, but he could hear his father's voice in his head telling him he was a fucking lunatic to allow a vampire to deliver his babies and keep his mate out of danger.

"Adam?" Evangeline came to, but before he could answer, she let out a moan and reached for his hand, squeezing it hard. "Ow!" she yelped, squeezing her eyelids tight. "Oh, God! It hurts, it hurts, it hurts."

Adam felt his head reel and his throat close. He put a warm hand on her forehead, wishing it were cool and let her squeeze the other. "I'm sorry, baby. I'm sorry. It'll be over soon. I'm right here." How the hell could he have done this to her?

She opened her eyes as the pain subsided. Her gaze disoriented, but again the contractions took over her body and she arched back against the pillows. "My, God, is all this normal? Why does it hurt so much?" Evangeline muttered through clenched teeth.

"You're doing great, Eva. It'll be over soon, honey," Dr. Moros soothed.

"I'm not *doing* anything." Evangeline panted as another pain came fast once more.

Good God! Adam had never felt so incredibly helpless in his life. He wished he could bear it all for her. It was killing him to see her in so much pain. He leaned his face closer to her, whispering words of comfort.

Relaxing a bit, she gave Adam a feeble nod. Even in agony she was worried for *him*.

Adam turned a tense face to Dr. Moros. "Can we give her something?"

"Unfortunately, no. It's too late. She's almost ready to start pushing."

Adam heard the front door open, footsteps, and then voices downstairs. The Fighters had sensed his fear for Evangeline, their emotional bond stretching out across the entire town. They were just as concerned as he was now, pacing through the house.

Evangeline gripped his hand hard again, her nails digging into his skin. This time she screamed louder and then followed it with a curse. "Fuck, Fuck, Fuck!!!"

Adam lost it and snarled at the doctor, eyes shifting. "DO SOMETHING!" His voice was animal-like now.

The bedroom door jerked open and Jason came in.

"Perfect timing," Dr. Moros uttered as he began moving Evangeline toward the edge of the bed. "I take it you're the beta?"

Jason nodded.

"Good. You need to get your leader out of here," he said calmly as he lifted Evangeline's knees up.

"Fuck you! I'm not leaving her!" Adam had the insane urge to rip the doctor in pieces.

"You're not thinking clearly and that's understandable, but I'm pretty sure she's dilated ten centimeters by now. You can't be here when I check. By the way you're looking at me right now for touching her legs, I won't have hands to deliver these babies." The doctor was getting angry now. He spoke to Jason.

"He's going to be trouble once I..." He nodded toward Evangeline's nether region.

"Come on, Adam," Jason said.

Evangeline's head angled back again and her cry shot through his heart. She was focused on her own pain and not listening to what was going on around her.

He looked wretchedly at her, his face strained and drenched with sweat. "I can't leave her."

Dr. Moros cursed. "Fine! Step away from the bed then. You," he shouted at Jason, "make sure you have a good grip on him. Remember, she's delivering *two* babies."

Adam stepped as far away from the bed as he could, never taking his eyes off Evangeline. Jason came to stand next to him, ready to grab him if he should make a move toward the doctor. Jason kept his eyes respectfully on the floor, but he was going through almost the same pain as he was. It was probably not a good idea for two werewolves to be in the same room right now, but he was not leaving Evangeline. At least Jason still had a fairly leveled head at the moment.

"Okay, Evangeline, we're going to start pushing. Can you hold your legs up for me?" The doctor placed her hands under each knee and showed her how to lift them once she began pushing. "Right. Just like that." He brushed his hand over her brow and Adam made a mental note to shoot this doctor and then go to medical school.

He should be doing it. He should be taking care of her and helping her right now. He was the one who caused this. But no, he was sitting on the windowsill like a dumb ass because he couldn't control his temper.

He couldn't remember when Jason put a restraining

hand on him, but his beta's grip was tight on his shoulder. Adam noticed then he was half standing, apparently about to attack the doctor.

Evangeline was pushing now, holding her knees back toward her head as the doctor counted back from the number ten. "You're doing great, Eva. Keep going. Three...two...one."

She let down her legs with a loud huff, breathing hard, her body drenched now.

Adam got up, shrugging Jason's hand away and walked slowly to her. Dr. Moros gave him a dark look. "I'm fine. Let me help her." Adam's fury with the doctor had dimmed slightly as he watched his Evangeline work on her own to birth their babies. And just then, his concern for the woman he loved, who was giving him two children, overrode his jealous, overbearing nature. He knew the doctor wasn't going to hurt her. He was doing everything he could for her.

The doctor nodded. "Get on the bed and slide in behind her. Let her lean back against you, then you can reach around her and hold her legs up. Quickly, here comes another contraction."

Adam had detected the contraction coming too. Their supernatural keen senses warned it was coming. He slid in behind her and reached under her knees and pulled back as she tensed up against his chest, her nails digging into his thighs. His lips were at her brow and he whispered a silent prayer.

"There's the head! Come on, Eva! Five...four...push...here it comes!"

Adam watched in total wonderment as their baby's head came rising up in front of them, then shoulders, belly. "It's a boy, babe! A boy!" Adam didn't recognize his own voice as he shouted those glorious words.

"Come here!" the doctor yelled at Jason, who had turned to look out the window. He knew his friend wanted to give them privacy, but he wasn't about to leave his leader and his woman with only one doctor, albeit a quick and capable doctor, but a vampire nonetheless. It was as if Jason had been waiting to help. He rushed over, keeping his face on the doctor. "You're going to be our nurse today." He handed the baby off to Jason as soon as the baby began to wail. "As soon as we cut, place him down on the other side of the bed where I've put those sheets." He reached for a tool beside him and gave it to a stunned Adam. "Cut the cord quickly, the other one is ready to go." Dr. Moros reached down. "Don't worry, Eva, I'll put your second born right on you. You'll be holding them both in a minute."

Adam cut the unbiblical cord quickly and then reached for Evangeline's knees again, counting down in her ear. "Nine... You're amazing you know... Eight... That's it, baby... Seven... I love you... Six... I love you... I love you... I love you."

****

"How fruity is this? We look like a bunch of girls right now," Ramo said as he held Adam's son in the rocking chair in the baby's room.

Jason, Nick, Alex, Ramo, and Adam were all crammed in the baby's room. Adam was at the changing table, doing the swaddling thing Evangeline had shown him. Jason stood in the doorway while Nick and Alex both leaned on a crib.

"You're the one rocking, fool," Alex said.

"Screw you, he likes it." He nodded at the baby.

After holding the first baby, Jason was traumatized. He'd been scared shitless he was going to hurt the baby and therefore could not bring himself to hold Adam's other son. Ramo was the only Fighter who insisted on holding both the boys. Nick and Alex watched from the sidelines, too nervous their close proximity might harm the babies.

"How's Evangeline?" Nick asked.

Adam nestled his son in the crook of his arms. "She's okay. As soon as she held them both, she knocked out."

"You try popping out two babies and see how you feel," Ramo said indignantly, rocking back and forth.

Evangeline slept for five hours. Adam finally woke her to feed the babies. He'd tried to feed them simultaneously, but he couldn't manage.

"I'm sorry, babe, but I need help feeding them." Adam told her.

"It's fine, honey. You shouldn't have let me sleep so long. They need to eat every two hours, the poor babies."

"Don't worry, Ramo and I fed them two hours ago."

Evangeline looked relieved. "Thank goodness."

They lay in bed together, feeding their sons who took the bottles without hesitation.

"Would you object to a full time nanny?" Adam asked as he gently patted the baby's back.

"Absolutely not," she replied.

They laughed together.

Adam's smile faded and he watched her carefully. "I don't think I can survive that again. How are you feeling?"

She smiled weakly. Her face was pale, and she had dark circles under her eyes. As she smoothed her hair back from her face he noticed tiny red spots where her blood vessels had popped from all the pushing. "I'll be fine, babe. But, we need to discuss something important."

He tensed. "What?"

"If we don't hurry up and name these boys, your cousin is going to name them Ramo and Ramon."

****

In the King's Coven, a disheveled Cyrus stood looking out his bedroom window with a drink in hand, having just settled down from the fervent anxiety he'd felt all day.

A knock sounded on the door.

"What?" he called out, having no desire for company.

The door cracked and Jane poked her head in. "It's me, Your Grace."

"I know it's you. What do you want, Jane?" He continued to stare out at the river below.

"Um...I know you're...concerned for Evangeline. I wanted to know if I could check on her."

"That's not necessary. She's fine now."

"Are you sure?"

Cyrus turned his head to look at her and by the way Jane's face paled, he must have been a sight. "Quite sure."

She hesitated at the door. "Are *you* okay?"

"Goodnight, Jane."

****

Sprawled in a chair, she watched with unseeing eyes, completely and utterly detached, as Leonardo brought up their new play things. Instead, she thought of the woman who had just given birth to werewolves and felt a seething hatred surge like poison through her, turning her eyes blood red.

Chapter Eighteen

Evangeline fell into the role of mother with ease. Daniel and David were her pride and joy, her reason why she'd been brought to this earth. Adam and Evangeline could not stop looking at them. The boy's nanny was constantly shooing them away when the twins were asleep. To be sure, Lydia must have been sick to her stomach at how much they talked about the boys.

Adam had tracked down Lydia, who'd been a close friend of his mother's years ago. Evangeline had been amazed to learn the woman was three hundred and twenty-one years old. She had once been his mother's nanny and Adam's too. She'd moved to Arizona in the early seventies and had been living alone all this time.

They were extremely grateful to have her. In fact, she was a godsend. The woman could change a diaper faster than Dr. Moros.

The day after the twins were born, Evangeline and Adam had their first visitors aside from the Fighters, of course. As Adam predicted, grandma and grandpa could not resist. Evangeline and her father hugged for several tearful minutes and the moment Rachelle and Geoffrey saw their two grandsons, the tears were relentless.

As she walked her father to the door after hours of eating and cooing at the twins, she asked if everything was okay. She watched his reaction carefully. Geoffrey's face tightened for a moment, but then he said, "Everything is all right. I'm...I'm back on my feet."

She eyed him warily. "What about the debt?"

Her father gave her an odd look. "There is no debt, honey. Stop worrying." Then he kissed her on the forehead, promising to be back over the weekend.

She hardly had a chance to dwell on the subject. The days were filled with entertaining visitors, bathing and changing the twins, washing bottles, and rocking them to sleep.

They received packages in the mail from people she did not know. Adam told her they came from distant relatives or leaders of other packs. Several members of the Blacktail pack came to see their leader's newborn sons. Even Katherine came down one Sunday to spend the afternoon with the boys.

"I think I've taken your healing abilities for granted," Adam said one night.

After two weeks of no sex, Dr. Moros finally gave them the okay during her check-up. They both lay on their backs, breathing heavily with sated smiles. In an instant they were both out.

Evangeline dreamed of the jackal. She was in the woods near her parent's home, searching for her sons. Somehow she knew the jackal had taken them. She had to find them.

Eva.

Evangeline's eyes shot open. She waited quietly in the darkness. Someone was calling her name.

Eva.

She sat up. She had to stop it. The jackal. The

jackal took the twins. Her boys needed her.

Come, Eva.

Evangeline took the cover off and got out of bed. She reached for her velour white robe behind the door and put it over her naked body.

Please, Evangeline.

I'm coming. She had to move faster. Moving down the stairs quickly, she reached the entryway and grabbed Adam's keys. Outside, she started the car and drove straight to her parent's house. Parking a fair distance from the house, she got out and headed straight into the woods. The October night was cool and Evangeline did not realize she was barefoot and in a robe.

The jackal had her babies. She had to find them.

She moved deeper into the woods, totally unaware she'd begun to shiver.

"Hello, my dear."

Evangeline gasped as if she'd been doused by a bucket of ice cold water. Every hair on her body stood instantly on end.

She didn't know what was weirder; that she was outside in the woods with a robe on and had no idea how'd she gotten there or the fierce lady with the odd getup in front of her.

"My, you are even more beautiful up close," the lady spoke again in her deep sing song voice.

Evangeline shook herself. "What...what am I doing here? Who are you?"

The woman stared back at her with an odd, assessing expression. The woman's hair was pulled back in a severe bun and her hard green gaze sent shivers down Evangeline's spine. She wore a long velvet dress of midnight black and a draping necklace with a medallion on the end. Evangeline couldn't tell if she was thirty or fifty years old.

"I need to get home." Evangeline made to move, but the woman's next words made her freeze.

Leaning her dark head to one side, she said, "I'm sorry my dear, but you will not be going home tonight."

Standing frozen as the woman's words sunk in, she finally said, "I've had enough." Apparently her sleep-deprived self had been sleepwalking and landed in the freaking woods. Evangeline turned to go, walking in the opposite direction when the creepy woman materialized in front of her.

"Jesus!" Evangeline screamed. "What the—? What do you want? Just leave me alone. I need to get home." Before she could move, her body locked. Every part of her had become suddenly immobile. Suspended in a single position, Evangeline began to panic in earnest. She was no longer in a sleepy state of mind, but wide-awake in pure dread. "What's happening? Why can't I move?" she whispered.

"I had big plans for you, Evangeline," the woman said conversationally, her hands folded in front of her.

"Who are you?" she demanded, struggling to move any body part with no luck.

"That is the question, isn't it?" She laughed wickedly. "I'm the person trying to decide what to do with you since you've wasted your talent."

What? Evangeline was furious now. She was a mother and she needed to get home to her sons. Whatever this lady tried to do, Evangeline was going to fight tooth and nail. "Stop playing games. Who the fuck are you and what do you want?" Evangeline snapped.

A slow smile crept up her pale face. "Now there's the great granddaughter I want to see."

Evangeline flinched. "What?"

"You don't see a resemblance?" she asked expectantly, raising a thin eyebrow. "Mmm, I'm afraid I'm past my prime." She stepped closer to Evangeline. "I'm your great grandmother, dear, on your mother's side of course. Goddess knows good looks only run on one side of your family." She scoffed.

I'm losing it! Did she say great grandmother?

Staring hard at the woman in front of her, who freakishly looked like a peculiar imitation of herself, but with deliberate mistakes, Evangeline recoiled inside. This woman's nose was a bit longer and her mouth was wider than her own, but there was no mistaking the similarities.

Evangeline's mind was reeling. Her mother was adopted. Could this strange woman actually be related to her?

"Yes, Eva."

If Evangeline could jump, she would have. Good Lord, had she heard what Evangeline was thinking? "Are...are...you...a witch?"

She smiled again. "Very good," the woman said as if Evangeline were a child and just said two plus two is four. "My name is Cassandra." She smiled. "And I believe you are now figuring out what *you* are."

Evangeline was struggling to keep her mind clear. Evidently this witch could read her thoughts.

"Now don't fight it, sweetie. In fact, your thoughts may just be the only thing to keep you alive."

"You want to kill me?" Evangeline asked, real panic setting in with potency. She tried to recall what she knew about witches, but what she had read was from the werewolves' perspective. Witches had existed for centuries before the werewolves were made. During medieval times, the werewolf spell was the witches' curse of choice. It was completely irreversible. What the witches had not anticipated was the werewolves' ability to procreate at a very high rate.

"You can't blame me. The first healer in seven hundred years and she's run off with a werewolf and given birth to two cubs." The woman's face turned hard now, veins poked out over her forehead and her eyes became red. "No descendant of mine should have ever allowed this to happen."

Pure terror washed over her now as she watched this woman grow angrier by the second. She understood instantly the predicament she was in. If this actually were her great grandmother, and every fiber of her being told her it was, then would she harm her mother for "allowing" Evangeline to get involved with werewolves?

"Unfortunately, my granddaughter is a fool. However, she did produce a healer so I won't be harming her any time soon."

Evangeline stared intently. "I'm a witch?"

The woman's arched eyebrows shot up again. "Yes, and one with extraordinary potential."

She didn't know how to process this information. Deep down she'd known she was…something different.

Her great grandmother took a deep breath. "Witches can do many things, sweetie, but heal. You, however, possess a rare gift."

"Why would you kill me then?"

She shook her head at her. "Evangeline, there has

not been a healer for centuries. You have been blessed with the gift and your insipid mother was to keep you from harm's way. I was confident you'd be safe in this dull town, but now look at you."

Evangeline was confused.

"You mated with a werewolf and delivered his offspring. Having children weakens your powers and by extension, weakens *you*. You're virtually useless to me now."

Evangeline filed this away for later. Right now, she had to get the hell away from this witch and back home. She forced herself to not think. There was no way she was going to trust this nut.

Her so-called great grandmother inspected her up and down. "Let me see."

In a flash, Evangeline's robe was evaporated from her body. She was completely naked in the cold woods and couldn't move. *"Ah!"* she shrieked.

"Mmm…" Her great grandmother murmured. "The resemblance is uncanny." She circled Evangeline, staring carefully as though she could see beyond skin. "I'm amazed you have regained your figure, although your breasts seem to be a bit swollen. Nevertheless, your powers can be the only reason you've managed this." She came around to peer into her eyes. "You are a fighter, my dear, but I'm afraid your time is up. The damage has been done."

Please, God. She couldn't die. She couldn't leave Adam and their babies alone. They needed her.

Evangeline was about to plead for her life when a roar echoed in the night and a dark, huge figure leaped in front of her, knocking her great grandmother off her feet, and smashing her onto the ground.

The witch let out a deep wail, fighting futilely at the werewolf who pinned her onto the ground. It wasn't Adam. This wolf's mane was black, streaked with gray. It was Jason.

Evangeline suddenly noticed she could move her limbs. Jason's attack must have lifted the woman's enchantment.

Evangeline ran to the nearest tree for cover, not knowing what to expect. She was shivering now, her teeth chattering in the cool night. She fought to see in the darkness what was happening and to her horror, heard a dramatic, snake-like voice, casting a spell in a strange language. "NO!"

Running closer to see what was happening, she saw Jason's large form suddenly lift off from the ground. He was twitching and contorting oddly, screaming in agony as his body gained more height.

"Stop!"

The witch stood and Evangeline could see her eyes were red and there were three dark, crimson slash marks across her chest. Cassandra continued her chanting, her arm outstretched, torturing Jason suspended in mid-air. The minute she was done, her arm cut through the air and she slammed Jason hard into the bark of a tree. He fell a good twenty feet and lay lifeless in the dirt.

Shivering uncontrollably, Evangeline stared wide-eyed at Jason as his body transformed back to man.

He's dead. He's dead. He's dead.

Her grandmother spoke with fury, clutching the gashes at her chest. "You pathetic fool! You're all pathetic!" She looked at Jason on the ground. "Mutts running around like they're the center of the universe, vampires creating realms." She turned back to Evangeline. "They are puppets, my useless descendent, *puppets.*"

Evangeline was shaking uncontrollably.

"I shouldn't have sent my jackal after your dog. I should have sent it for *you.*" Evangeline was horror-struck. The woman paused dramatically, her voice ringing in Evangeline's ears. "You're not worth my time." She arched her shoulders back and her chin jutted out. "You'll die a horrible death, my little idiot."

Evangeline could not look at her. The witch had murdered Adam's best friend right before her eyes and it was all her fault. He had come here to save her and now he was dead.

"Go, then. Live the rest of your days as a whore to a dog."

There was a gust of wind. Evangeline turned a tearful face to the place her great grandmother had been standing, but she was gone.

The realization she was alone now brought back her senses. "Jason!" She ran toward the Blacktail, crouching over him. His long hair covered his face, and she brushed it back, caressing his cheek as the tears continued to pour.

She had to check for a pulse, but finding out he was truly dead was like watching him die all over again and her body shook violently as she wept. Slowly, with unsteady breaths, she pressed her ear to his massive chest. He was still very warm. Was it a good sign? And suddenly, she heard the wonderful sound of a feeble heartbeat.

Evangeline inhaled sharply and shot up to stare hard at his face. She grabbed for his wrist and checked for a pulse there. It was weak, but still going.

"Jason? Jason, can you hear me?" she said. Her voice strained with fear.

He didn't move.

Trembling hands covered his body and she knew he was alive, but for only so long. Looking back only months ago in similar surroundings, she lifted her head to the heavens and thought cynically, *some fucking déjà vu!*

****

The sound of his phone beeping woke him out of a deep sleep. The annoying tone told him he had a phone call or text.

Adam reached for it in the dark with a curse. Who the hell was calling now? Didn't everyone know he had two infants in the house and sleep was a precious commodity?

When the little light on his phone came on he turned to check it didn't glare too bright on Evangeline.

"Babe?" He reached over when he didn't see her and realized she wasn't in bed. She must be in the boy's room.

He got up, pulling on his boxers to go help Evangeline. "Shit." His addled brain remembered he had a message. There were two phone calls from Jason and a text. *Get to the woods by the Wolcott's now! Trouble!*

"What the hell!" Adam dashed into the hall and into the boy's room to let Evangeline know he had to step out. His sons were both sleeping peacefully, but their mother was not there. Running down the stairs, he searched around in the living room, kitchen, but she wasn't there.

He checked his phone to see if she'd left him a message but there wasn't one. With a sinking feeling, Adam ran outside fully prepared to shift and trek like mad to the woods. At least then he could check if Evangeline had gone to her parent's house. The instant he set foot outside his eyes slammed on the most terrifyingly disturbing sight, and his heart plummeted to the pit of his fucking gut.

Jason's large naked body climbed up the front stairs with an equally naked Evangeline, cradled in his arms, her cheek lay on his chest and she appeared to be sleeping. One of Jason's hands held her thigh and the other was precariously close to her breast.

Several things went through his head at once, but before he could entertain one of them, he lashed out. With a ferocious growl, he snatched Evangeline from his beta's arms. Adam panted hard as he glared at his best friend, baring his teeth, fuming with anger and betrayal.

Jason spoke fast. "A witch took off her clothes and tried to kill her. I tried to help, but she cursed me. When I came to, Evangeline was lying on the ground. I came straight here." Jason stared dead into his face, avoiding Adam's naked lover lying still in his arms. "I don't know what's wrong with her. Nothing is broken and as far as I can sense there is no internal bleeding."

Adam calmed some. There was no reason not to trust his best friend, but fuck… How the hell was he supposed to react to his lady in another man's arms, naked? He slowed his breathing and looked from Evangeline's pale face to Jason's, grasping the situation.

Jason misunderstood. "I had to check her for

injuries, but I swear—"

Adam shook his head at him. "Were you hurt?"

Jason flinched. "Don't worry about me, it—"

"It matters. Were you seriously hurt?"

Jason gawked at him. "The witch pulled some torture shit on me, yeah, but the last thing I remember is being knocked into a tree. Who the fuck cares? I'm fine! Not a scratch."

Adam's face drained of all color. "Because she healed you."

"What? Why would the witch—"

"No. Evangeline healed you." Adam rushed her inside and up to their room. "Call Dr. Moros." He called over his shoulder. "He's back in Boston, but I need him here as fast as possible."

After two hours of watching her sleep, Adam woke her up anxiously. "Babe? Babe wake up!" He sat next to her hip, shaking her shoulders gently. "Eva!"

Lids opened over brilliant green eyes. "Are you okay? How do you feel? What the hell happened? Why the hell did you go to the woods in the middle of the night?" His voice was rising as she stared all around her, collecting her bearings.

She whispered frantically, cutting him off. "Jason? Is he all right?" She started to get up and called again, "Jason?"

Adam pushed her carefully back down. "He's fine."

Her face told him she didn't believe him and then there was movement at the door. Evangeline looked straight ahead, her expression turning from apprehension to relief.

"Jason!" She released a deep sigh and shut her

eyes, leaning back against the headboard. "I was so scared she'd...I thought you were..." She heaved a shaky breath.

Turning to look at his friend, he saw Jason staring solemnly at Evangeline. It was the first time Adam had ever seen his friend really look at her. There was a haunted look in his eyes now and the emotion emanating from him was clear. Jason was full of gratitude and remorse. Evangeline had saved his life, but at a price.

He shocked Adam again by addressing her, something he had never done. His voice was wrought with severity. "You shouldn't have done it."

Lifting her head slowly, she looked at Jason, her face grim and Adam saw a new woman now. A woman who was mother and mate and he couldn't be more in love with her.

She had risked her life to save a member of his pack, his best friend, and he knew they would all be eternally grateful to her. She said weakly, "Don't," shaking her head at him. "Do you honestly think I could have left you out there?"

"You'll never know how incredibly thankful I am for what you did, but,"—he glanced at Adam—"I should have sacrificed myself for you. Not the other way around."

"You did."

Jason said nothing and simply glared at the floor.

Adam turned to her. "How are you feeling?"

"Just tired. How are the boys?"

"They woke up when you got home, but Lydia got them back to sleep." Concern for her was making his head throb. He could sense her body's weariness as if she were a wilting flower. "Why were you in the woods, alone, in the middle of the night?" Adam tried to keep his voice calm, but he sounded severe.

"I was sleepwalking. Although…I guess it might have been a part of the spell."

Adam listened to her with forced patience, gripping her hand in his.

Evangeline stared listlessly at nothing. "I was dreaming about the jackal. I thought it had taken the boys and then someone was calling me. Then all of a sudden I was in the woods and this woman was talking to me. She said she was a witch and my great grandmother. Her name's Cassandra and she was really angry with me for having the boys." Evangeline took a deep breath. "She said I was a gifted witch, but I'd ruined my powers by giving birth."

Adam's skin was on fire, but he needed to hear everything. "Go on."

She flushed slightly. "My robe disappeared in thin air and she studied me…said I was a fighter, but…" She closed her eyes, inhaling and exhaling hard.

"But what, babe?"

Evangeline looked at him now, her face grave. "But, I would die anyway."

Adam's eyes flashed and his nostrils flared. He moved his head toward Jason, but glared at Evangeline's legs under the covers. He didn't want his countenance to upset her, but anger poured through him like lava. "Thank God you were there. How did you know where to find her?"

There was a pause until Adam turned all the way around to see if Jason was still there.

Jason stood motionless. The nervous energy around

him was peculiar.

"What?" Adam urged.

"Cyrus called me."

Both Adam and Evangeline stiffened, but he was sure he was the only one with roaring in his ears.

Jason offered answers to questions both he and Evangeline were thinking. "Her blood...you know...he could sense she was in trouble. He called from London, just said Evangeline was in trouble and for me to haul ass." Jason sensed Adam's next question and hesitated before he spoke. "He told me to tell you,"—Jason stared at Adam—"he wouldn't call you if you were the last man on earth and his entire coven was on fire." Jason turned to Evangeline. "And he told me to tell you he was mistaken."

Fucking prick! Mistaken about what?

Jason shrugged.

Adam felt his body burn with hatred for the fucking king, but a reluctant part of him was grateful the man could still sense when Evangeline was in trouble. Jesus, if Jason hadn't gotten there in time...

He turned and saw Evangeline gazing lethargically at the foot of the bed and felt it then. She wasn't telling him something, but he wasn't about to pressure her now after all she'd been through.

He bent and hugged her firmly to him, kissing her tenderly on her lips, cheeks, forehead, and back to her lips. "Get some rest, my love. If Dr. Moros isn't here in the morning, we're going to the hospital."

Evangeline was about to protest, but then gave up, a sure sign something was wrong. Moving down into the covers, she looked over at the door again. "I'm so happy you're okay, Jason."

His beta nodded.

"And Jason?" Evangeline called.

He looked to her, warily.

"Thank you for saving *my* life."

Chapter Nineteen

Dr. Moros returned Adam's call immediately the next morning. He was back in Boston, busy as ever, but would return to Wilmington in a day or two. He advised Adam to take Evangeline to the hospital, which Evangeline had downright refused, convincing her mate she was just fine.

The truth was, she still felt weak and tired. The lies began to pile on top of each other then. "I think I'm getting a cold from walking around naked in the woods," she told a concerned Adam the next day.

Having no desire to get the boys sick, Lydia took the twins to the Wolcott house while Evangeline tried to regain her strength. "Please go with Lydia, honey. I don't want the boys to feel neglected," Evangeline told Adam later.

"I just called, they're sleeping. I'll check on them in a little while. I want to make sure you're okay."

Evangeline forced a smile and lied once again. "I'm feeling much better. I think if I eat, I should be fine." It felt strenuous to even talk. Fact was, she was feeling a hundred times worse. The effort she was making just to stay awake in Adam's presence made her woozy.

He brought her a sandwich and soup in bed and told her to get some rest. She slept the entire night away and woke up to a note on Adam's pillow.

Checking on the boys. Be back soon. Love you.

Evangeline sighed, thankful Adam was with their sons. She got up warily, her body aching in places she didn't know existed. Her legs throbbed under her weight as she limped into the bathroom. Bathing was no easy task. She washed her hair and body in slow, feeble movements.

Too tired to dress, she threw on her old purple robe and walked down to the kitchen, not bothering to turn on the light. The gray sky outside cast a gloom in the kitchen, which felt fitting.

She started the coffee maker and took a cup out of the cabinet. As she waited for the pot to fill, she sat at the kitchen table and stared out the window to face the truth of her condition in quiet solitude.

She was dying.

Evangeline took a deep breath, fixing her tired eyes on a single leaf barely clinging to the branch it hung from.

The truth should have made her scream, cry, go completely hysterical, but all she felt was a raw numbness as she stared out at nothing, listening to the coffee brewing on the counter.

Her great grandmother had been right. Giving birth had weakened her, and healing Jason had sped up the process of her impending end. She couldn't blame her children or Jason, though. She wouldn't. No one was to blame. Given the chance to go back, she would have done the exact same thing. Evangeline loved her children unconditionally and there was no way she could ever live with herself if she'd let Jason die.

Her mind sped back over the years. She should have known this gift of hers would eventually kill her.

She passed out way too much for someone who can heal. Hadn't her recovery after she'd healed Adam taken almost two days?

Oddly, she wasn't afraid of death. She was scared for her children and for Adam. What would they do without her?

Pity, the likes of which she had never known filled her, making her choke on the wretched sensation. Instead of the past, it was the future she would never know flashing before her eyes now. She saw her boys taking their first steps, uttering their first words, heading out with back packs on their first day of school as Evangeline and Adam watched fondly with matching wedding bands on their fingers.

Anger came then, flooding her to a boiling point. Her head throbbed at the injustice of it all. She had only just found true happiness. She was incredibly lucky to have experienced what she did in the past few months, finding love, having two healthy baby boys was a blessing. Why would God take this away from her so soon?

Her body seemed to vibrate with fear. She let silent tears fall without moving and just then, she didn't feel like the twenty-two-year-old woman she was. She felt ancient.

How on earth would she find the strength to tell Adam? As big and strong as he was, she knew this news would kill him. She wondered, with a sense of dread, if Adam would be capable of taking care of the boys after she was gone.

God! Never in a million years did she think she would die so young.

The doorbell rang. It resounded in her ears, but

Evangeline didn't stir. She debated answering it, knowing if it was Adam, he would have just walked in. She didn't want company right now. All she wanted was to suffer in peace and be left alone.

The doorbell rang again and then she heard three hard knocks.

Evangeline rolled her eyes and hung her head back. Getting up gingerly, she walked toward the door. Fighting the urge to tell whoever it was she was dying and to leave her the hell alone, she wiped the tears from her cheeks and neck and attempted a brave face.

The bell rang two more times, but she was too tired to even tell them to wait.

With a dizzying effort, she opened the door.

"Evangeline!" The ferocity on the man's face made her recoil slightly.

Staring hard at the tall figure, her eyelids feeling extra heavy, she wondered if she were dreaming. "Cyrus?"

He stared with wide eyes, his hands gripping the sides of the doorjamb. "Invite me in," he demanded.

"What?" She mumbled. What was he doing here?

"Damn it, Evangeline, invite me in," he repeated.

She stared confusedly at first, then, "Oh." Vampires had to be invited into a human's home, but this was a wolf's home, she thought. Evangeline noticed Jason stood behind Cyrus. Apparently, he'd convinced the beta to let him on the premises. Since there was no wooden stick in his chest and his head was intact, Jason must have disabled the security traps to let Cyrus pass.

Jason's eyes were stern. "You don't have to let him in. You know Adam wouldn't—"

Cyrus didn't look at Jason, but he spoke through gritted teeth. "I told you I'm not going to hurt her or your fucking alpha. Something is wrong. She's..." Cyrus paused at the look Evangeline gave him. He spoke to her now. "Just let me in."

Evangeline nodded weakly and whispered, "Come in."

Jason made a face and followed Cyrus in.

She knew Jason would have never let him near the door if Cyrus hadn't given him the heads up the other night. Evangeline hoped Adam would see this point of view. Cyrus was clearly concerned for her and had no intention of hurting anyone, at least she hoped. She was too weary to think straight.

Needing to sit down, she walked stiffly to the living room, very aware of Cyrus at her back. Reaching the sofa, she sat down as if she were ninety years old.

Cyrus hovered over her. "We need to talk."

"Okay," she said, leaning her head back to look at him.

"Alone."

"Whatever," Jason said. He stood leaning in the doorway, his arms crossed.

"Feel my fucking emotions, wolf. Am I going to hurt her?"

Jason didn't answer.

Evangeline had had enough with the male testosterone to last her a lifetime, a very brief lifetime, she thought bitterly. "It's okay, Jason. We're just going to talk."

Jason gave her a long, assessing look, and then sighed. "Holler if you need me. I'll be right outside." They stared for a moment. The night they had saved each other's life had formed a strong bond between them. Not to mention she was his alpha's mate and mother to, possibly, the future alpha. His loyalty to her was heartwarming.

"Thanks, Jason."

He nodded at her and walked out. She heard the door close behind him as he stepped onto the porch and she could almost picture him texting Adam right now.

"He's lucky he saved you the other night." Cyrus muttered looking toward the door then back to her. "You look like hell."

She gave him an exasperated look. "Thank you. Did you send Jason away to insult me?"

"No." His tone was deathly serious. For a moment, she thought he was about to touch her, but then thought better of it. "It's happening much faster than I thought." He walked away to sit in the armchair facing her.

Evangeline stared blankly at him. Folding his hands, he rested his elbows on his knees, studying her. "What do you mean?" she asked, but comprehension wormed its way through her. "You knew about my powers, didn't you?"

He nodded. "Not at first. It took a while to figure out what you were after I'd tasted you. The night of the summit confirmed my suspicion when I saw how fast you'd healed. I knew the night we met, though…"

"That I was dying?" she said a matter fact, her voice a mere whisper so Jason wouldn't overhear.

"Yes." He leaned closer to her. "I sensed it the night I first saw you at the fundraiser, but I couldn't be sure. Then, you came to dinner and I heard the odd beat of your heart and I knew something was very wrong." He paused then and a look of anguish washed over his features.

She knew he was thinking of the night he'd fed from her, making her pass out.

I'm so sorry, my love, Cyrus spoke in her head.

She shook her head at him, her eyes becoming heavier by the minute. "You shouldn't call me *my love*."

"I will call you whatever I want," Cyrus snapped.

Evangeline laughed weakly. "I knew you'd say that."

The king stared longingly at her, his shoulders and arms tense.

"Thank you for calling Jason."

He said nothing.

Fiddling with the ties of her robe, she said, "I got your message." Looking up at him through her lashes she asked, "What did it mean?"

His eyes were sad and his lips were stiff as he spoke. "I made a huge mistake letting you go. I knew you were dying and I just let you walk away with—" His face contorted as he broke off.

Shivering, she remembered how angry he was. Evangeline felt strangely guilty. "I'm sorry I hurt you."

"You were mine." Cyrus wasn't about to spare her feelings. He knew she was feeling guilty and he wanted her to bask in it.

It was odd, but she no longer felt the hatred for him she'd clung to for so long. The night he'd let her go had somehow changed her feelings. She sensed there was a tender side to Cyrus, although she'd never say it aloud. "I can't help…" she started.

He sat up straight, rolling his eyes. "Spare me the speech about how in love you are with the mutt. I did not come here to listen to that shit."

"Why are you here?"

Ignoring her question, he asked, "Where is he anyway?" He looked around, his fingers drumming on the armrest. "I'm surprised I don't see the pups padding about too." He added, looking down at the floor then.

She gave him a warning look. "Adam is with the boys at my parent's house."

Cyrus gave her a curious look. "I understand sending the litter away, but why the hell would he..." Understanding dawned and he looked at her astonished. "He doesn't know, does he?"

Before she could answer, Cyrus stiffened, his head whipping to one side and she knew he'd heard something she did not.

Adam appeared a moment later in the doorframe as quiet as a ghost. He paused there, stock-still, his face completely devoid of emotion as he stared at the back of Cyrus' head.

Evangeline tried to say something immediately to set things straight, let him know Cyrus was only here out of concern and nothing else, but the look on Adam's face chilled her to the core.

Adam tilted his head back slightly as if he were pondering how to toss Cyrus out of his house and sauntered into the room in slow, calculating strides, his fists clenched tight. He only glanced at her for a second, noting the robe she wore. Clearly he was pissed at her for letting a vampire into a werewolf's home, and then he turned his full attention on Cyrus.

Too late, she thought warily that it would have been decent to put on some clothes when Cyrus arrived, but she was too weak to go up and down the stairs.

They must paint quite a picture sitting casually in Adam's living room with her in a robe. The only thing missing were cups of coffee, but then she remembered the house smelled of the fresh pot she'd just put on.

What was wrong with her? How could she invite the Vampire King of North America into an alpha's house? She must be losing it, because she was too tired to dwell on the issue.

Evangeline did not have the strength to watch these two go at it. She found her voice, as weak as it was, "Babe, it's okay," she began as she stood up wearily, swaying as she did so, but Adam's eyes were locked on Cyrus. He put out a hand to stop her from explaining.

Adam's voice was like ice. "The only reason you're still alive right now is because you tipped off my beta about Evangeline." She had a view of his broad back and every muscle looked taut with tension. "You have ten seconds to tell me what the fuck you're doing here and get out."

Cyrus stood up and slipped his hands in his pockets, glaring mutely at Adam. Evangeline couldn't help but notice Adam and Cyrus were almost the same height. Adam was just an inch or two taller and much wider than Cyrus' leonine frame.

"Really? You're just gonna stand there?" Adam turned to Evangeline now and her expression must have given her distress away. Adam's brow softened and he became instantly alarmed. "What is it?" He glanced accusingly at Cyrus. "What's wrong? What did he do?"

Evangeline felt her throat constrict. Staring into Adam's concerned face now made her mind go blank. What was she supposed to say? She knew she had to tell him the truth, but not right now, not in front of

Cyrus. This was private.

"Tell him, Evangeline." Cyrus' voice cut into her brain and she flinched.

Adam growled at him. "What the fuck is going on?"

Evangeline's head was whirling. She couldn't find her voice. Adam stared intently and she could only imagine what was going through his head. She was panicking with guilt for not telling him the truth, but evidently, Adam's acute sense was only picking up on the guilt part.

God, she needed time to think, time to find the words.

"Tell him, or I will," Cyrus snapped.

Evangeline saw Adam's eyes widen with betrayal. His jaws were pronounced as he bit down hard. His chest began to pump hard. He was jumping to the wrong conclusion, she thought. *Say something, stupid!* She couldn't let him think something was going on between her and Cyrus.

"Fine!" Taking his hands out of his pockets, Cyrus stepped closer to Evangeline and Adam. "With all your keen senses dog, you failed to notice the one most important thing about our lovely Evangeline."

Evangeline felt like a bright light just went on in the room. Shaking her head, she spoke up, "Cyrus, don't, I…" She tried to cling to the light, but it began to fade in and out.

"I was a fool to think she would be safe with you. Now look at her."

Evangeline's voice rose. "Cyrus, shut up!" The room was closing in on her. Everything around her was becoming hot and dark.

Cyrus ignored her, glaring at Adam who looked like he was about to pop several blood vessels in his head.

"She's *dying,* you fuck, and only I can save her."

Chapter Twenty

"I'm so sorry, Adam," Dr. Moros said.

Adam stood in the doorway of their master bedroom. His arms were folded tight in front of him, locking the pain within himself, trying not to let the angry beast free. It would not do Evangeline any good to phase right now. "I noticed she had an odd heartbeat, but she seemed fine. *Christ!*" His voice did not sound like his own. The second the bloodsucker had uttered those words his heart had burst into a million pieces. There was a non-stop deafening ringing in his ears.

"Her condition has always been peculiar, but I'm afraid healing others and,"—the doctor shifted uncomfortably—"childbirth were just too much for her body." Adam saw Dr. Moros take off his glasses and pinch the bridge of his nose. "I truly wish there was something I could do, Adam, but it's out of my hands."

Adam felt the icy pain sear through his chest. His head throbbed with the finality of the doctor's words. Becoming dizzy, he wished the world would just swallow him up whole. He did not want to exist anymore. His agony far outweighed the suffering he just barely sensed from the two werewolves downstairs, and scarcely heard the anguish howls from the rest of his pack outside. No one could imagine the pain he was going through. Bond or no bond, they couldn't possibly feel the way he did right now.

"Adam?"

Dr. Moros' voice was starting to irritate him and he didn't answer. Adam stared at Evangeline's pale face as she slept. Her cheekbones were more pronounced now, her eyes deeper in their sockets. He had caught her when she'd passed out in front of him and carried her to their bed. What had he done to her? This was his fault. He should have never taken her from her home. If she had never met him, she wouldn't be dying right now at the age twenty-two.

Adam shivered at the thought of never knowing her. Even in this little town they had managed to never cross paths. He was a recluse for starters and back and forth to Chicago. She'd been away at college for four years before she moved back home. They didn't exactly mix in the same circles, but it would only have been a matter of time before they'd met. They would have run into each other eventually. He just sped up the process by kidnapping her. As sorry as he was for scaring her, he would not change anything. He'd saved her from marrying the king and given them two beautiful children.

"Adam, I know her family well. She doesn't have much time. Let me break the news to them and bring them here. They'll want to say—"

"No."

The doctor took a deep, frustrated breath.

"Adam, I don't want to argue with you, but the longer we wait—"

"I'm not ready," Adam said.

"With all due respect, it's not up to you."

"How long—" Adam cleared his throat, but could not manage to get rid of the lump and didn't finish the question.

The doctor nodded sympathetically. "It's hard to tell. It could be a couple days or in the next hour or so."

A loud and wretched noise made them both jump slightly and Adam realized it had come from him. The half man, half wolf yelp had been uncontrollable. Looking at the doctor, he could only imagine what Moros saw because the man's face was frozen. Adam was squeezing his arms to himself, leaning heavily on the doorframe. He felt the beads of sweat begin to pour and the nausea in the pit of his stomach. "In…an…hour?"

The doctor could not respond, his face stunned as he stared back at Adam.

He vaguely sensed the vampire king step up behind him, forgetting Cyrus was there. Funny, how his hatred for his enemy did not surface at all. He couldn't remember how he felt about the guy just then. There was only a slight recognition he was a vampire and he wasn't supposed to be here. Weren't they enemies? Adam couldn't remember. It felt like a lifetime ago.

"We need to talk, Perez."

Moros spoke up. "Your Grace, I don't mean to be rude, but this is not the time."

"It's important." The king ignored the doctor.

"Adam, you don't need to stress yourself any further. Go and sit with Evangeline. Your Grace, can we speak downstairs?"

Cyrus sighed. "George, you can stay while Perez and I talk if you shut up."

There was a pause and then Adam heard Cyrus call him by his name.

"Adam."

His given name on the vampire's lips sounded strange. He turned to look at him.

What he saw in the king's eyes made him curse his creator, for there could be no other person responsible for the injustice of this life. Cyrus' expression spoke volumes and Adam instantly understood what the man wanted to discuss. He should have known this was the reason why the king was here. There had to be another way.

Adam turned to face Cyrus fully, leaning his back against the doorframe, though, for support. "I can't..."

Cyrus spoke fast. "But you will."

Adam narrowed his eyes at him. "Will it work?"

"What's going on here?" Dr. Moros cut in.

Adam saw Jason and Ramo step up to the second floor landing and stop behind the king. They had been listening in as well.

Cyrus' voice sounded almost genuine now. "He won't let her die, George, and neither will I. The only way to save Evangeline is to change her."

Adam nearly keeled over in front of all the men. He heard Ramo curse and the doctor's intake of breath. Jason's hands came up over himself to squeeze the back of his head. Regret and shame oozed out of his beta, but it would have to wait.

Adam repeated his question. "Will it work?" As outrageous as the thought was, he couldn't help but cling to the possibility Evangeline would live.

Cyrus' features strained as he stared at Adam. "It has to."

Standing in the hallway, Adam was overcome with grief and bafflement. There they were...three werewolves and two vampires. Contemplating changing the reason for his existence into an immortal enemy.

Enemy?

There was no way he would consider Evangeline his enemy. She would still be Evangeline, wouldn't she? She'd just have subtle differences.

"Think on it, but don't ponder too long," Cyrus said seriously. "She'll still be Evangeline." Adam jerked slightly. He felt like Cyrus was in his head. "Don't focus on the negatives. As a vampire she'll live longer, till eternity, in fact. I bet that kept you up at night, knowing you would one day outlive her."

Adam shivered. He had wondered about it, but he didn't expect to really deliberate on the fact this early on as Evangeline was so young. Even so, he knew what he would do when the time came. The solution was clear. He'd end his life with her. He just didn't expect it would happen so soon.

Cyrus continued on. "She'll never grow old, she'll be stronger, invincible. What's more, she will be my ward. Therefore, the vampires on this continent wouldn't dare hurt her or her children."

Daniel and David. The mention of his boys brought him round his stupor. It didn't matter what he wanted. Their boys needed Evangeline. They needed their mother. To take her away from the boys so early in their life when he could do something about it was downright cruel.

Adam looked at his cousin and best friend. They were focused on him. He read the weariness they felt, but also a small sense of hope, the same hope keeping him standing right now. Jason gave him a look, that seemed to say, *You won't be able to live without her. There is no other choice.*

Ramo looked like a ten-year-old boy who'd just flunked a math test. "Hey," he muttered miserably. "It might be kinda hot."

Adam turned back to Cyrus. "The choice is hers. If she agrees." He looked away from the king, abhorring to leave Evangeline's fate to Cyrus Stewart.

****

The muffled sounds near the door is what kept her in an odd state of alertness. The dreamlike sensation made her jump whenever the voices grew higher.

Damn her weak body!

Evangeline wanted to scream at the top of her lungs. It wasn't fair. She couldn't move. Her body had been reduced to a useless lump on their bed. She couldn't even roll over onto her stomach, the way she liked to sleep, and the thought of it brought a tear down her cheek. Feeling sorry for herself, she forced her eyes open to stare dejectedly at the ceiling. How long would she be like this before the selfish bastard upstairs took her?

That's right. I'm talking to you, the Almighty who has nothing better to do than rip mortals from the world before their lives can actually begin. Just wait till I get up there. I have quite a few bones to pick with you.

Evangeline's rant at the big guy upstairs was interrupted by footsteps coming toward her.

Her eyes instantly found the blue of Adam's and she cursed inwardly. She would give anything right now to get up off the bed and jump into his arms. Again, pitiful tears ran down her face.

"Baby, don't cry." Adam sat on the bed and carefully laid his head on her chest. "Please don't." His voice was strained.

This was killing him and she knew it. Forcing herself to stop, she opened her eyes wide enough to dry them out.

She struggled to speak to him. Every word she uttered made her dizzy with weakness. "The…babies…"

Adam lifted his head to stare raptly at her. His eyes were red-rimmed, his brow tight with tension. "They're fine, honey. You're parents are spoiling the crap out of them." He laughed with little amusement. "Lydia is getting annoyed."

Her weak smile only made his face tighter.

Evangeline stared into blue eyes that melted her very soul, and felt a flare of hope spread through her. Adam's strong and beautiful face held more for her than he would ever imagine. She saw her best friend, confidante, lover, and if she miraculously lived through this wretched ordeal, hopefully one day she would make love to him again as his wife.

A look of anguish twisted his features as he shivered over her. He bent his head to compose himself, gripping the bed sheets on either side of her. There was something he had to tell her…no…ask her, but he was struggling.

Evangeline tried to lift her hand to console him, but it was way too heavy. She lifted her index finger instead and nudged the inside of his wrist.

Adam looked up. He was under some control now. A steady resolve surrounded him. "I understand why you kept this from me, but all the same, I wish you would have told me sooner."

"I…I…" Evangeline started in an aching whisper, but he held up his hand to stop her, and smoothed her hair back from her forehead.

"Don't, baby. It's fine. We can argue about this later." He let out a rough cough and glanced away.

She stared.

Adam took a deep breath and continued. "The doctor can't do anything and we're out of options...medically speaking." He was shaking now, jerking the bed beneath her. "I don't want to pressure you by declaring all the things you need to live for...the decision is yours...I can't be the one..."

She nudged his wrist again to urge him on, hating her body for growing weaker and weaker by the second.

"Cyrus has offered to turn you."

A leap so fierce and potent jolted her dying heart. Had she heard him correctly? Somehow she found the strength to utter the word he was fighting with. "Vampire?"

Nodding, he read her reaction carefully. After assessing her expression he went on. "It's completely up to you, but you need to make a decision fast, babe. I hate pressuring you like this, but it's the only solution we have." He paused. "I'll understand if you don't want to do it."

He misread her hesitation. She was thinking why hadn't she thought of this herself? There was no decision to make. God had heard her fit of anger and He was giving her another chance at life, not the life she knew, but an altogether new one where she was part of the living dead, but who the hell cared. Evangeline would be alive with Adam and the boys. That was all that mattered.

Sure, they would have issues to contend with, but what family didn't? Evangeline could only see the bright side of the situation. She would live longer now with her werewolf family. They wouldn't have to worry about her because she would be nearly invincible. It was a perfect plan, but…

Evangeline's excitement wavered as she stared at Adam. She whispered the agonizing question, barely moving her lips, but she knew he would hear her. "Could you still…love me…after?"

Adam's face contorted and he held her tightly to him. "God, baby, of course I'll still love you. I don't care if you come back a hyena. We'd make it work. If this is something you're willing to do then you have my total support."

She saw the sincerity in his gaze and breathed in shakily. There was so much to consider about this entire situation, but she knew she was out of time.

He noticed something in her expression. "Will you… I mean…" He looked haggard.

Staring deep into his eyes, she whispered as strongly as she could. "Yes."

Letting out a profound sigh, he hugged her, resting his head in the crook of her neck as he whispered, "Thank you, thank you, thank you."

They had to work fast. She felt herself slipping away and she fought to hold on. There was something she needed to do first, though.

Evangeline tapped Adam's hip to get his attention. He looked up. "What is it?"

She let out another shaky breath, trying to control her nerves. "Take me…outside." Her eyes gestured to the waning sunlight in the window. He knew instantly what she wanted.

Adam nodded slowly with a far off look in his

eyes. He came off the bed, pulling the covers down and lifted her gently into his arms, positioning her so she was nestled comfortably with her head on his chest.

The men outside their door looked eagerly at them as they appeared in the hallway. Adam met Cyrus' solemn eyes. "She wants to see the sun. We'll be back soon."

Cyrus nodded. His face, usually disciplined, now softened as he stared at Evangeline.

She met his gaze briefly before her lids gave way from the effort of keeping them open for so long. She let them fall, saving their strength till they were outside. It would be the very last time she would see the sun and what better way to do so than in Adam's arms.

When she opened her eyes again, she was seated on Adam's lap on the back porch steps overlooking the wide, grassy backyard. The sun was low as it descended in the western sky. Adam stared off thoughtfully, as if he too would never look upon the bright orb ever again.

There was a vague sense she should be more saddened at the reality of never seeing the sun or daylight again. She'd never lie out under the sun on a beach, or take her kids to the park on a Saturday afternoon, but it all seemed so trivial now. Evangeline would trade a million days in the sun for one evening at home at the dinner table with Adam and the boys.

He was still trembling as he held her and it filled her with immense joy to know he would not have to worry about her for long.

Adam looked down at her in surprise. "Baby, you're missing the sunset."

Evangeline realized she had barely glanced at the sun and was staring avidly at him instead. She shook her head once. "You're my sun now."

Adam's jaws flexed hard and a tear spilled rapidly down his cheek. He pressed his lips firmly on hers, barely containing the tremors going through his body. Coming up, he pressed his forehead to hers. "I love you so much." Whispering in her ear, he promised, "I'm going to make you the happiest vampire in the world."

If she had the strength, she would have laughed. She couldn't wait to laugh with him again.

It was time.

Uttering her last words to him as a human, she said, "Let's do this."

****

Cyrus wondered if he would have to fight the three werewolves blocking him out of his way. Adam's beta and his punk cousin stood slightly behind their alpha as Adam stared him down.

"You know," Cyrus said, casually, "if you phase right now and attack me, I can't help her."

"You're not the only vampire here," Adam said coldly.

Dr. Moros flinched, then said awkwardly, "Uh, Adam, I'm not sure I could."

"Why not?" Adam barked at him, but it was Cyrus who answered.

"Because I am his sovereign and if his mouth comes within three feet of Evangeline I'll cut out his fangs and feed it to him."

Moros gave Adam an exasperated look and gestured mockingly to the king with a hand as if to say, *That's why.*

Cyrus ignored the doctor. His eyes were watching Adam carefully. The man looked like he would explode any second now and sure as shit those dogs behind him would explode with him. "We're wasting time. Move!" he demanded.

Adam held up a hand. "Let's get something clear. If she doesn't live through the transformation, you're dead. Got it?"

"Fine, now get out of my way." Cyrus stepped forward, passing the wolves.

"I'm staying too." Adam started to follow him.

Cyrus spun around fast to face him again. "The hell you are!"

"You actually think I'm gonna leave her alone with you?" Adam asked, incredulous.

Cyrus leaned closer, seriously pissed now. Speaking roughly through his teeth, he uttered back in his face, "You actually want to watch me get into bed with her and sink my teeth in her throat?"

Adam lunged at him and smashed him hard into the wall. In his haste to get to Evangeline, it hadn't occurred to him to bring reinforcements. It was thoughtless on his part, but he hadn't come to fight with the wolves. His only concern was for Evangeline. Cyrus would love to go toe to toe with this mutt, but there were more important matters right now. He stared hard at the dog, breathing up in his face. "You done?"

The doctor spoke up again. "Adam, I have to agree with the king. This is definitely something you don't want to see." Moros stood a few feet away, not daring to come close to Adam.

Ramo chimed in. "Adam, I'm picturing it and even *I* want to fuck the guy up. You won't be able to handle it. Let's go downstairs."

Cyrus spoke to all of them, but didn't take his eyes

off Adam. "No. You all need to leave the house. I'll have to take her underground after I've drained her."

Adam snarled and punched through the drywall an inch from Cyrus' head. Debris and dust rained down on both of them. Cyrus rolled his eyes. The guy was being unreasonable, but he was within his rights. Still, if he didn't move...

"What do you mean underground?" Adam was shaking harder now.

He sighed. "We don't have time for a rundown on vampire transition."

"The quick version then."

"Fuck." Irritated, Cyrus pushed Adam off him. "Look, in order to complete the transition she has to spend an entire day underground with her maker. I don't want to physically put her in the ground so I think we can find a crevice under the floorboards in the basement. I know who built this odd-fucking house and I know the basement isn't cemented. Now I'm done talking. Get out!" Cyrus turned and stepped into the bedroom. He closed the door behind him, but not before catching Jason, Ramo, and Dr. Moros restraining a red-faced Adam. As soon as the door clicked shut, a growl wrenched loud in the hallway and he heard several pops.

Something told him Adam wouldn't dare open the door. He can have his conniptions, but he knew what was best for Evangeline.

Cyrus surveyed the room and resisted the urge to scoff at their "master bedroom." The air was warm, almost stifling. No doubt the wolf was emanating heat like a furnace. The poor girl must be boiling. He turned to look at Evangeline and froze. For an instant he thought he was too late. Her face was paler now as she lay on her back, stock still on the bed. The image was horrid. Then he heard the extremely faint thump of her heart and breathed again.

Suddenly afraid, he crossed the room toward her. She looked so terribly fragile. What if he drained her and she didn't survive the rebirth?

Her eyes opened then as he approached the bed. Heavy lids blinked over those lovely eyes, and she gave him a small, tired smile.

Cyrus nearly crumpled to the floor. She had never looked at him like that and his deadened heart melted. What he wouldn't give to see her smile every day. If it all worked, he just might decide to order her to his side every evening to give him an alluring smile. She wouldn't have a choice as his ward. He was looking forward to enlightening the wolf on that particular aspect of maker and ward.

"Why...smiling?" she asked in a raspy whisper.

"Because you're going to live, my sweet, and I get to save you." He sat down at her hip and gazed warmly at her.

Blinking at him, she said, "You look...different."

"Mmm..." He reached up to caress her cheek. "I'm sure I resemble the cat who got the cream."

She shook her head. "Look..." Evangeline hesitated. "Good."

He frowned at that. He had a feeling she was going to say *human*.

She looked away toward the window, her chest beginning to rise and fall in quick succession, her nerves taking over her.

"Easy, love."

"Will...will it hurt?" Her voice broke on the last word.

"No, it will not hurt." He took her chin between his fingers and turned her face toward him. "You have to trust me, remember? All you have to do is relax in my arms and let me do the rest."

She nodded at him and a tear slipped down her cheek. "I'm scared."

A foreign pain ignited inside his chest. He reached down and lifted her off the bed, repositioning them so he lay back against the headboard with Evangeline cradled on his lap. Making her as comfortable as possible, he tried to soothe her. "Don't be afraid, Evangeline. I won't let anything happen to you. You may even like it. It will feel like you died and went to heaven." He winked at her, but she would soon find out how literal those words were.

Smirking at him, she asked, "You'll stay?"

"Of course. You know how the process goes, don't you?"

Evangeline nodded again and their eyes held for a long moment.

Evangeline knew a lot about his race and he was sure she was thinking about the rebirth. "Everything is going to be fine." Her body temperature was beginning to cool down thanks to him and she relaxed more. Cyrus began to rock her gently.

They were not married and she belonged to a werewolf, but somehow he had found a way to make her, his. If he couldn't have her in name, at least they would be bonded by blood. By many standards this was much better. This had been his long-term plan anyway. Had they been married, he would have changed her eventually. It was what human and vampire couples did. At least this way he didn't have to convince her to change.

"Close your eyes, my love."

A wretched howl shot through the night, making Evangeline flinch. "Adam."

Cyrus cursed in his head. The bloody mutt always had the worst timing. "It's all right. He'll be fine. He's with his pack. Just focus on calming your nerves."

He continued to sway them side-to-side for a long while, his eyes on her gorgeous face. She stared off toward the window thoughtfully and then closed her eyes. Soon, she began to drift off as he'd hoped. Cyrus reached up to brush strands of hair away from her neck and a tightening built in his chest.

There was no reason to be so attached to her, but he couldn't help the way he felt. He thought briefly of his wife when he was human. She had been nothing like Evangeline and yet he'd loved her. Could his damned heart have fallen in love again after all these years?

Dimly aware this would be the only time he'd hold her in his arms, he wasn't letting go until she was reborn as his vampire. The urge to make her his was overwhelming, and he was exhilarated she was his first and only child. He prepared himself, letting his fangs take shape. His eyes were fastened on her throat and his body shivered with excitement. He was going to save her and taste every ounce of her blood. They would be connected for eternity and his eyes took shape, turning silver at the thought.

Cyrus brought her up closer to his face, inhaling her wonderful scent. In a slow caress, he ran his nose and mouth over her brow, down her cheek and along her neck where her pulse beat weakly.

Savoring the moment with great concentration, he sheathed his fangs into her skin.

Evangeline let out a shocked moan, and her hand gripped his arm. Cyrus ran a soothing hand over her back and she relaxed, but she held onto his arm, her weak fingers lightly massaging his bicep. She was not in pain this time. In fact, he knew she was feeling a very delightful sensation now, one she could have felt the first time had he been gentler and she'd been a bit more willing. Pain, tension, stress; all her worries oozed out of her and left her experiencing a profound high.

Consuming her in slow pulls, he relished the taste of her blood. The sound of her heart slowing unimaginably more made him focus on his task more seriously. She was dying in his arms and he began to panic. He had to finish. If he stopped now, she would die for sure. He had to drain her completely and reseal the vein. His venom coursing through her would bring her back to life. With steady determination, he concentrated on drinking her in.

The instant her hand fell from his arm, her heart beat for the last time.

****

In the cold autumn night, Adam felt the world halt and a vast light go out. He sank to his knees, stunned, as his pack that surrounded him in a protective circle, sang his suffering in earsplitting howls.

Chapter Twenty-One

Evangeline's body was cold in his arms, colder than his own.

They lay frozen under the house for God knows how long. Cyrus had been in and out of sleep, checking on her every five minutes. He didn't know what time it was, but thought it might be late afternoon. His watch was on his left wrist, which was stuck under Evangeline's waist.

He was on his back, with Evangeline in the crook of his arm. They lay on the thick comforter he had taken from their room and faced underneath the floorboards of the basement. It was cold and damp, but as he was always cold it hardly mattered and Evangeline couldn't feel a thing.

Anxious for her to wake up, he tried to remember the first initial sensation when a newborn vampire wakes from the dead. His maker had been there to supply him with blood from his vein, which completed the process. Cyrus remembered being completely out of it, not knowing or understanding what the hell was happening to him. At least Evangeline knew what was coming.

Although, he should have told her they would be waking up together in the dark. She might know the process, but a reminder would have been nice. A newborn needed to stay as far away from the sun as possible and underground was the perfect place. Cyrus only hoped this spot was good enough.

A tickle on his side made the hairs on his nape stand.

Evangeline was stirring.

He didn't move or make a sound as he stared down at the top of her head on his shoulder.

She came up slowly, but with lithe precision, her hand exploring from his abdomen to his chest as though she'd never seen a man's torso before. Evangeline lifted her head, and their eyes met.

Silver irises replaced the olive green in a perfect porcelain face. He laughed nervously, feeling slightly frightened at the intensity in her expression. It startled him and barely contained a shiver. It was as if she were looking at him for the first time. The hunger in her eyes made his immortal blood boil.

"Welcome back, Evangeline."

Her mouth opened and Cyrus' groin tightened as he gazed in pride at her glorious new fangs hanging lower than the others. They were perfectly sharp and the tip of her tongue tested their points in measured strokes.

Moaning deep, he said, "Come here, my sweet." He moved his collar to the side, having loosened the buttons of his shirt hours ago. "I have exactly what you need." Lifting her on top of him so she straddled his hips, he groaned at the feel of her. Pressing a finger to his vein, he said, "Right here, my love."

He bent his head back to expose his throat, grasping her by the back of her head with one hand and squeezing the fabric of her robe at the small of her back with the other. She struck hard and he nearly came in his pants. Fuck, this was better than he imagined. He was rock hard in his pants, poking the skin of her thigh. He watched as her robe fell off her shoulders.

"Oh God, yes, Evangeline!" he cried. The feel of this woman drinking him was like nothing he'd ever experienced. It was the first time he'd let another taste him. Female vampires had tried in the past when they were together, but he'd never let them, refusing to share his blood with some passing fancy.

Now, Evangeline Wolcott lay atop him, her hands gripping his shoulders, her body writhing with every pull she took feeding her hungry body with his essence. The moment was too good to be true. His head swarmed from exuberance.

Let her never stop, he thought. Every inch of his body was aware of her. His skin was on fire and for the first time in all his years as a cold blooded vampire he felt great warmth at his core with their joining lifeblood.

She was his.

Evangeline was finally his. The beautiful truth filled him with unimaginable elation.

He refused to think of the wolf and his pups now. To him, they were far off in another world. He, Cyrus, was experiencing a miracle, bringing this incredible woman back to life. This was the last of the process. She would drink her fill of the vampire who drained her and renew every part of her body with his energy.

As a newborn vampire, she'd be hungry often, and unfortunately for him she could only get so much nourishment from his blood. Her real source of sustenance would have to be human or animal.

He cursed in his head. The thought of her

replenishing her body with the wolf's blood bugged the fuck out of him. Irritated that the mutt kept slipping into his head, he repositioned them. Moving carefully as to not disturb her work, he rolled her onto her back. Her movements down there were driving him insane and he needed to put a little space between them.

Cyrus remembered how he'd felt drinking his maker's blood.

Vertigo hit him hard and reluctantly he pulled back, trying futilely to disengage her fangs from his throat. Evangeline held onto him, refusing to let go. "Evangeline, you'll suck me dry." *Fuck!* Ok...wrong choice of words. His hard on twitched between them and this time he was right between her legs. Her robe had crumpled higher around her waist and despite her new blood type, she was warm down there, warm and wet. She must have realized their precarious position because she froze on his neck, pulling away slowly.

Evangeline leaned her head back on the comforter and stared avidly at him in extreme befuddlement.

He gazed back at her, his tongue suddenly leaden. The urge to soothe and explain to her what was going on in her new form just floated out of his head.

There was a tightening in his chest. A balloon the size of Texas was about to burst inside him. This must be like what a mother felt the first time she laid eyes on her child, only it was different, very different. This child was not one he had fathered with another. She was his alone, a product of his love and desire for her. She was a part of him now, in every sense.

Cyrus had ignored his true feelings for her before and for good reason, but now, it was inevitable he face it.

He loved her.

In every way possible, he loved her. There wasn't anything he wouldn't do for this woman. She was his ward and underling. For all intents and purposes, she was his to command, but Evangeline had him wrapped around her finger.

The amount of blood she'd obtained was enough to sate five vampires, but her eyes were still shining bright. Her body was trembling beneath him and she rubbed his arms hard, begging for something. The need in her expression was heartbreaking. She was overcome with an intense desire, one no human or vampire could ignore.

It was his blood coursing under her skin, yearning for the most ultimate of sensations.

Closing his eyes in defeat, he thought, *Why fight it?* Her nails were digging into his back and she was breathing hard.

Cyrus opened his eyes to take a mental photo of the look on her face. She did not know what she craved, but he did.

"*Bloody hell*," he whispered, his face tight, and began to move. His hips drove forward between her thighs in slow rhythmic movements. Cyrus kept his pants securely fastened. He wasn't suicidal after all. His ward was aching and it was his duty to take care of her.

He didn't know whose need was greater, his or hers, but it didn't matter. They both had to find release. The aching expression on her face was a clear indicator she was in pain.

The feel of her sex against him made his head reel. Her lips were parted as she gazed at him, and it took every ounce of restraint not to taste them.

Thrusting harder against her, he felt her go rigid, her expression confused as she stared at him with wide hungry eyes. There was little time left. She was coming slowly to her senses, but her body still necessitated the release it shuddered for.

"Stop!" she said, in an agonized whisper, pushing against his chest.

Cyrus pulled back instantly, unable to control his release. Violent tremors rocked through him making him go dizzy.

When he could, he opened his eyes to look at her. Evangeline was in shock. She was gasping, her chest heaving rapidly, but of course her odd heartbeat was now gone. Her vampire venom now circulated her blood.

"Are you sure?" Cyrus gazed at her in concern, amazed she was able to control herself. "You're in pain. Let me—"

"No." Her body trembled beneath him. "I'm fine." She shifted under him, trying to avoid any further contact. "Please…"

"Damn it!" Cyrus rolled off her to lie on his back and stared up at the moldy plywood. He spoke without looking at her. "I'm sorry. I couldn't help myself." His voice was clip and stern. "And for a moment there neither could you."

From the corner of his eye he could still see her puffing away with her hand on her chest as if waiting to feel a pulse. She lay there staring straight ahead for a long while. He wondered if she'd lost her ability to speak in the process of the transformation.

"Say something," he demanded, still not facing her.

Her voice, always beautiful, was now an octave

higher. Her singsong tone resonated in his bones. "Will it always be like that between us?" she asked anxiously.

His jaw flexed. "No." Evangeline was worried she had no control over her body. "I wouldn't worry about it if I were you. Your reaction to me was based on the transformation. Your human blood runs through me and my vampire blood runs through you. The initial bond between a creator and his newborn is quite powerful." She was nodding her head, remembering the affects from all her studies. He turned to look at her and she met his stare. Her eyes were back to their lovely green and he smiled possessively. "Your senses are heightened now. They were particularly heightened when you woke up. It's only natural for you to become aroused when you feed, especially when you feed from your maker."

Her face was grave. "We can never do that again."

"I'm sorry," he said again, but was he? It's not like they had really fucked. His damn pants were zipped and buttoned. Still, he could understand she'd feel guilty for what they'd done, but he sure as hell wouldn't.

He sighed heavily, irritated. Her love for the Blacktail ran deep. Otherwise she would have never been able to stop herself as she did. Cyrus had been right. She had profound strength and a small part of him, a very tiny fraction, was actually proud of her. Her other supernatural side must of had a hand in too, giving her the power to control her urges. His ward was going to handle her transition just fine.

Evangeline turned to stare up again at the floorboards, an apprehensive look on her perfect skin.

"You look amazing. How do you feel?"

Pondering for a moment, she said, "Physically, I

feel like a million bucks, a little hungry, but fine. It's just…" She searched for words. Her hesitation told him she was fretting over seeing her wolf again. "I have to see him."

"Whenever you're ready," he said immediately, but cringed inwardly. He did not want to part from her. Jealousy over Adam was tenfold what it was before. How the hell was he going to let her go to him? How the hell could he walk away from her again? He hadn't really thought that far ahead, too caught up in the moment.

"I'm ready now. Is it safe to go up?" She fixed her robe around her.

He nodded mutely, but thought *not likely*. "I'll go first." He cleared his throat. "Calm yourself. Your emotions are still a bit…telling."

Her hands covered her face in real mortification.

Cyrus sighed and popped the loose floorboards to climb up into the basement. "Let's get this show on the road."

*****

The voices in his head wouldn't shut the fuck up. The room spun around him and the floor tilted like he was standing on the deck of a ship.

Adam leaned forward with his elbows on his knees, his head in his hands, relishing and hating the effects of the pills and alcohol his pack had given him.

They had run all night together, trying futilely to take his mind off of what was happening at home. At daybreak they had practically dragged him to Ramo's place and tossed back at least five bottles of tequila. Ramo had given him some pills too and he'd taken them without question, but since then he'd been hallucinating and hearing disturbing voices in his head. He heard Evangeline's cries as she'd given birth, his pack's howls, Cyrus' yells as he'd slammed the door to their bedroom on his face and his father's antagonizing put downs at his willingness to turn Evangeline into their greatest enemy.

It felt like years had passed since he'd left last night. When the hell would they come up?

Jason had reluctantly dropped him off a few minutes ago and Adam had stumbled in and plopped into the armchair in the living room where he sat now. He had insisted on going home to see her when she woke up. He knew his beta waited outside to make sure for himself Evangeline was okay.

Adam mulled over the past few days and again he came to the awful truth he'd fought against all last night. This was his fault. If he'd never taken Evangeline she would be alive and well now. She would have married that freak, but at least she would have been healthy. Cyrus couldn't get her pregnant so she would have been able to stay human.

His father suddenly reared his ugly face in his mind, scoffing at him. Adam rubbed his eyes with the palms of his hands, attempting to clear them. His mind jumped from turmoil to turmoil and his stomach rolled with anticipation. He was anxious to see her. He needed her, needed to see she was alive and going to be okay. Somewhere in the far reaches of his befuddled mind he knew she was okay. He'd have felt it if she weren't.

A vision of Cyrus slamming his bedroom door in his face flashed before his eyes. Adam tried to center his attention on the big issue, which was Evangeline's health, but he couldn't control the perverse working of his brain. What was Cyrus doing with her right now? Did he have his arms around her? Jealousy stabbed through his wretched heart at the thought of him lying beside her.

As much as he'd asked his pack all morning none of them would tell him what a vampire transformation consisted of. Either they didn't know or refused to enlighten him. He'd been too wasted to look online and he'd left his phone at home.

"You actually want to watch me get into bed with her and sink my teeth in her throat?" Cyrus' words made his stomach jolt for the millionth time.

God, what was wrong with him? Cyrus was saving her, but leaving her alone with the bloodsucker was pure, unadulterated torture. He winced. Bloodsucker was a rude name to describe a vampire, a term he'd used for as long as he could remember. Adam couldn't imagine referring to Evangeline as one and yet, that was what she'd become. Interestingly enough, it wasn't Cyrus being a vampire, which bothered him so much anymore. It was the fact he was in love with his lady that pissed the fuck out of him. Knowing he was alone with her right now, doing God knows what to her.

So Evangeline was now a part of the supernatural. So what? He knew she'd probably find her new life fascinating when all this blew over. Adam just couldn't shove the nagging feeling this would not be the end of the Adam/Evangeline/Cyrus triangle.

The sound of clapping wood made him jerk his head up. It came from downstairs. Jason had warned him not to go down there. His fucking second had actually threatened him. The movement from down there echoed in his head and it was though an invisible hand had materialized and slapped him into focus.

His heart was hammering in his ears, but he controlled the spasms running through him with the help of the drugs still in his blood. Instead of getting up to meet them at the back end of the house, he stayed where he was, glued to the chair. He sat back, a bit slouched with his head bowed, eyes on the open doorway of the living room. He tried to relax his composure, but the nagging feeling grew, turning his would-be calm position to a menacing crouch. He gripped and released the arms of the chair, counting every excruciating second.

Two pairs of footsteps hit the stairs.

His chest constricted and he squeezed his eyes shut at the sound of her dainty feet. An array of emotions swiveled inside him.

She was alive. Thank God, she was alive and walking to him right now. He couldn't move though. The tension in his body only increased with every passing second. Something was wrong. He felt the nervous panic in the pit of his stomach.

A door creaked along with the footsteps now, and he heard the rustle of fabric. Adam pulled in an unsteady breath and froze.

It took Adam about half a second to register in his muddled brain the scent wafting toward him. The instant he realized what it was, Evangeline and Cyrus appeared in the doorway.

He took a cursory glance at Evangeline. Her eyes were wide with panic, but she looked amazing. He wanted to go to her and hold her in his arms and a small part of him actually hesitated to take in the realization she was going to be fine, but fury, hate and tequila won over. A burning, red haze filled his eyes.

"YOU MOTHERFUCKER!" Adam lunged across the room in one graceful leap, tackling Cyrus. They landed hard on the floor of the foyer, cracking the hardwood beneath them. Adam clasped his hands around his throat, choking the shit out of him. "I fucking trusted you!" His voice was sheer animal, a ferocious growl. Hauling back his fist, he landed a fierce blow to Cyrus' head.

"Adam, please—"

He vaguely heard the angelic cry behind him. "She trusted you? How could you do it? I'll fucking kill you!" He was spitting with rage as his fist met Cyrus' face again.

The door slammed open and he felt more than saw Jason's readiness to fight.

"No!" Evangeline screamed.

Adam's grip slackened at her protest, giving Cyrus the chance to throw him off, landing a swift kick to his stomach, and tossing him into a wall.

They got to their feet at the same time, crouched and poised to pounce.

Before Adam could make his move, Evangeline jumped in between them. She faced Adam with her hands up, her back to Cyrus. She was the most frighteningly, beautiful thing in the world.

Evangeline's limbs were strong as ever. Every movement she made was executed with grace and care. Her body, always slender and lithe looked healthy and firmer. She faced him warily. Adam realized in his fury she was protecting him. *Cyrus.*

Seething, he spoke to her. "Tell me you're not protecting him?"

Evangeline seemed to have noticed her posture and straightened up some. "Please, Adam, don't. He saved me. Please don't do this."

He spoke through his teeth. "Move, Evangeline!"

Tears began to fall down her perfect cheekbones. "I c—can't," she stuttered.

Adam lifted his arm and punched through the glass window beside him. He shouted in agony. "He fucking raped you! MOVE!"

There was a loud growl, a shudder, and then several pops. Too caught up in their shit, he hadn't noticed the bomb in the doorway.

Jason exploded. Shards of clothing ricocheted around the foyer. He crouched down, snarling, ready to kill.

Evangeline screamed. "NO! Jason, stop!"

Adam was thankful at least one of them could shift. He had to wait till all the pills he took were out of his system, which wouldn't be too much longer.

Adam and Jason advanced carefully, waiting for Evangeline to get out of the way.

Stunned, Adam watched as she braced her arms outward, shielding Cyrus from them. Cyrus put a restraining hand on her arm as she backed them up against the far wall.

"What the hell are you doing?" Adam's eyes were wide on hers.

She was crying hysterically now. "I can't let you hurt him."

Adam shifted his gaze to Cyrus. "Are you going to hide behind my mate like a coward or are you going to fight me like a man?"

Glowering, Cyrus said, "It's useless, Adam. Even

if I order her to move, she won't." His eyes turned grave. "She'll die for me if she has to."

All the breath in his body was cut off. He stood frozen, glaring at the scene before him. Evangeline was panting and shivering, protecting the monster behind her.

"I'm sorry, Adam, but I can't let you hurt him. I'm trying to move, but my body won't allow it." Her face was a mixture of pain, confusion, and terror. "I want…but…I can't… Oh, God!"

"What the hell is this?" Adam barked, his head throbbing.

Cyrus managed to move her to the side. "I'm her maker. In many ways our connection is more powerful than any father/daughter or husband/wife. She'll obey my every command and protect me by any means possible."

Adam's head reeled. "Son of a bitch! You sure took advantage, you prick!" He stepped closer, but Evangeline moved in front of him again.

Cyrus' jaw clenched, but he didn't reply.

Evangeline said in a small voice. "Adam, he didn't rape me."

At her words, Adam stiffened, absolutely stupefied.

Her face was tormented. If Cyrus hadn't taken advantage of her...

Had she consented?

He stared at her in shock. "No," Adam whispered in betrayal, his bloodshot eyes piercing into hers. The tears continued to pour down her face and a tiny fraction of his soul was relieved she could still do this very human act. She stepped toward him, warily. Her sorrowful expression told him all he needed to know.

He couldn't speak, couldn't think. There was no way she'd betray him. And yet, he honed in on her emotions.

There it was.

Evangeline was filled with guilt, shame and, to his horror, he felt the stunning urgency of her arousal. She was fighting it, but it engulfed her.

Jesus Christ! She didn't! The room tilted beneath him.

"Careful, Evangeline," Cyrus uttered behind her.

"He won't hurt me," she said.

"The way he is looking at you would suggest otherwise. Give him some space," Cyrus warned her.

Adam didn't hear a word of their exchange. He stared dumbfounded at the woman he loved as the truth of her words rang loud in his head.

He didn't rape me.

"Adam, please let me explain. It's not what you're thinking." Evangeline was about two feet from him.

There was a loud roaring in his ears. *It's not what I'm thinking?* Shit, he couldn't even *think* straight right now. He focused on the signs blaring at him in the face. The scent of the king's release and her profound guilt was in the air. Evangeline sobbed and the prick behind her just stood there watching him. *What the fuck am I supposed to think?*

He saw Evangeline flinch and take a step back from him and realized he'd shouted his words.

She looked down, her cheeks burning red and spoke to everyone, but him. "Will you please go and give us some privacy?"

Cyrus stepped forward and Jason snarled, baring his teeth at him. "I'm not sure that's wise, Evangeline."

Cyrus actually looked concerned for her, like Adam would really hurt her.

As if the guy was reading his mind, he said, "You're upset..."

Big fucking understatement, cocksucker!

Cyrus continued to speak to him, but Adam could only stare, dejectedly at Evangeline. "Believe me when I say, we do things we would otherwise think better of when we're in a state." Adam caught Cyrus glance at the back of Evangeline, an odd expression on his face.

He looked Cyrus in the eye, his voice eerily calm. "I'm nothing like you. Now, you have five seconds to get off my property before I stake you in the fucking head."

Evangeline let in a sharp breath.

Adam looked down at her. "Jason won't hurt you, but he can restrain you." His voice was like ice.

She recoiled, petrified at his words. "Cyrus, please go. I'll be fine."

"The best place for you is in the transition facility. You need to—"

"I need to speak to Adam, please, just go." She turned to look at him and then faced Jason. "Adam, I know I have no right to ask you, but will you please ask Jason to wait a few minutes so Cyrus can make it home safely?"

Adam let out a harsh laugh. "Believe me, if anyone is going to attack your precious maker, it'll be me."

He wished they would all leave. He wished he could phase. He wished he had more of those pills. It wasn't a good idea to be around him right now. He felt like he was a bomb, ticking down to the last second. Maybe Cyrus was right. Could he control himself around her?

Cyrus didn't move. The vampire was visibly struggling with himself, staring hard at Evangeline with a longing expression. He must have said something to her telepathically because she shook her head.

He couldn't take it anymore, and let out a growl deep in his throat.

The king closed his eyes in defeat and turned toward the door. Before he left, he spoke again, standing in the doorway with his back to them. "Remember, wolf, I'll know if something happens to her." Then he was gone.

Adam looked at Evangeline smugly. "How touching. Are you sure you don't want to run off with your lover...make sure he makes it home okay?" he finished mockingly.

"Please don't act this way. He's not my lover."

His temper increased impossibly more and he stalked forward, towering over her till she was backed into a wall. "Not your lover? So are you telling me he had a wet dream?"

"Stop! Just listen to me. You're jumping to the wrong conclusion."

"Your little tryst is written all over your face. DON'T LIE TO ME!" His eyes flashed and he knew they burned yellow now. The pills were wearing off. Behind them he heard the low warning growl of his beta. Adam didn't turn, but he spoke to him. "You need to remember who you answer to, J. Phase back and leave." He heard Jason's heaving pants and then the cracking of tendons as he morphed into his human form.

Adam's face was inches from Evangeline's. Silent

tears continued to fall. Her brow was creased as she looked at him pitifully and whispered, "We didn't. I swear we didn't. It was the whole transition and the feeding." Flushing, she looked down, hiding her face. She muttered, "He kept his pants on the entire time."

He lost it. Both hands came up and punched through the wall on either side of her head. She jumped, but to her credit she didn't run away from him. He was destroying his entire house and he didn't care. Hell, if she left him, he'd happily burn the fucker down.

Adam stood, hovering over her, shaking with rage, with his hands in the wall, his forehead pressed against hers. He felt trembling coming from behind him and realized Jason was about to phase again. Looking over his shoulder, he commanded, "Get out."

"Adam—"

Speaking menacingly through his teeth, his eyes bright on his second, he uttered, "You know I won't hurt her. This is personal. You need to leave."

"You're not like him, Adam. Listen to what she has to say." Jason's eyes bored into his. His second knew him too well and he cringed at the reference to his father. If he wasn't like his abusive father, then why did he have the woman he loved pinned to a wall?

"I've got this, J, just go," he said automatically. Knowing, despite what Jason thought, he could never physically hurt his mate.

There was a long quiet moment as Evangeline and Adam stared at one another, then he heard the front door close quietly behind him.

He felt Evangeline's hands come up on either side of his face and he flinched. Her hands were freezing. For a second the feel of her icy skin on his relieved the massive hangover creeping up on him.

She snatched her hands back. "I'm sorry."

"So, what's the story you two came up with?" he snapped.

"There is no story. When I woke up, I fed. The rebirth made me feel...things. I had no control over myself. I nearly drained him." Evangeline's face twisted in pain and she pushed back against the wall, her fists clenched at her sides as though she were struggling with some invisible force.

He ignored this, and spoke obsessively. "I need to know everything." The perverse need to know alarmed him. "Did he kiss you?"

"No," she uttered through clenched teeth.

Good. He stared possessively at her lips. "Where did he touch you?"

"Please, Adam. Don't do this. It's over."

He moved closer to her and she turned her head to the side, squeezing her eyes shut. His breath was hot on her cheek. "From my understanding you fucked with his pants on." He looked down at her robe. "Did your robe come off?" he asked menacingly.

"No." She writhed against the wall. "He never entered me. He didn't touch me."

"Just dry humped you, right?"

"Please, let this go. I told you, I couldn't help myself. The initial blood bond does something completely out of my control, but I stopped it. I was able to hold back. You have to understand how a newborn vampire feels when they awake. It will never happen again. I don't have to feed on him." She moaned and finally moved, ducking under his arm and crossing the room in a flash, stopping with her back to the front door.

Frozen, he took in her new, incredible speed. "Going somewhere?"

He stalked her and she put her hands up to ward him off.

Adam's voice was cool and threatening. "Are you afraid of me now?"

"No. Adam, please don't get close to me. I'm getting…" Her eyes darted to his neck.

Lifting his brows, he thought, *Holy shit…she's thirsty.*

"I'm not sure it's safe to be around me." Evangeline trembled.

"I'm not sure it's safe to be around *me*, babe," he countered. There was definitely something wrong with him because he ignored her warnings. He couldn't let it go. "Did you like it, Evangeline?"

"Stop!"

"Did he make you feel good?" This time his hands came up on either side of her with much less force, laying his palms gently on the door.

"You're angry right now and I understand, but please listen to me. I love you, Adam. That has not changed," she said, gazing up at him.

Speaking through his teeth, he leaned in closer, his mouth an inch away from her face. "Do you have any idea what I went through last night? Do you have any idea how messed up I was thinking about what he was doing to you and to have one of my worst nightmares come true? Do you think I enjoy knowing you laid with my enemy for nearly an entire day? IT MAKES ME SICK!"

Adam heard her fangs elongate before he saw

them, his focus totally on her glowing eyes. Stunned, he gaped at the woman before him. Evangeline's olive green irises flashed silver the moment he'd screamed in her face.

He was speechless.

She whimpered, only just realizing her fangs were out. Squeezing her eyes tight, she clamped her mouth shut, turning away from him.

"No," he said, instantly. "Open your eyes."

She shook her head. "I don't want you to see me like this."

"Do it, please. I need to see." His voice was remarkably calm now, smooth. Something about seeing her this way dazed him at the moment. He tilted her face gently toward him.

Her lids opened slowly, revealing crystal, silver eyes. He'd stared upon eyes like this when facing his enemy, but somehow those feelings associated with those awful experiences didn't conjure up now.

Adam struggled hard with words to describe the way he felt just then. It was as if she were a magnet pulling him toward her. He couldn't move away from her even if he'd wanted to. She was amazing.

If this was how vampires compelled their victims to feed from them, then it sure as hell worked. Only, she didn't look like she was trying to compel him.

He was so unbelievably confused by his reaction to her. Vampires were the enemy and yet here he stood, gazing avidly at the most beautiful creature in the world. "Did I cause that?" he asked curiously.

Evangeline opened her mouth to speak, and then closed it, hiding her fangs.

Again, he was fascinated and reached up without

thinking, brushing his hand over her mouth and pulling at her bottom lip. His thumb ran over a fang, riveted. So sharp were they he pricked the padding of his finger in a second. Evangeline hissed and sucked eagerly on his thumb.

Adam hardened instantly, his arousal kicking out, demanding to be set free. Completely spellbound by her, his chest heaved as he watched her suck on him.

She jerked back, covering her mouth with her hands. "God! I'm sorry. I'm so sorry."

Adam shook his head at her. "Here" He tilted his head to the side, exposing his neck.

Comprehension dawned on her striking face. "What? No—"

Nodding, he grasped the back of her head, pulling her toward his vein. "I want you to," he said deeply. There was no reason other than he needed to be a part of her, a part of her transition. If she had the king's blood in her, then sure as shit, she was going to have her fill of his. She tried to pull away from him, but he only gripped her harder. "Do it, babe."

Evangeline couldn't resist their close proximity. With a sharp intake of breath, she bit him.

Adam couldn't help groaning. He braced a hand against the door and held the back of her head with the other. Her arms were wound around his torso, squeezing him as she drank him in. The initial puncture stung, but quickly subsided. Jesus, this was amazing.

The headache coming on completely evaporated, all tension drained from his body. He was floating in the clouds, while tiny sparks emanated from the pit of his stomach and spread outward through every limb.

Her body moved against his, making his head reel.

Clamping his jaws together, Adam chased away the ugly images of her and Cyrus out of his head. "You're mine, Evangeline." His voice was unrecognizable, savage even. Although, he was at her mercy right now, he felt incredibly possessive. His hands moved of their own accord and untied her robe. He slid inside grabbing her waist, pulling her toward his hips.

Adam was about to explode. The feeling of vulnerability and greed did the craziest shit to him. Undoing his pants quickly, he sprung free, spread her legs wide and wound them around his hips. Sliding inside her in one powerful thrust, Evangeline came instantly, her body pulsating around his shaft.

Unsheathing her fangs, she licked the puncture wounds at his neck and leaned back to look at him with her shining eyes. "You're mine." He repeated in a growl, wolf eyes riveted on her, as a vicious need overcame him, and he began fucking her hard.

There was no way he could hold back. His supernatural strength ruled his body now. Her cries echoed in the foyer as he pounded her against the door. The selfish urge to claim was far stronger than any moon heat. He was blinded by lust, rage, jealousy and fearsome love for this woman. The animal within him had taken over as he thrust harder and harder, banging her against the wood.

The instant he spilled himself inside her, reality hit and he froze.

Several truths flashed into his head at once and he staggered back, stunned.

Evangeline is alive.

She's a vampire.

He just came inside her, but they will never have

any more children.

She'd been in his enemy's arms.

She was devoted to her maker and evidently, would die for him.

She's alive and a vampire.

And he just violated her after returning from the dead.

She's alive and he'd abused her.

I'm a fucking bastard!

The pounding headache hit him in full force and he felt dizzy.

"Adam?"

Stepping away from her, he closed her robe and zipped up quickly. "I'm sorry. Jesus, I'm sorry." She'd gone through hell and back and here he was, giving her shit when he should be welcoming her back from her near death experience with open arms.

He stepped further away from her, shaking his head. "I'm sorry…I…I need some time."

Adam turned and walked through the house and out the back door. The cool air hit his face and he inhaled deep, hoping as he stalked off she would one day find it in her heart to forgive him and prayed to God she didn't leave him.

Chapter Twenty-Two

The damp, ominous chamber that had been her prison for so long now felt like a sanctuary. The black, moldy stone walls surrounding her on four sides were a sort of comfort at the moment. It was a tiny room, located underground and no bigger than her bedroom at home. She thought of her room now, a room she had seriously taken for granted and longed to lay in her queen-sized bed with her down comforter and plush pillows.

She shoved the memory of her bedroom aside. Too many times she'd allowed herself to miss and it only brought on added pain. Too late, her thoughts had begun to spiral once more and she lost herself in self-pity. Why was this happening to her? What had she done to deserve this?

The sounds of the sordid people in the house coupling and chanting echoed down to where she was being kept. She pictured their repugnant stares and her stomach lurched, dreading the moment they would drag her back up again.

She was in a living nightmare.

Her natural body heat was the only thing keeping her warm, since her clothes had been taken months ago. Still, every now and then she'd get the chills and huddle in the corner, rubbing her hands over her sore arms and legs.

Sitting with her back to the cold wall, all sense of hope, minimal, yet still there, lingered in the far reaches of her mind. Will they find her soon or had they given up? Did her brother think she was dead? The terrible thought had come to her weeks ago. It had to be the only reason why no one had come looking for her.

They all thought she was dead. She would forever be a prisoner in this god-forsaken place begging for death to actually come. Her mind had already begun to hallucinate. She could only imagine what she'd turn into after years of being locked in this depressingly cold room. She'd rather be a corpse than an insane inmate, wasting away in her enemy's clutches.

Not for the first time her mind focused on the face, keeping her sane as she whiled the hours alone. She thought of the golden eyes boring into hers, holding such enduring strength.

Shuddering violently, weak tears falling down her cheeks, she whispered desperately into the hollow darkness. "Please find me, Jason...*please*."

****

It was two o'clock in the morning. Evangeline paced the living room in her favorite jeans and a white t-shirt. She was on her third cup of hot, steaming coffee. There was no need for caffeine. She had more energy than an Olympic runner at the moment. Caffeine was useless anyhow. She drank simply for the taste, to keep her hands busy, and, she thought pitifully, to keep her body temperature warm. She didn't want to freak out Adam again. Evangeline would drink twenty pots a day if it kept her body warm for Adam and the boys.

Stalking to the window, she felt anxious over seeing her family. She'd called her parents earlier, letting them know she was on the mend and they'd get the boys tomorrow. It had been way too long to be away from them.

Would her sons notice?

Evangeline shivered with unease. Will they notice she smells differently? She fought back tears as she thought of her boys falling asleep to the beat of her heart. Would they recognize her without a pulse or would they be frightened of her?

She stared at her reflection in the windowpane. Her features were the same and yet more pronounced, the skin a far lovelier color it had been before was now a shimmer of pale porcelain. Her hair was fuller and shinier too. She looked like she'd just come back from a day at the spa, but she felt like the weight of the world was on her shoulders.

This vampire transition plan had its ups and downs. She was very thankful to be alive and truth be told, she really did feel wonderful. Her body could now do things that were never possible before. Always tired and weak as much as she'd fought it, but now, she was healthier than ever.

Her family aside, she was looking forward to testing her new abilities. And Cyrus had been right. She was going to have to spend a couple weeks in the transition facility soon. There was no way she was going to take a chance living as a newborn vampire with her family without some help.

Sharp, new ears picked up his footsteps coming from the meadow just south of the house. He was in his human form, but she knew he must have phased when he'd left. Adam needed some time and it was understandable. She hoped a few hours had done the trick, because he was going to have to face her now, like it or not.

Evangeline walked through the kitchen and opened the back door. She'd hardly spent time in the yard since moving in. Looking around now she thought it needed a woman's touch. The grass was mowed, but there were no flowers in sight.

Adam sat now on an old wrought iron chair, leaning one arm on a matching table. It was the only outdoor furniture in the wide yard. It was obvious there was no use for the large backyard being a werewolf when he had the woods to run around in.

He faced away from the house, his head bent low, contemplating the frozen earth. She stared longingly at his broad, muscled back. An icy tightness welled inside her and she prayed everything would be okay. It had to be.

She stepped to him slowly and before she could reach him, he lifted his right hand over his shoulder, holding it out to her. She took it. His warm hand held hers in an agonizing grip and he brought her fingers to the side of his face. Without looking up, he asked softly, "Can you ever forgive me?"

"Oh, Adam." She came around and sat in front of him on the empty chair, taking both of his hands in hers. "There is nothing to forgive."

He stared at her silently, his face grim. Then he shook his head. "The way I reacted was—"

She cut him off. "Understandable. I don't blame you. If the situation were in reverse, I would have been just as angry." It was true. She'd rather him scream and shout than ignore her or repress how he felt. What she'd done with Cyrus was despicable. At the time there was no way to stop herself and thank goodness he understood. She'd like to think she would understand if Adam were in her shoes, but selfishly, she knew she'd put him through the ringer.

His eyes were roaming all over her face. "You look radiant," he said.

Shaking her head, she began to protest.

"No, you do. I know it's a little too late to say this, but you have no idea how damn happy I am you're sitting in front of me right now," Adam said, shuddering slightly.

She gave him a small smile. "It's not too late."

"You scared the hell out of me, babe."

"I'm sorry." Trembling too, she thrilled at his endearment. Did this mean they were going to be okay?

"It wasn't your fault. This whole thing is on my shoulders." He gripped her hands tighter. "Everything."

Staring at their clasped hands for a while, she said, "I could have been honest with you about the transition." She paused, not for affect, but because she dreaded this topic. "I knew what some of the side effects of the rebirth were and I didn't tell you."

Leaning forward, he rested his elbows on his legs. It was his turn to contemplate their hands. "You knew there was a chance that could happen?"

She nodded. God help her, she would do it again if it meant living a healthy life with her family.

Taking a deep breath, he said, "You were right not to tell me. I don't think I could have left you with him, if you had. Anyway, you could barely speak at the time. How could I expect you to give me details about turning into a vampire?"

She shrugged, her face etched with worry. "I hate

this is between us."

Adam leaned his head back as he considered this. His neck was thick and long and she ached to kiss him there. "It doesn't have to be," he said, softly.

Breathless, she looked at him hopefully.

He let out an unsteady exhale. "Do you love him?"

"No," she said instantly, then, "I...not like that."

His brows drew downward. "Then how?"

How on earth was she going to answer this when she was still discovering her feelings for Cyrus herself? "It's not love really. I can't exactly describe it. I don't love him like a lover. Cyrus told me it was the initial bond that made us ...and I won't feel those feelings again." She struggled to go on. "But, now I feel like he's a close relative of sorts." She was staring off to the side. "I've read about the relationship between a maker and his ward and it can be very close."

He tensed.

"But there is a difference. I am not his wife. I'm mated to you. Somehow I know *this* makes a difference. We will never grow together and it's not like he needs me around as I hold no real value to his coven."

Adam swallowed hard. "He can command you to his side."

She knew it took all his strength to say that without losing control. Her brow furrowed as she spoke. "I won't pretend he won't do so on occasion, but he also has his pride. If he summons me, it will be for good reason, not to spite you."

Adam pursed his lips as he listened to her.

"He knows how much I love you and our family." She hesitated. "Cyrus has softened toward me now because in a lot of ways I am like his child. He won't do anything to you or take me away from you because he knows it would kill me."

Adam stared before he spoke again. The shadows behind his eyes sent a thrill through her body as he asked, quietly, "Do you still love me?"

Her expression softened. "Of course I do. Can't you feel it?"

Jaws tight, he nodded. "I don't deserve you."

"Yes, you do." She kissed his hands, noting how warm they were on her lips and she frowned.

Adam ran the back of his forefinger over her mouth. "Your lips are cooler than your hands."

Pulling back, she said, "I was holding a hot coffee cup. It brings up my temperature." Looking at him apprehensively, she asked, "You're...you're not repulsed by me?"

He gave a small chuckle and her insides lurched with delight. "Why would cold repulse me?" Adam reached over and lifted her in his arms, setting her on his lap. He held her close and they sat for a while, letting their bodies adjust to their temperatures. "This works," he said. "You'll keep me cool and I'll keep you warm."

A silent tear slipped down her cheek.

Adam bent and kissed her long and hard, warming her lips with his. When he came up, he brushed the tears from her face. "Why are you crying?" Adam soothed, questioningly.

"I was so nervous how you'd react to...to this." She gestured to herself. "God, I have fangs now. I even bit you."

"Because I told you to," he said as a matter of fact.

"Evangeline, you're still you. You're what matters. I don't care about the fangs or the cold and shit... I really didn't mind the biting."

Giving him an exasperated look, she said, "I won't do it again."

"If you need to feed, yes, you will. I'm probably the best person to feed from. I heal fast and I sure as hell don't want you compelling some stranger."

"I've read eating rare meat can quench the thirst," she offered.

"Great, I love red meat, but you'll also get nourishment from me. No arguments."

She looked at him skeptically. "I can't believe you're being so great about this."

"Can't you?"

Smiling, she said, "All right, I guess I can. You're amazing, you know?"

He blushed and bent his head, staring avidly at the place her heart stopped beating. Swallowing, he rested his hand there. "I heard it, you know. I heard it beat for the last time."

She let out a long breath. "Adam..."

"I'm not saying I'm going to miss it. I was terrified I'd lost you for good." A horrible look of anguish flitted across his face. "And now you're in my arms. You're going to live for as long as you want." He buried his head in her hair and whispered, "Thank you. Thank you for coming back to me."

Adam and Evangeline sat quietly together in the cool autumn night for over an hour before either of them spoke. There was so much to be thankful for and they took time to simply be happy.

Adam took a deep breath. "We're going to have to

talk about your other supernatural side eventually."

She looked at him cautiously. "I'd almost forgotten." Then she giggled. "It's not every day a werewolf finds out he's mated to a witch/vampire."

He smirked. "Can you magically make us some steaks?"

They laughed and the feeling felt wonderful.

"I wonder if I can still heal," she thought aloud.

"No!" Adam stopped smiling, glaring at her now.

She stared back. That would be something she'd test out on her own.

"Evangeline," he warned.

"I'm sorry. It was just a thought." She gave him a quick kiss. In the same instant, Evangeline straightened, remembering what her great grandmother had said after nearly killing Jason.

"What's wrong?" he asked, concerned.

Evangeline looked off toward the far meadow. "Something my great grandmother said." She thought hard, her fear for Jason overshadowing the memory. "She made a point to shout out how vampires and werewolves ran wild and they, or I should say, *we* are only puppets. I didn't give it much thought then, because my mind was on Jason, but now when I think about it...Adam, I honestly don't believe the King's Coven started all of this. I don't believe they killed Tyson," she added cautiously. "I have a feeling my great grandmother is the one pulling the strings. The jackal that attacked us was really meant for you. Cassandra was furious I had gotten myself involved with a werewolf. My guess is she either put a spell to make the jackal's bite posionous, or she conjured up the jackal herself."

"You mentioned this before, at the summit." Adam was thinking long and hard too. "It doesn't make sense, though. Why, after all these years, would the witches start trouble?"

"Well, no doubt werewolves and vampires put together outnumber the witch population, or so I imagine."

He was quiet for moment. "The guys and I will look into it," he said, attempting to dismiss the subject.

"You know what this means though?"

"What?"

Hesitating before going on, she said, "I can help you, now. I won't feel so useless."

His eyes narrowed at her.

"I want to help you find your sister."

Adam's expression softened and he stared for a long while before responding. "I really don't deserve you."

"What do you mean?"

"Nothing." He shifted her closer to his chest. "Babe, as thoughtful as you are, I don't want you getting mixed up in all this business. Remember, my pack and the vampires still have scores to settle. You're going to be a registered vampire and it will be common knowledge who you are."

"So what? I have strengths now and I'm an excellent researcher. You can put me on rotation with your pack."

Adam was getting a little frustrated. "Eva, I just got you back from death's door. I'm not going to put you in danger so soon after—"

"What danger?" she cried.

His jaw tensed and his arms were like steel around

her. "Think. You're the Blacktail alpha's mate and the Vampire King of North America's ward. If my pack or the King's Coven didn't start this mess, witch or not, someone else did." Adam was beginning to tremble. "In our selfish need to win you, Cyrus and I made you our enemy's number one target."

Evangeline stilled. "Oh."

He looked as though he regretted telling her this. "I don't want you to worry. I'm not going to let anything happen to you."

She traced her finger over his forearm. It was her attempt to soothe him. "I'm not as scared as I should be."

Adam shook his head at her, exasperated. "Right. Remember when you tried to outrun a werewolf?"

She peeked up at him, grinning. "I bet I could outrun you now."

He smiled boyishly. "You're on, but first things first."

"Mmm?" she murmured softly.

"I need you to promise me a couple things."

"Within reason?" she asked, cautiously.

He gave her a stern look. "Within *my* reasoning, yes."

Smiling, she asked, "What is it?"

He held her tight. "Promise me you will never keep anything as important as your health from me again, no matter what it is. If you're thirsty for blood, I want to know. If you stub your toe, I want to know. Do you understand?"

"Yes, honey. I promise." She smoothed his stubble on his cheek. "And the other?"

Blushing slightly, he continued. "Now, you know

we're mated under werewolf law."

Evangeline nodded.

"I know it wasn't your idea...the boys weren't planned, but they are a blessing." His eyes brightened at the mention of their beautiful twins.

She smiled, excited she'd get to see her sons in just a few hours.

"Nonetheless, you didn't ask to be mated to me." He went on, his voice warm. "I want us to be joined in the human tradition too." His eyes smoldering, he said, "Marry me, Evangeline."

Joy leapt inside her and she shrieked, *"Finally!"* then laughed out loud, rocking forward on his lap.

Adam laughed too, shocked. "Were you waiting for me to ask?"

Evangeline blushed. "I confess, I have been. I've even daydreamed about it. I am, or was, human after all."

He stared, dumbfounded. "I'm a complete idiot."

She kissed him, hard, molding her lips to his. Her hands gripped the back of his neck, holding him against her. They moved together with perfect precision.

Adam pulled back slightly. "So does *finally* mean *yes*?"

"Yes, it does. Although, technically you didn't ask, you demanded, *alpha*." She inhaled, taking in his wonderful scent, wanting desperately to taste him again.

Smirking, he said, "Occupational hazard." He kissed the tip of her nose. "Now for the second promise."

She looked up. "That wasn't it?"

"No silly. That choice was yours, of course. Now

you've agreed to marry me, I need you to promise me one more thing." Adam reached up to hold her face in his hands, his blue eyes shimmering on hers. "Promise me you will never leave me." The intensity of his words set her frozen heart on fire.

"Adam Perez,"—she snuggled into him, her mouth finding the crook of his neck it longed for—"you're stuck with me till the end of time."

A word about the author...

Julia Laque holds a B.S. in Education and an M.A. in School Administration. As much as she loves teaching, her true passion has always been the written word.

An avid fan of love stories, Julia writes gripping romance with memorable characters. She lives in Chicago, Illinois with her family.

You can visit Julia's website at:

www.julialaque.com

Thank you for purchasing
this publication of The Wild Rose Press, Inc.
For other wonderful stories of romance,
please visit our on-line bookstore at
www.thewildrosepress.com.

For questions or more information
contact us at
info@thewildrosepress.com.

The Wild Rose Press, Inc.
www.thewildrosepress.com

To visit with authors of
The Wild Rose Press, Inc.
join our yahoo loop at
http://groups.yahoo.com/group/thewildrosepress/

38870644R00187

Made in the USA
Lexington, KY
28 January 2015